THORNTON BROTHERS
BOOK ONE

Touched
SABRE ROSE

ISBN: 1717584624
ISBN-13: 978-1717584625

1

GABE

My alarm went off and I fumbled under the sheets until I felt the smooth surface of my phone, swiping to stop the incessant ringing. It was early, too early, despite the sun being high in the sky. My head throbbed and the swell of the waterbed brought waves of nausea. It took a while for the memories to wade through the murkiness of my brain, but finally, flashbacks of the night before hit me with a vengeance.

The boss was going to kill me.

Ten minutes passed as I lay with my head buried beneath the covers before my alarm went off again, screaming that I needed to get ready for work. Swiping it silent, I forced my eyes to focus on the too bright screen. Two missed calls. Was Tyler ever going to give up?

Tossing the covers off the bed, I lay in a pool of sun streaming in through the open curtains. It was warm. It was comfortable. And all I wanted to do was close my blurred eyes and fall back into that blissful state where my head didn't pound, my mouth wasn't dry and the memory of the night before didn't exist.

Yesterday was the two-year anniversary. It was why Tyler was calling. It was why I drank three-quarters of a bottle of vodka by myself.

It was also why I ended up fucking Kate, something I promised the boss I wouldn't do. She was sick of losing staff. But despite never promising any of them anything, they threw themselves at me. And yet, I was the one branded a player. A man-whore. An arsehole. And I had only just turned twenty-one.

My phone rang and I stared at the screen in disgust. Tyler. Again. When were my family going to get it through their heads that I was done with them?

Bracing myself, I knew I may as well get it over and done with. "What?" I answered.

"Can you talk?" my brother asked.

"I answered, didn't I?"

"I thought you'd be at work."

"My shift starts soon. What do you want?"

"Are you coming this weekend?"

Sitting up, I shielded my eyes from the glare of the sun. "Is Jake home?"

"Not until the end of the year."

"I told you the only reason I'd come home was to see Jake."

"Dad is expecting you," he said.

"Dad can kiss my arse."

Tyler let out a deep sigh. "It's the two-year anniversary." He said it quietly, but his voice held the hint of a threat.

A knot of emotion caught in my throat. I wanted to yell at him and ask how the fuck could I ever forget, but instead, I took a deep breath and forced myself to sound calm. "And?" I replied.

"For fuck's sake, Gabe. Can't you just get over yourself for one minute? His death affected us all, not just you."

I took another deep breath, pushing away the memories. "Anything else?" Dragging myself out of bed, I started sorting through the mess of clothes lying on the floor.

I expected a lecture on how I was letting the family down. How my lack of attendance at family gatherings was an embarrassment to Dad. How I needed to get my shit together. But instead, Tyler, the fucking perfect son, just sighed again.

"No one blames you, Gabe."

There were so many things I could have said, so many other people who could share in the blame, but I knew there was no point in bringing up any of it. Clark was gone. Nothing could bring him back.

I let silence be my answer.

Tyler tried again. "It would mean a lot to Dad if you came."

"It would mean a lot to me if you left me alone."

"I can't do that. We are family."

"Fuck family."

I hung up.

For nearly two years I had avoided them. That wasn't about to change.

With only minutes before I was due to start my shift at the café, I dragged myself through the shower, ran a brush through my hair and stumbled out the door, pulling a t-shirt over my head that clung to my still-damp skin.

The boss was there to greet me when I walked in five minutes late. I was improving. Flashing her my most winning smile, I hoped to avoid a scolding. It must have worked as she merely narrowed her eyes and tapped the skin of her wrist.

Jordan, the new girl, came out from the storeroom and smiled at me shyly. When she started a couple of weeks ago, the boss warned me I wasn't allowed anywhere near her. I didn't bother to explain that it didn't matter if I went near her or not, rejection in any form meant they ended up hating me. Then leaving.

The cafe was busy and I spent most of my time at the coffee machine, trying not to let the gurgling of the steamer or the clinking of cups drill into my thumping head. My stomach churned from the mere scent of food so Jordan took any orders to the tables.

A couple of hours before the end of my shift, my mates wandered through the door. "I'm taking my break," I yelled to Mark in the kitchen. A grunt was the only reply I got.

Checking that no customers were watching, I jumped over the counter and slumped into the seat beside Drew.

"You good?" he asked.

"Apart from feeling like someone took a shit in my mouth and a thumping headache, I'm great," I replied dryly.

"You drank a lot," Drew replied.

As if I wasn't aware.

Stefan wiggled his eyebrows. "So," he drew the word out. "How was she?"

"Not here," I warned, glancing around the café before remembering the boss had popped out. "It shouldn't have happened. It was stupid. I was stupid."

"And yet you keep doing it," Drew said.

I threw him a withering glare as Stefan nodded over to where Jordan was preparing our drinks, every now and again flicking her eyes over to our table. "What about that one?"

She was pretty enough. I didn't really have a type, but if I did, she probably wouldn't be it. All angles and straight lines, no curves. But then again, I said the same thing about Kate. My type usually depended on my need, and my need depended on my mood, so that could change. The need to laugh, the need to be wanted, the need to forget, they all required a certain type of girl.

Glancing over at Jordan, I shook my head. "The boss has already got me on warning since the last one walked out. There's no way I'm going near her."

"That's what you said last night too," Stefan said, his smirk overtly obvious.

Kate had come on strong, and at first, I ignored her, but when she caught me at a weak moment, right as I was in the middle of attempting to drown my memories with vodka, well, things happened. She wasn't impressed when I told her it was a one-off. She didn't realise they were all one-offs. Now, I just had to hope she didn't tell the boss. Or leave. Maybe I should have played it nice for a few days.

"Hook me up with this one then, would you?" Stefan said.

Drew rolled his eyes. "Could you be any cruder?"

"You're on your own," I told Stefan. "I'm staying well away. I need this job."

Translation: I needed the money. Supporting myself was harder than I expected. Still, I'd discovered I didn't need much. A roof over my head, food in my stomach, beer for the fridge, and gas for the jeep.

Jordan made her way over to our table, tray laden with drinks. She smiled brightly and placed them down, her eyes flicking to mine shyly. I smiled politely and stared at my coffee. She made good coffee.

"Are you getting up to much tonight, Gabe?" She clasped the empty tray close to her chest.

Stefan made the most of my hesitation and held out his hand. "I don't believe we've met. I'm Stefan." She shook it hesitantly as I looked down at the table and tried not to catch her eye. But it felt awkward after a while so I introduced Drew, still barely looking up at her. He didn't bother shaking her hand. I could tell from the expression on his face his head was still too twisted up in Haleigh to even register another girl. He had just been dumped. Again.

"Actually," Stefan piped up when he realised I wasn't going to answer. "We're heading for a game of pool after Gabe's shift. You keen?"

I shot him a death glare and kicked him under the table.

Jordan's eyes flicked to mine. "I'm not that good at pool."

"I'll teach you." Stefan winked.

Ignoring his flirting, Jordan turned to me. "Can I hitch a ride with you?"

She wasn't as shy as I initially thought. I couldn't think of a decent excuse while she stared at me all doe-eyed and hopeful. "Sure," I muttered.

Hugging the tray closer, she flashed a smile at the others. "Mark will be over with your food shortly."

"Thanks," I groaned to Stefan as soon as she was out of earshot.

He laughed and sipped his coffee from the spoon. "I'm not too proud to ride on your coattails."

Stefan didn't need to ride on my coattails. He did well enough without dipping his stick into my work environment.

Mark, the cook, waltzed over with our dinner. Three plates piled high with nachos. They weren't on the menu. Too pub-like, Mark said, but he made them especially for me and the boys. Didn't charge us, either. It was something of a tradition for a Wednesday night.

Mark dumped the plates onto the table and slumped into the empty chair beside me. "Your break is almost up, Casanova."

I raised my eyebrows. "Casanova?"

"Jordan was grinning like a Cheshire cat. I'm assuming you had something to do with that?"

"No, I did not," I replied grumpily and stared hard at Stefan.

"Poor Gabe." Stefan stuck out his bottom lip before stuffing his mouth full of nacho chips and cheese.

"It would be different if he actually had to try," Mark said dryly.

"Hey." I blinked indignantly. "What are you implying?"

"I'm implying," Mark said, helping himself to Drew's plate, and getting slapped in the process, "if you actually had to put the effort in like the rest of us, your success rate wouldn't be so high."

"So you're saying I'm just a pretty face?"

Mark pinched my cheek and grinned. "It's not just your face."

"I'll have you know I'm a very nice person, thank you very much." I knocked back the last of my coffee. It was hot and felt like I had swallowed a fireball.

"Yes, you've got a lovely personality, Gabe," Mark said, rolling his eyes and smirking at the guys.

His words got to me more than I let on. It was true. Girls often liked me before I even opened my mouth. Sure, they didn't stop liking me after, but it wasn't the same thing. I knew that their attraction usually had very little to do with me. It was simply genetics. Not that I was complaining.

"I'm pretty sure if you went outside your little bubble of adoring girls, the results would change."

"I've seen him pull women of all sorts, and they've never turned him down. It's sickening really." Stefan talked with his mouth full and Mark screwed up his nose in disgust.

"I don't pull anything." I pushed my chair back and stood. "Break's over. I'm going back to work."

"All I'm saying is," Mark said, leaning over to the others, "has he ever been successful when it wasn't the girl who made the first move?" Mark took a chip from Stefan's plate and popped it into his mouth. It crunched loudly as he bit down.

All three of them looked up at me expectantly and I scowled. "I may not have had to try, but that doesn't mean I couldn't get any girl I wanted. I can be very charming," I said, trying to distract from the fact that Mark was right. I had never put effort in. Well, not for a while, anyway. There was one girl, but it was complicated.

"So, you'd be up to a little challenge?"

I folded my arms. "Name it."

"I will pick a woman and you have to woo her."

"Woo her?" I snorted.

"Fine. Fuck her. Is that better?" Mark raised his eyebrows and looked at me blankly.

"That's a bit lame, isn't it? And not all that nice."

"So, you're going to renege on the challenge?" Mark asked.

"Fine. I'll 'woo' someone." I felt a little tug of guilt. I'd slept with plenty of girls before but never for a bet. I should've told Mark to take a flying leap, but there was something in the way he looked at me, in the way he challenged me, that meant I couldn't refuse. I'd slept with a few girls who turned out to hate me when it didn't go any further, what was one more?

"What's the bet?"

"Five hundred," Mark proposed.

Money. Shit. The one thing I no longer had much access to. I wasn't expecting that. I thought it would be more along the lines of doing the dishes for a week or having to walk down the main street buck-naked. "Five hundred is a lot."

"If you think you can't do it…"

"I never said that." I knew he was taunting me but I took the bait anyway.

"Fine." Mark began to look around the room slowly, weighing his options.

"Now?" I asked, a little worried at who he would pick. The café wasn't too full, and there was a good mix of women about, but I had no idea what he had in mind. Knowing Mark, it wasn't going to be the blonde sitting in the corner who had been eyeing me up for the last half an hour.

"That one."

He nodded to a woman sitting alone at a table, staring down at her phone. She was older than me; late twenties, early thirties maybe. Not that I had anything against older women, I just wasn't expecting it. She was attractive at least. Long brown hair pulled back into a messy bun and decent curves to her shape. She was dressed plainly in worn jeans and a slightly crumpled shirt. Nothing flashy. Nothing that really made her stand out from the other customers dotted around the café.

"Easy," I said, and grinned at Mark.

"We'll see." Mark winked at the others. "Well, off you go."

"Now?" I got a sense there was something he wasn't telling me.

"Yes, now. She won't be still sitting there tomorrow. People tend to leave cafés at some point."

The three of them watched, smirking, as I tucked my hair behind my ears, and approached her table. She hadn't noticed me yet. Her eyes were still glued to her phone. I was nervous, but I wasn't about to let the boys know that. If only she would look up, then I'd be able to better gauge my approach. But just before I got to her, my boss, Peta, flew through the door, all flying hair and shopping bags, and over to the woman at the table.

"Sorry I'm late," she said, hugging her.

"I'm used to it," the woman replied, looking away from her phone and grinning at Peta.

"Oh, I forgot to mention." Mark came up behind me as I stood frozen in the middle of the floor, unsure how to proceed. "She's the boss's best friend and your new workmate." He chuckled.

I turned away from the two women now talking animatedly at the table and looked at Mark determinedly. I wasn't about to give up. "Give me a week."

Mark's eyebrows lifted. "A week?" He shook his head, amusement tainting his smirk. "Heck, I'll give you a month. It's still a safe bet." He started to walk back to the kitchen, but then turned, rubbing his fingers together greedily and laughing. "You'd better start thinking of some smooth chat-up lines because she starts working here tomorrow."

2

LAUREN

I was supposed to be preparing for my wedding. Instead, I was starting a new job, a new life. Rather than the nervous flutter of excitement at the thought of walking down the aisle, I was thumbing through the clothes in my wardrobe and trying not to let my eyes slip to the bolt of white lace shoved in the back.

Just wear what's comfortable, Peta had told me the day before when I met her at the café. I hated it when she did that. She knew better than to give me such vague instructions. Comfortable was my favourite pair of tracksuit pants and an old t-shirt. Comfortable was my pyjamas. Comfortable was not trying to decide what to wear on my first day at a new job.

I sighed and flicked through the clothing. It fell into three categories: office wear, dresses, and lazy slop. Peta had provided me with a white shirt and baby blue apron, but the rest of the ensemble was up to me. I tried to think of what the staff had been wearing, but I hadn't actually taken any notice. And even though I'd frequented the café often when it first opened, thanks to the recent events in my life, I had never actually met any of the people that worked for my best friend. The people about to become my workmates.

In the end, I pulled out a black pencil-skirt and wiggled it up over my hips. It was too tight, and the slight pouch of my stomach stood out, making me look like I was at the beginning stages of pregnancy. The pre-wedding diet had long been discarded. I tried untucking the shirt and pulling it down to hide the small bulge, but then it just looked scruffy. I tucked it back in and grunted at my reflection. At least the apron would cover it. Already I was stressed, and I hadn't even arrived.

I slipped on the most sensible pair of high heels I owned and walked to the kitchen to collect my handbag and keys. Smudge meowed and looked at me expectantly.

"I've fed you already."

He meowed again, a howling, painful meow, and walked over to his food bowl which was still filled with the biscuits I had placed down earlier. He looked up and blinked slowly.

"There is still food in your bowl." I reached down and shook the bowl, hoping the sound of the biscuits would somehow convince him to eat. Smudge ignored the shaking and wandered over to smooch against my leg.

"Bugger off," I said grumpily and nudged him away with my foot. One leg of my black pantyhose was left covered in white hair.

"Arsehole," I muttered under my breath. Smudge blinked indignantly and meowed again, refusing to give up on whatever it was he wanted. I gave up trying to figure out what.

Smudge was an arsehole. There was no other way of explaining him. The mixture of black and white on his coat made for an adorable kitten, but as he grew, the adorable kitten was replaced by a demanding, annoying cat. I think Derek had assumed that a kitten would somehow replace my loss, but instead, all it did was emphasise it. And even though it was Derek who adored the stupid thing, somehow, I ended up with him. Apparently, his new apartment didn't allow pets. But I suspected it probably had more to do with the fact that pets required looking after and Derek was used to being looked after. He didn't do the looking after.

I felt a momentary wave of guilt over moving Smudge with my foot and bent down to pat him. He hissed and backed away.

"Smudge," I cursed and hissed back. Smudge and arsehole had become synonymous in my vocabulary.

I arrived at the café ten minutes early. I couldn't stand being late. The man behind the counter looked me over slowly.

"Lauren, isn't it?"

I walked over and held out my hand. "Hi."

He took my hand, shaking it for slightly longer than what was comfortable. "Mark. I saw you yesterday over there with the boss." He nodded to the table we had sat at the day before. "You're starting today, right?"

"Sure am," I said, giving him what was probably something between a smile and a grimace.

"Peta won't be long. She had to pop out. Just have a seat and wait."

He kept looking at me, an amused expression on his face, as he served the customers that flowed through the door. I glanced down at my outfit, certain something was wrong; a stain on my top, or a ladder in my pantyhose, but I couldn't see anything.

Peta opened the café two years ago and it had quickly become one of the most popular ones in town. Decorated in creams, light blues, and natural woods, she aimed for the feel of something thrown together, a quaint cottage style. Hence the name: The Cottage. With mismatched chairs and tables, odd collections of tea pots, china cups and bold lettering on the wall, it certainly had that thrown-together holiday-home feel, but somehow, the entire effect looked like something out of a magazine. The food was divine too. Peta had never trained as a chef, but her skills were unparalleled. I used to feel embarrassed whenever she came to my place for dinner. My attempts at cooking felt meagre and basic compared to hers. The opening of the café had met a sudden bump when Peta discovered she was pregnant with her third child, but with her husband at her side, that woman could do anything.

"Hey you," Peta said, coming up behind me and wrapping her arms around my shoulders. She planted a kiss on my cheek and then frowned as she looked down at my legs pressed tightly together and ankles neatly crossed. "I said comfortable, Ren. It looks as though you can barely walk in that."

Peta was dressed in plain black pants and her blonde hair was pulled back in a no nonsense pony tail.

"Comfortable is sweatpants or pyjamas. I didn't think you would want me turning up in either of those."

"Comfortable is being able to move easily. Do you not own anything other than office attire?" She frowned and looked me up and down. "It will have to do for now, though I suggest a pair of comfortable pants for tomorrow."

"I don't own any comfortable and presentable pants," I said, mentally taking a note to go shopping before work tomorrow. "You should have been more specific. I thought I had to look, you know, business-like."

Peta sighed and rolled her eyes. "It's a café, Ren, not an office." She sighed again. "Never mind, let's get you sorted."

I followed her behind the counter and out into the kitchen where she introduced me to Mark, the man who had greeted me earlier.

"This is Lauren," she said to him, offering no further explanation.

He looked at me, still with a slightly amused grin on his face, and nodded. "We meet again." And then he dropped the smirk, grunted and turned back to where he was hand-mixing some dough on the bench top.

"You'll get used to his moods," she said, then she turned back to the cook. "Won't she, Mark?" She playfully shoved him and he flicked a small piece of dough over his shoulder in her direction.

"I was at that counter for half an hour, Peta," Mark said, finally turning around to face us. "Half an hour. You know how much I hate serving. My heart belongs in the kitchen."

Mark was in his forties, maybe. He was short and his hair was thinning. Fine stubble trailed over his chin and his glasses sat lopsidedly on his face. He didn't really look like a cook but, then again, I didn't know what a cook was supposed to look like.

Peta held up her hands. "I was as quick as I could be, Mark. It's not my fault that staff called in sick today." Peta turned to me, explaining, "We like to have at least four staff on at all times, more if we know we're going to be busy. That way there's at least one to man the register, one on coffee, one in the kitchen and one to serve and gather dishes. Today, two staff called in sick and we've been under the pump. Usually, Mark is a sweetie," Peta said as we exited the kitchen. "Well, when he wants to be," she yelled over her shoulder.

The last job I had was a personal assistant for my fiancé who was a real estate agent. I was used to making phone calls, photographing houses, and filling out contracts, but the constant flow of information I received over the next hour left my head spinning. All the buttons on the cash register looked the same, and the required number of shots for the multitude of coffees on the menu caused a fine sheen of sweat to form on my forehead. And we hadn't even got to the food. Give me commission percentages and contracts over that stuff any day.

Peta laughed at my dazed expression. "Don't worry, you won't be expected to remember everything, I just want to give you the full rundown."

"I'm not sure if I'm up to this, Peta," I said as a familiar wave of anxiety began to flutter in my chest. I liked knowing things. I hated floundering around and having to figure things out as I went.

"You'll be fine," she said. "You always stress over things and they always turn out fine."

Not always, I wanted to say, but I kept my mouth shut and smiled. "I hope you're right."

"Of course I'm right." She shrugged then winked. "Just ask Shrek."

Shrek was Peta's husband. Of course, his real name wasn't Shrek, it was Dylan, but his wide smile, small ears that poked out from his head, and closely cropped hair earned him the nickname as soon as the movie had come out. I'm not sure if Dylan appreciated it or not, but since everyone picked up on it, he was left with little choice but to accept it.

Shrek was a stay-at-home dad to their three boys while Peta ran the café. She had recently increased the hours from closing at four to staying open until nine, so in order for her to at least spend some time at home, she had offered me a job. Really, she was just being nice. She knew I needed the job, needed the money, and even though I had no idea what I was doing, she hired me.

"I just don't want to let you down," I said.

"Nonsense. You won't. Soon you'll be flitting about, wondering why you ever felt nervous."

"If you say so."

"If you ever need to know something, just ask. Someone around here will know the answer. Or they should."

"They're going to hate me on sight for coming in like this." I despised the thought of being the woman that only got the job because she was friends with the boss.

"On sight?" Mark called from the kitchen. "We hated you before we even saw you." He walked through carrying a tray of freshly baked scones. He winked at me as he placed each one into the basket by the cash register. The scent made saliva pool in my mouth. "I'm just yanking your chain. We've all got to start over again at some stage in our lives."

I threw Peta a frustrated look and she shrugged apologetically. She had obviously filled Mark in more than she needed to.

"We're a pretty tight bunch," Mark offered, noticing my look of annoyance before concentrating on his display of scones. "Perfection every single time." Slowly and deliberately, his eyes moved to the scones leftover from the previous batch. The ones he had placed down looked lighter, fluffier, and altogether more delicious.

Peta laughed. "Yes, Mark. You win. You are the scone king."

"It's the buttermilk," he said, sprinkling icing sugar over the golden scones.

My stomach growled loudly and Peta sighed. "You haven't eaten yet today, have you?"

I shook my head. Eating had become less of a routine and more like sporadic binging since Derek had left.

"Go on then, you can have one. Jordan will be arriving soon and then the afternoon rush will start, so you may as well grab something now while you can."

I needed no further invitation and grabbed one of the warm scones. I was just about to bite into it when Mark interrupted me.

"Oh, no you don't! Treat that scone with respect. I don't slave over a hot stove all day for you to merely shove it in your mouth hole." He walked into the kitchen leaving me with the scone half in my mouth.

I removed it and looked to Peta. "Mouth hole?"

Peta just grinned as Mark walked back towards us. "Yes, mouth hole." He took the scone out of my hand, broke a piece off and slathered it in butter. "Open up."

Hesitantly, but obediently, I opened my mouth and he popped in the piece of scone.

"Well?" he asked, hands on hips, waiting impatiently.

"Divine," I mumbled around the scone.

He nodded as though he expected no other answer and walked back into the kitchen.

Around quarter to three, a girl flew through the door, backpack half open with books and clothes hanging out slung over her shoulder.

"Sorry!" she yelled to Peta as she rushed past us to the storeroom that also served as the staff room.

"That's every day this week, Jordan," Peta yelled after her. After a few moments Jordan reappeared, cheeks flushed red and smoothing out her hair. She joined us behind the counter, undoing the bun on the top of her head and twisting her hair into a high ponytail. "Sorry," she said again, screwing up her nose. "I promise it won't happen again. Hi." She flashed me a smile. "You must be Lauren." She stuck out her hand and I shook it. "I'm Jordan."

I started to respond but Peta talked over me. "You said that yesterday." From the way Peta interacted with her staff, I got the impression that this was a rather laid-back workplace. She was telling the girl off, hands on hips, stern expression, but there was still a hint of amusement. "So what happened this time?"

"I swear I was on time when I left home, but when I was driving here, this person just walked out in front of me. It wasn't a crossing or anything, and I just happened to nudge him with my bumper. It wasn't anything really, but the police came and then the ambulance..." Her voice trailed off and she shrugged her shoulders apologetically, screwing up her nose again. "Sorry."

"You ran someone over?" Peta's voice rose in pitch.

"Well, I just gave him a friendly nudge, really. There was no need for the ambulance to come. It was just a precaution."

"Goodness knows what we are going to do with you, Jordan." Peta shook her head. "Did you hear all that, Mark?"

Mark appeared in the doorway just as the first wave of the afternoon rush started. He lifted one eyebrow and shook his head dismally.

Peta smoothed down her apron and turned to me. "Ready to man the register?"

"Now?" I said, my heart racing a little. It seemed ridiculous to be this nervous, but after spending months on the couch, wallowing in my misery, everything was a daunting experience.

"No better way than to throw you in the deep end. Jordan, you can be on coffee while I show Lauren the ropes. Mark, I'm afraid you're on food and serving until Gabe turns up. Looks like he's late too. Why do I keep hiring such terrible staff?"

Mark grunted and pulled on a clean apron. "Because you love us, boss."

The first person in line ordered a cappuccino in a latte bowl with no froth and no topping. I frowned and looked to Peta, whispering quietly. "Isn't that just a latte?"

"What the customer wants, the customer gets," she whispered. "Just smile, nod, and repeat the order. Smile and nod, it's my motto around here."

I stared at the buttons on the register until they made sense and keyed in the order. I looked back up to the customer, smiled, nodded, and repeated the order back to him. He grunted so I took it as correct.

I got flustered about fifteen minutes into the rush. There were people lined up all the way out the door and I could hear murmurs of impatience. I wasn't used to working under such pressure.

"Here," Peta said, moving me to the side. "Let me take over for a while, just until things settle down a little. Would you pop out the back and grab some more takeaway cups? They're in the storeroom on the left."

Grateful to be leaving the register, I walked away as quickly as my skirt allowed and headed to the storeroom. It was crammed full of boxes and silver bags of coffee beans, so I had to search through a number of boxes before I found the cups. Unfortunately, they were right at the top of a pile of coffee bags and rather difficult to reach, and I couldn't find a stepladder. Stretching on my tiptoes, I reached out as far as I could, but my fingers only just brushed the edge of the box. The fabric of my skirt strained as I stuck one leg out behind me for balance. I was in no way considered a short person, but the box was simply out of my reach.

"Damn it!" I muttered under my breath.

I wasn't even capable of doing a simple task like getting cups. I could feel tears gathering and growled, frustrated that something so small could undo me so easily. Hatred towards Derek for making me this way surged through me, but it was mixed with sorrow. I hated him, but I still loved him.

"Need some help?" a voice said behind me.

I jumped, surprised I wasn't alone and turned to face the newcomer.

"Hey," he said, reaching over me and lifting the box down with ease. He wasn't that much taller than me, but obviously tall enough. "I'm Gabe. Lauren, isn't it?"

I nodded numbly and took a deep breath to gather myself. "Yes, it's Lauren. Hi." I smiled and shook his outstretched hand. "Thanks for that." I nodded to the box in his arms as he placed it on the ground. He opened it and pulled out two sleeves of the cups and handed them to me.

"Sounded like you needed the help." He grinned, grabbed his apron off the hook and tied it around his waist, leaving the top part hanging, rather than looping it over his head. He was also wearing a black t-shirt rather than a white shirt like the rest of the staff. Maybe the rules didn't apply to him. His shirt was tight, but I wasn't about to complain. He was extremely handsome. But he was young, early twenties maybe. Shoulder length dirty-blond hair framed his face and sat tucked behind his ears. His blue eyes twinkled mischievously and he had a smile that made my heart skip a beat. I inwardly laughed at myself, unable to control my body's response. But he was extremely good looking in a scruffy, young, immature kind of way.

"Something funny?"

I shook my head. "Just been one of those days."

Gabe swept his arm towards the door and bowed dramatically. "After you."

I peeked out the door to the line of customers and took a deep breath. "Round two."

Thankfully, due to Peta at the register, the line of people were waiting for their orders, instead of waiting to order, and once Gabe got to the coffee machine things began to speed up. He worked swiftly, steaming milk and pouring the coffees while Jordan lined up the coffee shots. I kept myself busy taking orders to tables and clearing dishes, while Peta manned the register for the customers still pouring through the door. Around four o'clock the type of customers changed, and instead of business people lining up for their afternoon coffee break, the café became filled with teenagers, still in school uniforms, ordering iced coffees piled high with whipped cream and dripping with sweet toppings.

Peta pulled me aside as soon as there was time, and we took a seat at one of the tables. I was grateful to be off my feet as the constant flow of people meant I hadn't sat down for hours, something I wasn't used to. I was beginning to think lustfully about my old office chair.

"I didn't realise this place was so busy," I said as I slipped my shoes off under the table, hoping no one would notice.

"It's partly due to Gabe," she said. I looked at her quizzically. "Don't tell me you hadn't noticed him." She wiggled her eyebrows suggestively.

"Peta!" I said, shocked. "He's so young."

She shrugged her shoulders. "No harm in looking, is there?"

I shook my head and rolled my eyes. "You're terrible."

She laughed. "Look at you. You're blushing just at the mention of him. You can't tell me you hadn't noticed."

I dropped my shocked expression and laughed. Gabe, still working at the counter, stretched up to reach a flavour shot bottle, flashing the smooth muscles of his bicep. He caught my eye and winked.

"Okay, I might have noticed," I conceded.

"Might?"

I told her to hush as Gabe walked over carrying our coffees. He placed them down and winked again.

"Kate is sick today, Gabe." She cocked her head and looked at him expectantly.

"The fact that she is sick has nothing to do with me, I swear."
He held up his hands and blinked innocently, but his smile wasn't
so innocent. "Honest boss, I'm behaving."

Peta shook her head and shooed him away. "He's trouble."

I lifted an eyebrow and took a sip of the coffee. "Sounds
interesting. Spill, I need some distraction. My feet are really killing
me."

Peta glanced down at my shoes under the table. "Might pay to
add some flats to your shopping list. Anyway, Jordan is the third
girl I've had to hire in the past two months and already she's
showing signs of falling for him. And as for Kate, well, I'm not
sure what's going on there. Hopefully, she really is sick, but I have
my doubts. I've talked to Gabe about fraternising with the staff but
they follow him around like little lost puppies until, finally, he
notices them. Then, when he pays them some attention they are
left devastated when things don't go the way they had imagined."
Peta took a sip of her coffee as Mark plonked himself on the seat
beside me. "I'm just filling Lauren in on our local Lothario over
there."

His brows creased together. "I just don't see what they see in
him. He's all tousled and messy looking." Mark and Peta shared a
look and laughed. "You do have to admit he's good for business
though."

When I looked around the room, it was hard not to notice the
majority of eyes were trained on Gabe. And not just female. There
was something magnetic about him, yet he seemed oblivious to it.
Each time he looked up, people sat a little straighter, flicked their
hair and pouted their lips. Others either watched a little too closely
or puffed their chests out a little further.

"I suppose it does make up for his role in my staffing issues,"
Peta said, looking around at the full café. She tipped her coffee up

and drained it. Everything with Peta was done that way. She never sipped. She sculled.

3

LAUREN

That night I lay in bed and stretched my arms out across the wide mattress. It's strange how the heart could still long for the very thing that hurt it.

I met Derek when I was sixteen so I could barely remember a time without him. We were high-school sweethearts, and I followed him south, keen to get into the real estate business, once he realised his dream of living fulltime off the band was never going to come to fruition. I played with my photography business and he sat his real estate exams.

There were times I used to fantasise about being single. About the little things, mostly, like watching whatever TV show I wanted without a running commentary of how pathetic it was, or cooking nothing but eggs on toast for an entire week if I felt like it. Stupid little things. But when my fantasy came true five months ago, the reality was shit. My fantasy was supposed to stay where it belonged; inside my head.

Derek sat me down one night after dinner. I had cooked a meal I knew he liked, thanks to a recipe and constant on-call advice from Peta. Slow-cooked beef brisket, creamy mashed potatoes, honey-glazed carrots and sautéed cabbage. It may not have turned out quite the same as if Peta had cooked it, and it looked slightly like a Pinterest fail, but it was the effort that counted. At least, I thought it was.

He took my hands in his and looked deeply into my eyes as we sat opposite each other at the table. It happened often, these 'talks' of his, so I wasn't concerned. In fact, I wasn't even really listening. I was prepared for another speech on how I needed to get out of the house more and be more social, on how I needed to do something other than work, on how I needed to get my life back. But there was something different about this time. It wasn't the words that made me realise it wasn't one of his usual talks. It was the fact that he was nervous. Derek oozed confidence, even when he didn't have any. It was a particular talent of his.

He swallowed and took a deep breath before talking. "You know I love you, don't you?"

I smiled slowly as a flutter of worry passed over me. "Of course, I love you too."

"These past few years have been wonderful and I know the loss of the baby—"

I flinched at the words and tears came unbidden. It had been two years but the pain was still there. Tears were my body's unwanted response to the memory.

Derek dropped my hands and got to his feet. "See, this is what I'm talking about, Lauren. We can't even talk without you bursting into tears."

I couldn't help it then, the tears spilled over my eyes and trickled down my cheeks. I hurriedly wiped them away but they continued to fall and I stared at him through blurred vision.

"I can't do this anymore." He didn't look at me. "We don't belong together. You, me, we're too different."

I got to my feet and touched his arm gently. "I will be better." I plastered on my most convincing smile, though my eyes were still swimming with tears I couldn't control. "I promise. I will be better. I will try harder."

Derek was a far more social creature than I. He longed for a return to the days when I eagerly clung to his side, content just to be anywhere he was. But since that day, my desire for a social life had lessened. He thought I was depressed, and for a while, I was. For the first three months I could barely get out of bed. I didn't want to. But then I started working for Derek and threw everything into my job. It was my distraction.

But it wasn't enough for Derek, despite asking for my hand in marriage only months earlier.

"It's too late." He turned from me and sighed deeply, his shoulders rising and falling dramatically. "I'm leaving." His eyes drifted over to a suitcase sitting by the door. I hadn't even noticed it.

Derek was my everything. But I never realised just how much of my everything he was until he was no longer there. We had been together for thirteen years, and for the last year and a half, we had also worked together. Losing Derek didn't mean just losing my fiancé. It meant losing my fiancé, my job, my home and, it appeared, most of my friends.

But later that night after our talk, having decided I needed to see him again, beg him to stay with me if that's what it took, everything changed. I drove to the office, knowing that was where he would be, and walked in to find him on top of a fellow agent. Literally on top. As in, she was spread across the desk, legs wide and Derek was thrusting into her like someone possessed.

It was a lot easier to let him go after that.

My phone lit up and my mother's face crossed the screen. I let it vibrate, waiting for it to go to voicemail. After a few guilty moments with Smudge staring at me accusingly, I called her back.

"Hey, Mother," I said in what I hoped was a chirpy voice.

"Hello, Lauren. Hey is not a greeting. Hay is what cows eat."

I rolled my eyes, held the phone away from me and gave it the finger. Smudge stood up, turned, and sat back down facing the other way, disgusted by my behaviour.

"When are you going to get a real phone line, Lauren? I hate talking on these cell phones. They cause ear cancer."

"You're not talking on a cell phone, Mother, I am. There is no point paying extra for a land line."

"You had a land line with Derek."

"Yes, I did."

I fell silent until it grew awkward and she couldn't handle it anymore. "How was your new job making coffee? Your sister told me."

I closed my eyes and breathed deeply. "It was great, Mother."

"You're not very talkative tonight. Is everything okay?"

"I'm fine. Just a little tired, I've been on my feet all day."

"Derek misses you."

"Derek chose to leave, not me."

"But there had to be a reason. Men just don't up and leave their wives for no reason. Are you sure you won't take him back?"

"We weren't married. I was never his wife, and Derek doesn't want to come back." We'd had this conversation many times.

"What God has put together—" she began.

"Let no man put asunder. I know, Mother. But technically, God hadn't put us together, well, he hadn't yet."

"Well, I'm pleased you enjoyed your new job, even if I don't understand why you had to get a new one. You were so happy with Derek and he loved having you work for him."

With him, I wanted to correct, but held my tongue. "Look, I really am tired. I'm going to go to sleep now, Mother. Tell Dad I love him."

"I will." And then she hung up. It annoyed me how she never said goodbye. She simply hung up.

Flicking through my contacts, I sent my sister a text message.

Me: She still blames me. Thanks for telling her I started a new job.

Morgan: Hope your first day went well. Why don't you just tell her about the man-stealing-bitch?

Me: Because somehow it would still be my fault. First day was fine. Scary. No idea what I'm doing.

Morgan: You'll figure it out. You always do.

Morgan: Got to go. Madi is still on the phone with her latest crush and we told her to get off the phone half an hour ago. Going to go get my yell on. Talk tomorrow.

Putting my phone aside, I rolled over and pulled my knees tight to my chest, ducking my head under the blankets, feeling small in the big bed, and wishing I wasn't alone.

I wished I could be annoyed at the catch in Derek's breath as he slept. I wished that I had the warmth of someone close to me. I wished that I had someone to share the night with, other than a Smudge of a cat.

4

LAUREN

"Never steam the milk to above seventy degrees Celsius, unless, of course, some idiot demands it," Gabe said, holding the jug under the steam wand. The milk made a gurgling sound as it whipped around the edges, growing in volume as it became thicker and frothier. Once it reached the desired temperature, he knocked the jug on the counter and expertly poured it into the mug leaving a beautiful fern-like design on top.

Smiling, he turned to me. "You're up."

"How do you know when it's the right temperature?" I asked.

"I can tell by touch, but you get to use one of these." He reached into the cabinet below, pulled out a thermometer, and clipped it to the side. It was angled so it protruded into the middle of the jug. "Remember, don't let it get to seventy or you'll burn it. And someone's mouth."

I held the jug up to the steam wand and started the pressure. It spluttered and Gabe covered my hand with his and pulled the jug up higher. He tilted it until it was the right angle.

"There, perfect," he said. "You'll get the feel for it after a while."

It was unusually quiet in the café and Gabe took the opportunity to train me while there weren't any customers waiting. I watched the milk forming small, thick bubbles and kept an eye on the needle.

"Remember, we don't want much froth. We want it creamy for a latte, not frothy like for a cappuccino."

I concentrated on the milk and, as the needle approached the little red line, I turned the knob, placed the jug down on the counter, and wiped off the nozzle.

"There," I said, surprised at the satisfaction I felt over such a small task. Gabe slid the coffee cup towards me, a thick crema over the surface, ready for the milk. I poured slowly. It looked nothing like his, but it was passable.

"I think the tongue helped," he said.

"Huh?" I looked up to find him studying me, amusement twinkling in his eyes. He ran his tongue back and forth across his lips, mimicking my look of concentration. I couldn't help but become a little transfixed with the image of his tongue running over his full lips and laughed to hide it. I had found myself allowing the indulgence of stealing looks all day, claiming it innocent under the banner of being pure fantasy.

Gabe slid the cup closer towards him, examined it closely, and then he lifted it to his lips and took a sip. "Not bad for a first attempt. Next latte ordered you're making it." He put the cup back down and rested against the counter, crossing his arms. "You're well on your way to fulfilling your lifelong dream of becoming a barista now. Latte sorted."

"Only cappuccino, mochaccino…" I turned and looked at the board behind me. "And countless others to go."

"We'll concentrate on one a day and you'll get there in no time."

I turned to the sink, picking up the jug and washing it.

"No skirt today, huh?" Gabe asked.

"I went shopping this morning. Business skirts weren't cutting it for this job. There is a lot more movement required than sitting at a desk."

"Pity, I kind of liked it." I looked at him sharply, but he just grinned. "So, tell me, Lauren, what brought you here to join our little team?"

"Peta hasn't told you?" I said, dumping the now clean jug on the counter.

He shook his head and picked up a tea towel to dry the jug. "We do have dishwashers, you know."

"I took this job for the same reason that most people do. Money."

Gabe nodded. "I hear ya. What did you do before?"

I decided to skip the last couple of years. "I used to have my own photography business, actually. Mainly, it was just weddings for friends and family, portrait shoots, stuff like that, but I did have the odd commercial client."

Crossing his arms, Gabe leaned against the counter. "What made you give it up?"

I shrugged my shoulders and turned around, plastering a smile on my face. "Life."

"Ah, yes. Life. A common occurrence for most people."

"What about you?" I asked. "Is making coffee your life-long goal?"

He shrugged. "For now."

Someone cleared their throat behind us and, as I turned around to greet the customer, my heart sank.

"Hello, Lauren," Derek said, smiling.

"Hello, Derek," I replied flatly. She was standing beside him, arm looped through his. Flashes of her creamy white thighs burned in my brain. She smiled and ran her eyes up and down Gabe. I inched a little closer to him.

"Your mother told me you'd started working here," Derek continued.

Of course she had. She would have been on the phone to him the second I had hung up. Beside him, the man-stealing-bitch cast her gaze along the counter and into the cabinets of food. She turned back and stared at me as if it were somehow my fault the food didn't impress her.

"It's nice you have something to keep you occupied."

I seethed at his comment but bit my tongue. The man-stealing-bitch blinked slowly and smiled up at Derek. Her blouse strained against her chest, the material between the buttons gaping open to reveal scarlet lace under the crisp white. The same colour she had been wearing that night. I smoothed my apron and looked back up at him, taking a deep, calming breath. I had never told Derek what I saw. After the shock had subsided, I merely closed the office door and drove back home.

Derek looked good. According to my mother, he had started going to the gym and was signed up for some charity fun run, or something like that. I had tuned out. Whatever he was doing, it sat well on him. His face had thinned out a little, not that it ever needed to, and his shoulders somehow looked wider. His hair was a little longer than he used to keep it, and was pushed off his face, giving him a more stylish appearance.

"Would you like to order?" I asked, mustering up the most professional tone I could manage. I would not let him get to me.

"Straight to business, is it?" He placed his hands on the counter and leaned in closer. A flicker of annoyance passed over the man-stealing-bitch's eyes at the familiarity. "How have you been? I've been worried about you." I rolled my eyes and gritted my teeth. Derek frowned. "Please Lauren, we're adults here. Let's behave like it."

I bit back the reply on my tongue. "Would you like to place an order? I'm rather busy."

Derek looked around the nearly empty café. "Fine, but I'm trying to be friends, Lauren. It wouldn't hurt you to try as well. Two lattes."

I started keying in the order when the man-stealing-bitch added, "With soy."

"Soy?" Gabe asked, eyebrows raised.

Derek looked at him as though he had just noticed him for the first time and nodded. Then his eyes moved to the man-stealing-bitch beside him, and the way her eyes roamed over Gabe, and he frowned. I couldn't help but smile a little.

"That's what the lady said," Derek replied curtly.

"Each to their own, I guess," Gabe said.

"Human stomachs are not meant to digest milk from animals," the man-stealing-bitch said in her slow drawl.

A crease of annoyance appeared between Derek's eyebrows as he handed over the money. "Do you have a problem with that?"

"Lowers testosterone levels from what I've heard." Gabe held up his hands. "But hey, maybe that's your thing."

I couldn't help the snort that escaped, and Derek's frown deepened. "Real mature, Lauren."

Gabe pulled the carton of soy milk out of the fridge and made a display of pouring it into the jug, lowering the carton up and down dramatically like a bartender. As it swirled under the pressure of the steam, he placed the thermometer into the liquid and the needle rose up to seventy. Gabe didn't stop. He kept going until it almost reached ninety degrees. He winked at me and handed over the cup. "One soy milk latte."

Derek jerked the cup from his hand. "You can bring the other one over to the table."

"Yes, sir." Gabe saluted.

I watched as he walked away, one hand resting protectively on the small of the man-stealing-bitch's back.

Gabe hummed quietly as he wiped down the counter top and leaned close. "Something tells me they aren't going to want that second cup."

"Fuck!" Derek yelled. Another customer in the café looked up at him and shook her head, unimpressed with his outburst. "Sorry," he muttered.

"You still want that other one?" Gabe yelled across the café.

"Fuck you," Derek mouthed as he pulled the man-stealing-bitch up from the seat and dragged her towards the door. She struggled to keep up with him, moving as fast as her tight skirt and high heels would allow. I shuddered to think that I might have resembled that the day before.

"You okay, baby?" she drawled.

Derek was holding his hand to his mouth. "I should have known better than to try and act civil." He shot a death stare in my direction as he walked out of the door.

I turned to Gabe, trying to look appalled and shocked when secretly I was pleased. "What did you do that for?"

"I didn't see you trying to stop me."

I opened my mouth to say more but promptly shut it again. He had a point. Gabe looked at me, his eyebrows raised and grinning stupidly. "You won't tell on me, will you? He was a prick. Ex-boyfriend?"

I shook my head. "Ex-fiancé."

"Ouch."

"And the woman?"

"The man-stealing-bitch?"

"Sorry, my bad. And the man-stealing-bitch?"

"A fellow real estate agent," I said.

"Oh."

"Yes. Oh." I glanced down at the pale band of skin around my wedding finger which had held my engagement ring. Strangely, I didn't feel the familiar tug of melancholy. "We separated about five months ago."

Gabe pulled himself up to sit on the counter. "Sorry."

For the first time since Derek left, I shrugged it off. "Shit happens." I didn't swear often, it wasn't professional, but damn, it felt good. Maybe the occasional swear word would become part of the new me. The new, coffee-making, less professional me.

Gabe furrowed his brows but laughed. "Awesome, Forrest Gump." He shook his head, smiling. "Shit happens," he repeated.

It struck me that it was the first time I'd almost felt okay around Derek. Usually, when I wasn't around him, I was sad. And then, when he was around, I was pissed. Mind you, the man-stealing-bitch's extra wide smile didn't help. Neither did the way he kept glancing down at her stomach, like he could somehow see the little part of him growing inside her, despite the fact that her stomach was still as flat as it was when he informed me she was pregnant. Turned out that was why he left. She could give him the very thing I couldn't. I swallowed the lump growing in the back of my throat.

Peta bustled through the door bringing with her a rush of crisp spring air. "I just saw Derek and the man-stealing-bitch clambering into the Beemer. What on earth happened? Are you okay?" She stopped and dumped her bags onto the counter. "Did he upset you? What did he say? Whatever it was I hope you took no notice. How dare he come in here! Gabe, I might need you to change roles and act as security if he ever—" Peta wrapped her arms around me and squeezed hard.

I squeezed back. "I'm fine, honestly."

"Are you sure?" She held me at arm's length. "He was swearing his head off and muttered something about my staff." Peta frowned when she noticed Gabe sitting on the counter. "Get your arse off there."

"That's my cue," Gabe said, sliding off the counter and heading out the back. "I'm going to see if Mark needs a hand." He winked at me and held his finger to his lips.

Peta looked between us, the line in the middle of her forehead deepening. "What's going on?"

"Seriously, don't worry about it."

"But why was he so angry?"

I grinned. "Ask Gabe."

"Should I be worried?"

I laughed away her concern. "What are you still doing here anyway? Shouldn't you be home by now? Go!"

5

LAUREN

With each day of work, I grew more confident. Under the tutelage of Peta, Gabe and Jordan, I mastered each of the coffees and was soon flicking over the register with ease. But I kept well away from the kitchen. The only time I ever entered was to pass through to the storeroom. It was Mark's domain in the afternoons and evenings; only Peta was allowed to interfere, and that was only when he was in a good mood.

The other staff were nice enough. Gabe smiled at me a lot. He would catch my eye and hold my gaze just a little longer than necessary, and he took every chance to brush against me and lean in a little closer than needed. If I didn't know better I would have thought that he was flirting with me. Of course, I knew he was probably like this with everyone, lapping up attention wherever he could grab it. Still, I allowed myself to think about him sometimes. I imagined his naked body hovering over me, imagined what his lips would feel like pressed against mine. But I would end up feeling so guilty over these fantasies that I disregarded any attention I thought he showed me. Clearly, my fantasies were affecting my perception of reality. I was just missing Derek. Gabe was nothing more than a pretty distraction. He would never seriously want to be with someone like me, used and broken.

Peta said she noticed how much time Gabe spent around me, but I knew any attention I received was really out of pity. She warned me off him, but she didn't need to. I wasn't young and stupid. I knew what he was. Still, as Peta said earlier, there was no harm in looking.

But then something happened that changed my way of thinking and my feelings for him got a little confused.

It was a Friday night and Gabe, Peta and I were scheduled to close at the café. Friday night was the only night Peta worked late, letting Mark get home early. Mark did every close apart from the weekends.

Peta and I were cleaning down the food cabinet. She was wiping the outside of the glass while I stuck my head inside and awkwardly swiped at the panels. As usual, we were discussing reality cooking shows, an obsession for both of us, even if it was only Peta who cooked.

"I honestly think they are only keeping them there for the ratings," Peta said. "I mean, why else? It's not as though they can cook."

"They've got a lot better recently," I said, ever the defender of the underdog.

Peta stopped wiping and stared at me through the glass. "You take that back, Lauren Lees."

"Actually, it's back to Greer." For some reason, as soon as Derek and I got engaged, all of our friends stopped using my maiden name, my real and legal name and started referring to me by Derek's. At the time, it seemed sweet. Now it just sickened me.

Her eyes grew wide. "You've gone back to your maiden name?"

"It was never my name," I replied.

Gabe walked over and pulled himself up to sit on the counter, looking down at me squished awkwardly into the cabinet. "So? What did you think?"

"Of what?" I asked, pulling my head out of the cabinet to hear him properly. I stretched and arched my back, trying to work out the kink that formed from bending over for so long.

"Of Blood Too Sweet?"

Yesterday Gabe had been trying to convince me to watch one of his favourite TV programmes. A zombie, bloodthirsty, gruesome one. He relished telling me about how they plunged axes into the zombies' heads, and how bodies with torn and missing limbs pulled themselves across the ground. The information had basically gone in one ear and out the other.

"Aren't you supposed to be pushing a mop over the floor or something?" I said, putting my head back into the cabinet. "Isn't he?" I mouthed to Peta.

"I've finished." He leaned over and ran his finger across the glass, leaving a smeared mark. "You missed a spot." He grinned at Peta and she shoved him off the counter.

"There's the kitchen floor, too," she said.

"Finished that." He crouched down beside me. "So, did you watch it?"

I stopped cleaning. "Hmmm, let me think about it. Nope."

"You didn't even try? You might really like it and how will you know if you don't try?" He looked at me intently and twitched his lips. "Did you even look for it?"

I rolled my eyes and sighed, though a slight smile remained. "I'm not into zombies."

"How do you know?" Gabe stood, and stretched his arms into the air, lifting his shirt and exposing a strip of tanned flesh. "Are you just about finished?"

I shook my head, eyes trained on my work and not Gabe. "I've still got to empty the last load in the dishwasher and stack the boxes in the storeroom. I can't stand how messy it is in there. You're more than welcome to help, if you like."

"Nah, I'm good. It will give me enough time to hire the DVD."

He walked into the kitchen and Peta looked at me, eyebrows raised. "What does he mean by that?" she whispered.

Gabe popped his head back around the door. "What's your address?"

"Why?" I asked standing up straight.

"Because I'm coming around to make sure you watch it."

"Now?"

"No, in three weeks," he scoffed. "Of course now. What's your address?"

I told him, not daring to look at Peta, and he dashed out the door, yelling he would meet me there in half an hour.

"Now do you still think his attention is pity?" Peta asked, looking at me with her hands planted firmly on her hips.

"I honestly don't know," I said with my heart beating a little faster. I shook my head. "No. He's just being friendly. He's friendly with everyone. He's friendly with Jordan, with Kate, with you. Heck, he's overly friendly with Mark. Besides, he's just too young."

Peta chewed her lip and smirked. "Too young? Not sure if I would say too young. Young, but not too young."

"Stop it," I said.

"And how many times has he invited himself to Mark's or Jordan's place to watch a movie?"

"It's not a movie," I said quietly as my mind raced.

"Jordan has been trying to get his attention ever since she laid eyes on him and he's never shown her the slightest interest that could be construed as anything more than civil." She narrowed her eyes a little, pondering what she just said. "In front of me, anyway," she added. "But, my point is, there is no denying the attention he's been showing you."

"You're reading too much into it," I said, but at the same time, a little part of me hoped she was right. I pulled myself up straighter, suddenly feeling a little less second hand.

"Be careful, Lauren."

I snorted. "You don't need to worry about me. Sensible is my middle name. Lauren Sensible Le—Greer," I amended.

* * *

Smudge greeted me at the door and meowed painfully. I reached down and scratched behind his ears, feeling more affectionate towards him than I had done in ages. Gabe said he would be over in half an hour, but that was forty minutes ago. He would be arriving soon and I was in quite a dither. I didn't know whether to change or stay in my uniform. Usually, I would change into my sweatpants and slippers but I hardly felt that would be appropriate. For a second I allowed myself the indulgence of imagining Derek walking in and finding me in Gabe's arms. I relished the look of shock on his face.

The cushions weren't straight on the couch so I adjusted them, emptied the dishwasher, and put more food in Smudge's bowl. I ended up staring at the clock and wishing I had his number so I could text him and put it off.

By the time Gabe knocked on the door, I had convinced myself he wasn't coming and I was stupid for even allowing myself to get excited about it. There were years between us. I wasn't sure how many. He looked to be in his early twenties, so it was possible that he was only five or so years younger. Five wasn't bad. No doubt he just felt sorry for me and was regretting his offer of coming over.

He was probably standing outside the door, scolding himself for getting into this position. I took a deep breath and swung open the door.

"Hey, sorry I'm late," Gabe said, pushing past me and into the lounge. An intoxicating musky smell clung to him and I wanted to lean in and inhale. "The store I went to didn't have it, so I had to travel to the one across town."

With dismay, I noticed he had changed into a clean t-shirt and jeans. The shirt clung to him tightly, outlining the contours of his chest and shoulders, and his jeans hung off his hips just right. I swallowed and internally scolded myself.

Gabe plonked himself down on the couch and slid the DVD onto the coffee table. "Nice place."

I looked around the room as if I, too, were seeing it for the first time. It was nothing like the house I shared with Derek. A lot smaller, a lot older, but I liked it. It had character that our large, modern house hadn't. Even if the decor belonged in the eighties.

"Going for the minimalist look, huh?"

I hadn't unpacked all my stuff. Well, I only had half of it now and unpacking it was just depressing. Smudge sauntered into the room, tail held high. He sat in front of Gabe and blinked slowly.

"Hey, kitty." Gabe reached down to pat him but Smudge pulled his head away and looked at him indignantly. Gabe scooted to the edge of the chair and tried to pat him again. Smudge hissed but didn't move away.

"Sorry about him," I said and shooed the cat. "You want something to drink?"

"You got any beer?"

I grimaced. "Tea, coffee or wine, I'm afraid." I used to keep beer in the fridge. Not anymore.

"Give me a minute." Gabe popped up from the chair and ran out the door. I took the chance to pour myself a wine and sat on the couch. He returned with a half-finished six pack. "Want one?"

I shook my head and adjusted my shirt. I wished I had changed out of my uniform. It was quiet for a few moments as Gabe opened the beer and took a long gulp.

I felt the need to fill the silence so I asked, "Do you enjoy working at the café?"

"Lifelong dream."

"Have you ever considered anything else?"

"Your last name isn't Thornton, is it?" At my confused expression, he shook his head. "Never mind. Architecture, maybe. I never really considered it until I went overseas and fell in love with some of the buildings I saw, but my father is a building developer and I couldn't think of anything worse than pursuing anything even close to his line of work."

I briefly considered asking him who his father was, since Derek was in real estate and I might have heard of him, but then I decided I didn't want to know. There was no need to tie everything back to Derek.

"What sort of architecture?"

"Restoring abandoned buildings. I hate the modern rubbish my father builds, but I love old ruins. I figure, maybe, I could combine the two and use modern construction to help save old buildings. It's just an idea. At this stage, I'm too obsessed with the art of coffee."

I nodded, feeling even more nervous and anxious and stupid than before he arrived. "You don't have a lot to do with your family?"

"My family? Yes. When I can. My father? No."

"Is he the reason you went overseas?"

"You are nosy, aren't you?" he said, laughing.

Colour flooded my cheeks and I cursed my nervous chatter.

"Should I put the DVD on?" He didn't wait for my response and stood to place the disc inside the player. When he returned he sat himself down on the couch beside me.

I can't say I concentrated all that much on the programme. There was a plot though, which surprised me. I thought zombies were all about blood and brains. There was an awful lot of moaning. Gabe sat glued to it, laughing at the gore. All I could think about was how close his thigh was to mine and how good he smelled.

Smudge came back and sat beside Gabe on the couch. Gabe gave me a look of surprise when, after a few moments of a staring competition between cat and man, Smudge deposited himself onto Gabe's lap and started purring loudly.

"So what did you think?" he asked when the credits rolled after the first episode.

"Better than I thought it would be. I don't get the zombies though."

"You don't get them? There's nothing to get. They're zombies."

"But sometimes they can only stumble along and then other times they run. It doesn't make sense. They aren't consistent."

Gabe laughed. "The zombie genre isn't really about consistency. But I like to think of it this way; some people run faster than others, some people walk differently from others. Wouldn't it make sense that when they turned into zombies, the same would apply, making some fast and some slow?"

I screwed up my nose. "I suppose."

"But really, it pays not to think about those things. Just sit back and enjoy the gore. Keen for the next episode?"

I looked at the clock. It was after eleven already and bed was calling. I still wasn't exactly sure why he was here. Was there something to it, or was he just a friendly guy who was invested in my zombie education? "I guess," I said finally.

"So you didn't hate it, then?"

"I'll tell you at the end of this one."

Gabe picked up the remote and pressed the button. Taking the cushion from the edge of the couch, he placed it on my lap, pushed Smudge off and stretched out, resting his head on the pillow. I was surprised and a little confused at his boldness, but didn't complain.

"You really need a bigger screen," he said as it began.

I tried to concentrate on the TV but my eyes kept drifting from the screen to Gabe. He was so relaxed, so casual, spread out over the couch, his head resting in my lap. He watched the screen intently, chuckling each time a zombie was killed. He was tilted to the side so he could see the screen better, his arms folded across his chest and instead of having his hair loose around his face, half of it was messily pulled up onto the top of his head.

I was tense underneath him, conscious of every twitch of his muscles and completely confused about how I was feeling. And of how he was acting. I didn't know where to put my hands. I didn't know how to relax and watch the TV with this young man laid out on me. And I had no idea what was going on in his head.

The only man I had ever really had attention from was Derek, and I was so comfortable with him, I barely noticed how it made me feel. We had dated since we were teenagers and I thought we would always be together. But sitting there with my heart pounding in my chest so loudly I was afraid Gabe would hear it, I found myself feeling like a girl with her first crush. Nervous butterflies flittered about my stomach, my head... everywhere. But Gabe didn't seem to notice. He was so relaxed, so present in the moment, that I soon forgot to feel nervous and found myself engrossed in the programme.

Gabe yawned and stretched high once it was finished. His shirt rode up and I saw the hardness of his abs and the little trail of hair that disappeared beneath the waistband of his jeans once again. I was becoming unreasonably fond of that strip of flesh.

"I suppose I better get going," he said, standing and making his way towards the door. "We could watch more another time?" Maybe I imagined it, but he seemed almost hopeful.

"Sure." I pulled open the door and leaned against it, holding in a yawn as Gabe's gaze slipped from my head to my toes. He made no effort to hide the way his eyes trailed over my body and when he locked eyes with mine, I felt the heat in his gaze.

It made me want to shrink in on myself.

"Thanks," he said quietly. "I enjoyed tonight."

"Me too." My heart pounded in my chest. He leaned in like he was going to kiss me, but then walked out the door, leaving me wondering if I had just imagined it.

6

LAUREN

"Spill," Peta demanded, pulling me into the storeroom.

It was Saturday night and Peta and Shrek were out, without kids, for the first time in months. We were just finishing closing up when Peta called in to get the gossip on what happened with Gabe the night before.

"Nothing happened."

Peta narrowed her eyes. "Nothing?"

"I swear. Nothing happened."

"Start from the beginning."

"We watched TV. That was it."

"I don't believe you."

"I'm not in the habit of keeping secrets from you, Peta. Believe me, if something happened, you would be the first to know. I know it seems a little strange, but Gabe and I are friends, nothing more."

"Gabe doesn't do 'just friends'."

"I thought Gabe always did just friends and that was the problem." I grinned. "I'm hardly what you would call his type, Peta."

"And what would you know of his type? I just don't want to see you hurt again, Lauren."

"I'm not going to get hurt because nothing is going to happen. It's ridiculous to think it could." Already, I was scolding myself for the way I was thinking about him the night before.

"How has he been around you today?" Peta asked, still unconvinced.

"Fine," I assured her. Gabe had been acting the same way he always did, convincing me even more that he was nothing but friendly. The attention I kept noticing was purely in my imagination. Put it down to wishful thinking, or loneliness.

"I think I'll talk to him," Peta said.

Opening my eyes wide, I gripped onto her arm. "Please don't! Imagine what he'd think, what any of them would think if they thought I thought he was interested in me. Promise me you won't, Peta!"

Peta looked at me warily. "I won't say anything, but I'd stay away from him, Lauren. You don't want to be one of the many."

"Many what?" Jordan asked, opening the storeroom door.

"Exactly," Peta agreed.

"I'm confused." Jordan shook her head. "Anyway, Shrek is looking for you. That's not exactly what he said, but it was the general meaning."

Peta gave me a warning look before following Jordan back out to the café.

"For goodness sake, woman," Shrek said, grinning. "We get a night away from the kids, the first one in months, and you want to spend it here at work?" He walked over, wrapped his arms around her waist and nuzzled into her neck. "Maybe we should just go home? I'm sure we could find something to entertain ourselves," he said quietly, but not quietly enough for it to go unheard by the rest of us.

Peta peeled his arms from around her and pushed him away. "That's enough out of you, Dylan Wilton."

Gabe stood, mop in hand, resting his chin against the top of the handle. "What have you guys got planned?"

Peta groaned. "That seems to be the problem. We haven't been out in so long we've forgotten what to do without children. We had dinner, thought about a movie, but now it's too late for that."

"Thanks to you," Shrek added.

"Yes, thanks to me. Tell me, what do normal people do on a night out?"

"I don't know about normal people, but I'm about to meet the flatmates for some pool. Want to tag along? You'd be keen for a game, wouldn't you, Dylan?"

"I'm keen," Jordan piped up, raising her hand. "You can give me some more pointers." She smiled shyly at Gabe and twirled a strand of hair around her finger. So obvious. Gabe's eyes flicked to Peta and he shook his head and held up his hands.

"Can we?" Shrek looked to Peta, begging. "I haven't played in so long. Last time was with you and Derek, Ren." His smile froze. Peta had forbidden him from talking about Derek in front of me, even though they maintained some sort of friendship, strained as it was.

"You'll come along, won't you, Ren?" Gabe said, smirking at Shrek's nickname for me. And there it was again. That hopeful look. The one that made my heart skip a beat. The one that made me forget myself for an instant.

"Of course she will," Shrek answered for me.

"I haven't got a change of clothing," I said, looking down at my shirt, complete with coffee stains.

"You can borrow a top from me, if you like." Jordan reached for her backpack and pulled out a plain white singlet. "This will do, won't it?"

"I'm pretty sure it won't fit," I said, comparing the size of her chest to mine. She was petite. I wasn't.

"Personally, I think it will fit just nicely." Gabe grinned.

"Watch it," Peta warned, and Gabe held up his hands, mimicking surrender once again.

"Come on, Ren," Shrek begged. "It'll be fun."

"Such fun," Peta said dryly. "A nice romantic night out with workmates playing pool."

I took the top and walked into the storeroom to change. Jordan followed me and changed into tight black pants and a sparkly silver top. I enviously looked at her small hips and flat stomach. Thankfully, the top was long enough to cover my stomach. My breasts strained against the fabric, though, like they were trying to escape.

"I wish mine were like yours," Jordan said, looking at my ample cleavage. She pulled her two small breasts closer together, trying to plump them up, and sighed. If only she knew mine were lined with faint white stretch marks, my body preparing itself for something that never happened.

The bar was crowded, but thankfully the pool tables were free. Gabe's flatmates were already there and, by the look of them, had consumed a number of drinks. Gabe introduced me and the one called Stefan got his eyes stuck on my chest. I resisted the urge to cover up and kept my hands firmly by my side, instead of crossing them over my chest like I wanted. It would only draw more attention.

"Hey! Eyes up, buddy," Gabe said, cuffing his head playfully. "Want a drink?" he yelled over the music.

Shrek came up behind us and passed me a red wine. "Got it sorted," he yelled back. He handed Peta and Jordan theirs and returned to the bar to collect the rest, shouting, "This round's on me." The boys clunked their bottles together and tipped them back. Shrek snaked his arm around Peta's waist and kissed the side of her face. "Rack 'em up, boys!"

It was decided that Drew and I would play Stefan and Jordan on one table, while Shrek would take on Gabe, leaving Peta to take on the winner.

Drew was a good player and we won easily. Stefan was too interested in getting Jordan's attention, and Jordan was too interested in getting Gabe's to actually concentrate on the game. Gabe would meet my eyes across the table, and often I saw his gaze slip down to my chest as I leaned over to take my shot. Mind you, I think every man in the room was doing the same. I was tossing between feeling empowered, and feeling ashamed that I felt empowered. Peta even playfully slapped Shrek when she caught him sneaking a peek, but he just laughed it off.

"Not bad." Gabe walked over and stood beside me once Drew and I had won yet another game. "One on one?" he asked.

Jordan sidled between us. "I'll give you a game, Gabe. Though I'm sure you'll easily beat me."

"I asked Lauren," Gabe said firmly.

"I don't mind. Go ahead," I assured them after taking in Jordan's crestfallen face. She smiled triumphantly and took Gabe's hand, dragging him away to the furthest table.

"Do you think I should be worried I'm going to lose another staff member?" Peta sat down and leaned back against the wall, drink in hand. Shrek blew her a kiss from across the pool table. She frowned, then laughed and blew one back. "That man," she said, shaking her head.

I sat down beside her.

"He looks at you a lot." She nodded to Gabe, who looked over at that exact moment. He didn't smile this time, he just stared intently. "That is not a 'just friends' look, Ren."

I sighed. "Whatever it is, I'm ignoring it."

Peta raised her eyebrows then pulled them back into a frown. "Wise choice."

Jordan missed another shot and looked pleadingly at Gabe. He leaned over the table, mimicking the movement of lining up the ball, showing her what to do, then handed the cue back. She attempted the shot, missed the white ball again, and batted her eyes. Finally, he leaned over her and helped her take the shot. She clapped and jumped up and down when the ball went into the pocket.

"He's such a player," Peta said, shaking her head and hiccupping. The hiccups were a sure sign that Peta was reaching her limit of alcohol. She took another sip and some of it spilled down her shirt. "But," her eyes bulged mischievously, "he's a damn good-looking player though. Oh to be young and careless." She hiccupped and put down her drink before clumsily slapping me across the arm. "Well, I've clearly had enough." She swiped her hand over her glass, signalling she was out. "Stay away from him, Ren." She hiccupped again. "You're an attractive woman, just ask Shrek. He's mentioned it enough times. Did you know he tried to get me to convince you to have a threesome once?"

"Peta!" She had definitely had enough to drink.

"Don't worry, I told him you wouldn't be down for it. Not that I ever was." She held up both hands, swearing innocence. "Besides, Derek never let you out of his sight." She laughed and swayed on the seat. "Imagine that! Seriously though, a guy like Gabe would be lucky to get someone like you."

I patted her arm. I hadn't seen her this drunk in ages. Well, not in public, anyway. "Thanks, Peta. But I seriously struggle to see what Gabe would see in me, other than maybe racking up a root in another decade."

Peta snorted and slouched against my shoulder. "He's not that young, and I'd root you in any decade. You know, if I was into that sort of thing."

"Thanks. I think."

"I seriously should have stopped like three drinks ago."

"Nonsense," I scoffed. "When was the last time you let loose?"

"I can't even remember."

"Exactly. I'll go get you a drink of water. You'll feel better in no time."

I walked to the bar and Shrek took my place beside Peta. He wrapped his arm around her and pulled her close. As much as it hurt at times, I loved seeing them together. Shrek adored everything about Peta and wasn't afraid to show it. They'd had their fair share of drama over the years, Peta falling pregnant only weeks after they had met, and it was nice to see them so happy.

"You ready for that game now?" Gabe slid onto the barstool beside me. He followed the direction of my gaze. "They make a cool couple, don't they? How long have they been together?"

"They met not long after Peta moved down here. Maybe about eight years."

Peta followed me down south only months after Derek and I had moved here. Derek introduced her to Shrek and a couple of months later they discovered they were expecting their first child together. It was a shock to say the least, but they made it work.

"It's nice to see."

As the familiar pull of melancholy began to wash over me, Gabe stood, took my hands and pulled me to my feet. "Come on, let's go have that game." He started to drag me from the bar, but I pulled back. "I haven't got Peta's drink yet."

"What's she having?" he asked.

"She's onto the hard stuff. Water."

"Drew!" Gabe called across the room. Drew held up his bottle in response. "Grab the boss a glass of water, would you?"

Drew saluted and headed towards the bar. Gabe tugged on my hands again and dragged me to the pool table.

I collected the balls from under the table and racked them up. "Do you want to break, or shall I?"

Gabe grinned, and once again his eyes slipped to my chest. "Oh, I definitely think you should."

"Get your mind out of the gutter."

I don't know if it was the three wines I had, but as I prepared to take the shot I leaned over lower than I needed to, feeling a little thrill as Gabe's grin widened.

Derek taught me to play pool and I was good. I think Gabe was a little surprised. In no time, I was down to the eight ball. I lined it up precisely, planning to knock it off the rail and into the pocket, and was just taking the shot when Gabe whispered in my ear. "Don't miss."

"Hey!" I whirled around and punched him square in the arm as the ball missed its intended pocket. "You made me miss!"

He grinned and took the pool cue from me. "Guess we will just have to have a rematch sometime." He walked to the end of the table to take his shot.

But two could play at his game. I crouched at the end of his line of vision and leaned over.

Gabe stood and put his hands on his hips. "No fair."

"What?" I asked, feigning innocence.

"Your distraction techniques surpass mine." Gabe leaned over to take the shot again, biting his lip when his focus slipped from the ball to me. He blew out a long, slow breath and took the shot.

"You missed!" I yelled triumphantly.

"I was at a disadvantage."

I took the pool cue and made the winning shot before any further distraction techniques could be employed.

After a few drinks of water, Peta decided she was good to have a dance. We laughed over the ear-splitting volume of the music and reminisced about the time back when this style of life was common for us. Neither of us had been on the dance floor in years. Peta had been too busy with the kids and the café, and I had been too busy planning a life that was no longer an option.

"There you go," Shrek said as he came up behind Peta and pulled her close to him. He dipped in time to the music, grinding his hips against her backside.

"Someone's had a few," Peta yelled. Shrek never danced unless he was half-cut. Shrek whispered something in her ear and she smiled slowly. "We're going to take off," she yelled. "You okay to get home? Want to share a taxi?"

I shook my head. Drew was still over at the pool tables and Jordan, having finally given up on Gabe, had gone home.

"I'll get going too. It's not a long walk. I'll be good."

"You sure?" Shrek asked. He grabbed my hand and pulled me in for an embrace with him and Peta. "We need to keep an eye on you," he slurred.

"I'll be fine. I don't think Drew was drinking, so maybe he can give me a ride," I said, just to assure him. They said goodbye and walked away, caught up in each other.

Gabe wandered across the dance floor as soon as he saw them leave. A girl caught his arm as he walked past but he shook his head and pulled away. She pouted and tugged at him again, holding onto his hand, before walking her fingers up his arm seductively. A tingle of jealousy rippled through me and I shook it away. The girl was what I guessed to be his type, and a lot closer to his age. But Gabe pulled his arm away and shook his head more forcefully, nodding to me. Her look when she glanced my way was one of disbelief. She looked back to Gabe questioningly, but he had already moved past her. His smile grew when I held out my arms and slipped them around his neck. The music was fast but he danced slowly and sensually. His attention and the wine had lowered my inhibitions, and my body responded as he ran his hands down my back and rested them on my backside, drawing me close.

"Watch it," I warned, removing my hands from around his neck and shifting his grip to rest on my waist. He threw back his head, laughed, and said something that I couldn't hear over the beat of the music.

"What?" I yelled.

He said it again but I shook my head.

Leaning in close, he talked into my ear. "You're a tease."

The feel of his lips against my skin just about undid me. I glanced up and suddenly imagined everyone staring. Look at that woman draping herself over that young guy, I could hear them saying. Even if there weren't that many years between us, it looked like there was. Gabe looked young. His jeans were too loose and baggy, his t-shirts were too tight and his hair too long. I, on the other hand, looked every minute of my twenty-nine years, maybe more.

"I'm older than you," I yelled, close enough for him to hear but not close enough to touch him. I didn't trust myself.

"And?" He grinned wickedly.

"And, we're workmates."

"Peta's not here." He looked at me and bit his bottom lip suggestively. It was only the thought of being laughed at that made me take a step back. He held up his hands. "Ouch. Shot down. I'll keep my hands off, if that's what you want."

I nodded. It was a lie.

"Friends?" he asked as he backed away.

"Friends," I yelled back over the music.

He walked back over to the girl who had grabbed him before. She smiled willingly and wrapped her arms around his neck. They danced closely and I felt a little sick watching him as he slipped his knee between her legs and pulled her closer. I didn't know if I felt sick because I had almost behaved like that, or if it was because I wanted to behave like that. Either way, it was clear I needed to stay away from Gabe.

7

LAUREN

I woke to my phone vibrating. I searched the bed with my hand, not willing to open my eyes and let any light that may be lingering in my room into my head. I peered through my eyelashes at the screen.

"What?" I said once I found the answer and speaker buttons.

"You sound worse than me," Peta said cheerfully.

"And you sound much too chirpy to have consumed the amount of alcohol that you did last night."

"That's because it all exited my body rather forcefully in the wee hours of this morning. First time I have ever called in sick. Poor Mark. He wasn't impressed to be heading in on a Sunday morning."

"That bad, huh?"

"Let's not go there."

I dragged myself up in the bed. "Did you end up having a good night, though?"

Peta hesitated on the other end of the line.

"What?" I asked.

"Let's just say there were silk ties and handcuffs involved."

I laughed loudly and immediately regretted it when the surge of pain bounced around my head. "So Shrek had a good night then."

"He better bloody appreciate it."

Peta was known to be far more adventurous in the bedroom after consuming a few drinks than she ever was normally, and Shrek wasn't one to waste an opportunity.

"You get home okay?"

"I left not long after you."

"So Casanova kept his hands to himself?"

"I wouldn't say that, but he did find a more willing participant."

I still felt a little sick when I thought of him dirty dancing with that girl. Still, I shouldn't let it worry me. He was young and free, he could do what he pleased.

"The girls got home without being assaulted then?" Peta asked. I could hear her sipping on, what was no doubt, a strong coffee. The image of me bending low and taunting Gabe with my cleavage replayed in my mind.

I groaned. "Don't ever let me do that again."

One of the kids started to cry in the background. "Got to go, Ren. You okay to still go into work today?"

"Of course I am. A strong cup of coffee and I'll be good to go."

"Well, good luck dealing with Mark. No doubt he's in one foul mood. Talk tomorrow."

Thankfully, Gabe acted completely normal at work. He was his same chipper self, though he did insist on calling me buddy, or pal, or mate, every time we talked. I couldn't help be a little disappointed. Sure, he still flirted, but he made damn certain I knew he wasn't serious.

* * *

The following Sunday afternoon, I was mowing the lawns, headphones on, and singing at the top of my lungs, when the music stopped and my phone started ringing. It was a number I didn't recognise and I considered ignoring it, but in the end, I turned off the mower and pressed accept.

"S'up, buddy?" Gabe's voice said.

"How'd you get my number?"

"Peta gave it to me." Oh, great. Now I was going to get more questions and warnings from Peta. "Hey listen, I know you've got today off, and since it's such a glorious day, I was thinking of hitting the beach. You keen?"

"Um." I wasn't sure what to say.

"Look, before you protest, there is a group of us going, and I don't think I could handle it if you not only shot me down but also rejected my friendship. It would be just plain rude. So I'm not even giving you the chance to say no. I'll meet you at my place in twenty minutes. I'll text you the address. Later, mate." And then he hung up.

I stared down at my phone for a few moments, wondering what had just happened. It vibrated and a text message came through with his address. Immediately another popped through saying that they were going to a beach which was known for the most awesome sunsets and I should bring my camera.

I started to type a response, coming up with the excuse of wanting to weed the garden while the weather was nice. It sounded plausible if you didn't know me all that well. I hated gardening. But I hadn't finished typing when another text came through.

Gabe: Don't even bother trying to think of an excuse. Friends hang. You said we were friends.

I looked down at my grass-stained hands, my worn t-shirt and old sweatpants cut into shorts and decided a shower and change was needed. Afterwards, I pulled on a more presentable shorts and t-shirt outfit and twisted my wet hair into a messy bun. If he thought I would be swimming, he would be wrong. There was no way I was getting into a bathing suit in front of him and even less of a chance I would be going deep into the salt water. I had an irrational fear of sharks and wouldn't be swimming in the ocean for anyone. After I grabbed my camera gear and popped some stuff into my bag, I was already late, and I hated being late. But I needn't have worried as Gabe was in the garage punching a boxing bag while Drew held onto the other side for dear life. He didn't hear me arrive and I watched as his muscles flexed under his sweat-covered skin. Of course, he didn't have a top on, and of course, he looked magnificent, but I did everything in my power to look unaffected. Down the left side of his body, there was tattooed black writing, but I couldn't make out what it said. One thing was clear though. He spent a lot of time working out. The garage was filled with gym equipment and the half-finished body of some sort of old car.

"Oh hey, buddy," Gabe said when he finally turned around and noticed me. "Got your swimmers?"

I shook my head and plonked my bag on the ground, crossing my arms. "It's a glorious day, but the water would need to be near boiling point for me to get in. Hey Drew," I added when he turned to greet me.

Gabe squinted into the sun and I kept my eyes on his face. "And here I was hoping I could give you a ride on my surfboard." He smirked.

"I don't do the ocean."

"Perhaps I can change your mind." He cocked his head to the side and wiped the back of his neck with a towel.

"Doubt it."

Just then, another car pulled up and two girls stepped out. They were both wearing denim shorts with the pocket linings longer than the actual shorts and bikini tops. I could see the goose pimples on their skin from the cool breeze.

"What's she doing here?" Drew whispered to Gabe. The colour drained from his face and he dropped his gaze to the ground.

"Elise, Haleigh." Gabe nodded to them both then leaned over to me. "Elise is Stefan's latest. Haleigh is Drew's ex. Things may get a little awkward."

"Oh, yay," I said dryly. "Teenage drama."

"They're not teenagers," Gabe said.

"They may as well be," I replied.

Elise held up a large bag stuffed with towels and brightly coloured premixed cans of alcohol. "Stefan said we're going to the beach."

"We're planning on it, yeah," Drew replied.

"Mind if I tag along?" Haleigh asked, smiling coyly at Gabe. It was obvious what she was doing but Gabe seemed oblivious.

"Might pay to check with Drew," he replied and started to walk toward the house.

"She's with me, not him," Elise called after him.

"You coming?" Gabe turned to me.

Both the girls looked at me for the first time. They shared a look of confusion and then walked inside. There was nothing left for me to do but follow.

"Take a seat," Gabe said once we reached the lounge. "I'll be out in a bit."

Haleigh's eyes trailed after him and I felt like slapping her. I really did need to stop having the urge to slap other girls, simply because they noticed someone I had no claim on. Drew sat on a chair, a horrified look on his face, simply staring at Haleigh as she very obviously checked out Gabe.

The house was a typical boys' flat. Beer posters on the wall, a coffee table made purely out of empty beer cans, and the floor hadn't been vacuumed for, what I guessed, was at least a month. The TV screen took up most of the wall and there were bean bags planted in front of it, spilling little white balls onto the floor every time someone flopped onto them. I counted at least four drying racks piled with clothing, and a stack of pizza boxes in the opposite corner.

"Sorry about the mess," Drew said, looking around the room.

"Are you still coming to the beach?" I picked my way through the obstacle course of remotes, drying racks and bean bags to make my way to the couch.

Drew shook his head. "Not now."

"Don't let her ruin it for you, Drew," I said quietly. "Don't let her see you upset."

"But did you see the way she looked at him? She made it rather obvious why she's here, and it isn't me." He looked so forlorn sitting there. Placing his shaved head in his hands, he sighed deeply.

"Don't let her walk all over you, come to the beach and have some fun. It will be the best thing you could do."

"You think?" There was a little hope or anger, I'm not sure which, in his eyes.

"I know."

Gabe appeared back in the room wearing only a towel wrapped around his waist, his hair wet and dripping water down his back. He grinned as he walked across the room and leaned over me to grab a t-shirt from the clothes rack. He was close enough to touch. Close enough to lick. His scent was intoxicating. I couldn't keep my eyes off him and he knew it.

"You okay there, buddy?" he asked as he pulled on the t-shirt.

"Right as rain," I replied as he walked out the door, trying not to look at the way his shirt clung to the dampness of his skin.

"So he still hasn't won?" Drew asked.

"Won what?"

"Don't tell me you hadn't noticed his attempts at wooing you?"

"Wooing me?" I laughed.

"Stick to your guns. It's nice to see that he doesn't get the girl every time."

I laughed again. "It's not like that. We're just friends. I'm way too old for him." I lowered my voice. "Exactly how old is he, anyway?"

"Gabe? He turned twenty-one last month."

I swallowed again but for an entirely different reason. He was barely out of his teenage years, almost a decade younger than me. Right then, I wanted to leave. I wanted to get up, drive home, open a bottle of wine, and forget I had ever agreed to be friends with Gabe. Forget I had even met him. What was I doing, hanging with people so young? It wasn't me. I was used to cocktail parties and client dinners, not pizza and beer evenings at the beach.

I reached for my bag but Drew's hand shot out and grabbed my wrist. "If I'm going, you're going," he said.

I put the bag back down and settled into my chair. "Fair enough. But I'm only staying to give you moral support."

Drew grinned. "Thanks. I think you're the only one who is going to be able to convince me that I'm not still in love with her."

"I promise to keep you strong," I said with mock seriousness.

Gabe sauntered out of his bedroom, dressed in jeans and the still damp and slightly see-through t-shirt he had pulled on.

"Ready?" he asked me and tucked his hair behind his ears.

I nodded and my gaze flicked to Drew. "You owe me," I muttered.

There were too many people to fit into Gabe's black jeep so Stefan pulled up his car and pushed open the door for Elise. "Hop in!" he yelled over the thud of the music.

"I'm going to go with Gabe," Haleigh said to her friend.

"Then I'm going with Stefan," Drew muttered, making Elise get out so he could clamber into the backseat.

Haleigh looked at me expectantly, holding the door of Gabe's jeep open. "Are you coming?"

I was just about to climb into the back seat when Gabe pulled me back. "You can ride up the front with me." He waved for Haleigh to hop into the back.

"Beauty before age, I guess," Haleigh said.

"What the fuck, Haleigh?" Gabe said. "Forget to take your bitch-be-gone pills this morning?" He shook his head and slammed the front seat back. I hopped in and stared down at the floor wishing even more, I had just picked up my bags and left.

"Sorry," Haleigh mumbled. "It was just a joke. I'm sure, despite how you look, you're not that much older than us."

Gabe scowled at her in the rear vision mirror before turning the key. Immediately, we were blasted with Def Leppard through the sound system, which was clearly a lot newer than the jeep. It was just nearing the end of the song and Gabe turned down the volume.

"Sorry." He grinned and worked the gear stick into reverse.

"What was that?" Haleigh complained from the back seat.

"A song from before you were even born," I replied, then turned to Gabe. "I'm surprised you listen to them."

"Someone, don't know who, left this CD in my car and it's become my favourite. It's filled with rock hits from the eighties. I love it. They don't make music like that anymore." He pounded his hands against the steering wheel in time to the music as we cruised down the road.

The sound of distant gunfire and hovering helicopters filled the car. My eyes grew wide. "I haven't heard this in ages! My dad used to listen to it whenever Mother was out of the house. I love it."

"What is it?" Haleigh piped up from the back again.

"How can you not know this?" Gabe said, momentarily lifting his hands from the wheel to play air guitar.

"Probably because it's ancient," Haleigh grumbled. "Can't you put on something that was at least released after we were born? Or, most of us, anyway."

We ignored her as the lyrics started and we sang in low gravelly voices. "I can't remember anything…" I threw my head back and laughed, deciding to not give a stuff about what the little miss in the back thought.

Gabe turned it louder and Haleigh blocked her ears. I hadn't listened to Metallica in years. It seemed unbelievable to me at the time, but Derek had preferred softer music. He would have far rather listened to Celine Dion than ACDC.

"Does this song ever stop?" Haleigh whined.

"You should have gone in Stefan's car," Gabe yelled back to her. "He's into that doff, doff, dance crap. Would have been more your style."

We arrived at the beach and Haleigh and Elise immediately stripped down to their bikini bottoms, slathered on some lotion and laid out on their towels. Stefan and Gabe grabbed the surfboards that were strapped to the top of the jeep and pulled on full-length wet suits. I watched them as they ran towards the water and tried not to think about what could be waiting for them in the surf.

"You going to take some pictures? Gabe said you used to be a photographer." Drew nodded to the camera hanging around my neck.

"Sure am," I replied, taking in the surroundings.

It was truly beautiful. Out in the water, a tiny island stood against the clouded sky. The sun was poking through the clouds and streamed in bright rays that reached down to the water. I lifted the camera and took a quick snap of the boys as they ran, one after the other, into the water, their bodies nothing but dark silhouettes against the light. "Want to join me?" I asked, turning to Drew.

He lifted a bag. "Mind if I collect some shellfish while we're at it? I prefer to stay in water that doesn't go above my knees."

We left the girls sunning on the beach and the boys riding the waves and waded out to the little island. There was a walkway to the top with a lookout which I stood on and took photos of the people below. Afterwards, I followed Drew as he climbed over rocks and waded into the water to retrieve the tight, dark shells that held the shellfish.

"Twelve," he said triumphantly, joining me back on the rock. "That should do us nicely for a snack." He was soaked. His jeans were heavy with water and his t-shirt was dark up to his armpits. "Ended up going a little deeper than the knees."

"You look like you're frozen," I said, noticing the way the little hairs were standing up on the back of his neck.

"I'm all good," he said. "Want to help me gather some wood? We'll cook these babies up over a fire."

I had fun collecting the firewood with Drew. He was a nice guy and I could see why Gabe counted him as one of his best friends. I discovered he was a little older than the other boys and worked as a nurse down at the hospital. He had been friends with Gabe since school and spoke highly of him.

By the time the boys came out of the water, we had a fire, complete with a homemade grill for the shellfish, ready and waiting. The girls had pulled on some more layers of clothing and were grateful for the warmth of the fire. Stefan pulled out a box of beers and handed them around the group. Gabe refused because he was driving, and I offered to drive home so he could drink, but he shook his head. I took a beer and gulped down the neck. It was horrible.

Gabe pulled his wetsuit half off and sat beside me. "Get any nice photos?"

I took out my camera and flicked through the digital preview button. There were some good shots of him and Stefan surfing which excited them greatly. Even Elise and Haleigh murmured some sounds of approval.

"Just a couple more minutes," Gabe said, inching closer to me. "The sunsets out here are stunning."

A few minutes passed and I saw for myself what he meant. Gabe stood and held his hand out. "Come on, let's go get some shots." He pulled me to my feet and followed me around the beach as I crouched behind the dry grass, lay on the ground and climbed the sand dunes, getting the angles I wanted.

"So why'd you give it up?" Gabe asked after a while.

"Pardon?" I said, intent on capturing the last of the lingering light.

"Photography? Why'd you give it up?"

I let the camera fall around my neck. "I got pregnant."

"You've got a kid?" Gabe's eyebrows shot up, and I shook my head quickly.

"Miscarriage." It wasn't exactly the truth, but it was easier than telling the whole truth. "I went to work as Derek's PA after that." What I didn't tell him about was losing the baby, the depression, and the endless nights of tears. The way I was broken.

"I'm so sorry." From the way Gabe said it, I knew he meant it. He looked so sad yet so handsome with the last of the light from the sun setting behind him. I lifted my camera and pressed the shutter, blocking out the dark thoughts that started to invade my mind.

"It never really goes away, does it?" He reached out and took my hand. It was a sweet touch, as if, in the moment he needed to feel someone close by. He played with each of my fingers before letting them slip between his and fall to my side. "I lost my brother."

"I'm sorry."

"Two years ago."

"He must have been young." Two years. He lost his brother around the same time as I lost... I didn't want to think about it.

"Car crash. They reckon he fell asleep at the wheel."

I wanted to take his hand like he did mine, let him know I understood, I knew what it was like to lose yourself in sadness, but Drew took that moment to yell out to us.

"Grub's up!"

Gabe's demeanour changed in an instant. He smiled and tugged at my hand again, his sorrow not forgotten, but buried deep. "You like seafood?"

"Love it."

We joined the others and sucked the smoked muscles from their shells. They were juicy and sweet and everything that fresh seafood should be. Drew licked every one of his fingers when he was done.

"Worth getting cold and miserable for?" I asked.

"Totally."

8

LAUREN

"I think we're going to grab pizza for dinner if you're keen," Gabe said when we pulled into the driveway of his house. He turned off the jeep, the vehicle suddenly quiet.

I opened the door. "I think I'll just head home, thanks for inviting me though."

"You have something important to do?"

I shook my head. "I had fun. Thanks. It was…" I flicked my eyes towards the back of the vehicle. "Interesting."

The corner of Gabe's mouth tugged upwards. "Interesting? Not exactly what I was going for, but I'm pleased, buddy." He patted my leg. "Come on, I'll even let you choose the toppings. Well, one of them, anyway."

"Let me out, would you?" Haleigh pushed the back of my seat impatiently. "My leg is cramping."

I got out, tilted the seat forward and Haleigh climbed out from the back. She walked to the front of the vehicle and stretched down to reach her toes.

Stefan climbed out of his car. "Not half obvious, is she?" he mouthed as he walked past and slapped her arse.

She squealed and jumped high. The look on her face when she realised it wasn't Gabe was priceless.

"Who wants what?" Drew asked once everyone was inside. Drew was bombarded with suggestions, until, in the end, he held up his hand and walked out of the room holding the telephone. Gabe flopped on the couch beside me and Haleigh beside him.

"Want some?" she asked, tilting her beer bottle towards Gabe.

He shook his head and held up his own bottle. "I'm good, thanks." He turned to me. "You want something?"

"I might just get going," I said and started to get up from the couch. I felt out of place, like I was invading on the TV set of a teenage drama. I wasn't sure why I came inside in the first place. I had been intending on walking to the car, but somehow I managed to just follow everyone through the door.

"For god's sake, woman. Would you relax?" Gabe grabbed my shirt and tugged me back to the couch. "I haven't seen you relax yet."

I leaned closer and whispered in his ear, trying not to let Haleigh hear. "I just feel a little out of place."

"Who's making you feel like that?" He looked around the room. "Is it the girls? I'll get them to leave right now."

Haleigh glanced over and I gave her an apologetic smile. "No one is making me feel anything."

"So it's just you, then?"

I thought about it for a moment. "Yeah, I guess so."

Gabe stood and grabbed my hands, pulling me up from the couch. "Come with me," he ordered. "I've got something to help with that." He walked, dragging me behind him, into a room directly off the lounge. "Sit," he instructed, pointing to the bed. I ignored him and started to walk around the room, gazing at the walls. Every possible inch was covered in photographs. Old cars with rotten panels streaked with rust, castle ruins with crumbling walls and scattered leaves, weather-battered lighthouses and industrial buildings with broken windows and water-stained walls. The rest of the room was sparse, the only furniture being an unmade bed, TV mounted on the wall, and a dresser covered in coins and wrappers and receipts.

"These are good," I said, pointing at the photographs. "Did you take them?"

Gabe stopped fumbling through the top drawer of his dresser and looked over at me. "Yeah, they're nothing great though. Just a few snaps I took on my phone when I went travelling." He rustled through the drawer some more and finally held up a small plastic bag. "Here we go."

"Weed?" I asked. I hadn't even glimpsed any weed since I was about eighteen. There was a time when Derek and I tried it at a party, but I couldn't remember it doing much other than making me hungry.

"Weed, pot, marijuana, cannabis, take your pick. The green stuff that's known for relaxing people and letting them enjoy the moment."

I laughed and shook my head. "I'm not doing drugs with you."

"Who said anything about drugs?" He took some tissue papers out of the drawer and dropped a thick line of the green stuff along the centre. Rolling it, he licked the seal before offering it to me.

I shook my head again. "I'm good. Honestly."

"Suit yourself." One more fumble around the drawer and he pulled out a lighter. He opened the window and leaned towards the opening, lighting the cigarette. He sucked in, paused, and then blew the smoke out slowly. "You ever tried it?"

I sat down on the bed, surprised when I sunk deep. "You've got a waterbed? I haven't seen one of these in years." I jiggled up and down and the bed swelled in response. "I bet you weren't even born when these were popular."

"I'm not sure if you were even born when these were popular," he said, holding his breath in after taking a puff on the cigarette. He let it out in one hurried exhale. "I remember my mother having one though. She used to get me to lie in the middle and she would sit on the edge and bounce up and down so the waves rocked me. So, as soon as I could, I found one at a second-hand store and set it up. Awesome, isn't it?" He sat down, the water rippling under him, and held out the smoke.

"I haven't touched the stuff in years."

"Time to get reacquainted then. Come on." He wiggled the cigarette. "A little isn't going to hurt you, is it? You never know, you might just end up having some fun."

I held out for a moment and then relented, taking the tiniest of breaths, and coughing as I blew the smoke out.

Gabe lay back on the bed and I waited for something to happen, to feel lightheaded, or happy, or something. But nothing did, so I took another puff.

"Easy there, buddy." Gabe took the cigarette from me and lay it on the bedside cabinet, stubbing out the end with his fingers. "This stuff creeps up on you." He lay down slowly and tugged my shirt so I fell back on the bed beside him. I stared at the photos sprawled across his ceiling and smiled.

Gabe nudged me with his elbow. "You're smiling."

I grinned harder, seemingly unable to stop. "It appears I am."

"See that one over there?" Gabe pointed to a photo, and I followed the line of his finger to an image of a fallen clown face, once the top of a carnival ride. "It's from an abandoned theme park. It's like walking around a horror movie. Some of the roller coasters are still standing and I just walked around for hours taking pictures and feeling like I was the last person left on earth."

"And that one?" I pointed to an image of crumbled stones.

"That's someone's pet dog's grave after that earthquake we had up north."

"You were there?" I asked. The quake had devastated the people living in the area.

He shook his head and propped himself up on his elbow to look at me. "This was a few days after. My brother was part of the volunteer group that helped with the clean-up. I just tagged along after I begged Dad to give me a few days off school. He wasn't going to, but then Clark called him and told him what a tremendous opportunity it was to teach me the importance of helping out those in need and, next minute, I was on a plane."

"So did you learn the importance of helping those in need?"

"Nope. I skived off and took photos while Clark helped with the clean-up. He was most disappointed in me."

"Your dad?"

"Nah, Clark. He was one of those goody-two-shoes types." He snorted. "Goody-two-shoes. Where does that saying even come from?"

"It was a children's story about some poor girl who only had one shoe and some rich dude gave her another one and she was really grateful."

"Seriously? How do you even know that?"

"I have a love affair with Google."

"Google. It's a weird word."

"It's a misspelt number."

"How do you know that?"

We both laughed and said at the same time, "Google."

"What about your brother?" I asked, suddenly remembering what we had been talking about.

"What about him?" Gabe asked.

"Did he forgive you for skiving off?"

"We never really spoke about it. He found me in bed with his girlfriend a while later. It kind of overshadowed the skiving off thing."

"You what?" I picked up a pillow and hit him across the face.

He held up his arms to shield himself, laughing. "It was all her, I promise!"

"That's horrible. Your poor brother. It's a wonder he ever talked to you again."

He shrugged. "I was a little shit."

I stretched my arms along the surface of the bed and high above me. The water sloshed and rocked us. "And you're not anymore?"

"Let's just say I'm less shitty."

I'm not sure how long we lay there in silence, looking at the images on the walls, but when the doorbell rang, we both sat up abruptly.

"Pizza!" we said in unison.

I tried to act normal in front of the others but I had no idea how successful I was. Gabe appeared no different than he ever did, although, he did consume an entire pizza by himself. Rugby was on the TV and Drew became the most vocal and animated I had ever seen him. He yelled at the TV, as if, somehow, the players could hear and heed his advice.

After stuffing myself with as much pizza as my stomach allowed, I lay back on the couch and watched the game. I had never been into rugby but—probably with the help of a recently consumed substance—I quickly became enthralled. And thanks to listening to Derek's comments while watching previous games, I had a general understanding of the rules and found myself yelling at the TV almost as much as Drew.

The couch jostled as Gabe got up. I watched him as he walked towards his room and, just before he went through the door, he turned and looked at me. It was a long and lingering stare, and the intensity of it made my heart pound. His eyes flicked towards his room, and I was certain I saw a slight jerk of his head as if he were signalling me to follow. Then, he disappeared inside. I didn't know if I had just imagined him signalling or not. I sat on the couch uncertain what to do. Uncertain what I wanted to do.

The game became distant to the thoughts in my mind. Finally, after sitting on the couch for what could have been fifteen seconds, or fifteen minutes, I walked over to his room and opened the door.

Gabe had his back to me, staring out the window. He didn't say anything when I walked in so I shut the door and leaned against it, my hand still on the handle. There was something in the way he had looked at me. Everything, every emotion, every thought inside me, was heightened.

Gabe turned and locked eyes with mine, stepping forward until he was only inches away. I tried to keep his gaze but my eyes dropped to the ground as my heart raced. My mind was a jumble of confusion.

He took another step closer, close enough so I could feel the warmth of his body, but not close enough to touch me. He tilted his head and his breath danced along the skin of my neck.

Unbidden, my body arched towards him, offering itself before I even had the chance to refuse. Gabe raised his hand and, with his finger, followed the line of my skin from my collarbone and up the curve of my neck.

I burned under his touch.

As he trailed his finger along my jaw, my breathing quickened. He stopped under my chin and lifted it so I had to look at him. My mind was screaming, though I couldn't tell whether it was screaming for me to stop, or screaming for more.

He didn't waver, just looked at me longingly, waiting for my response, waiting for me to press against him. My lips ached for him to kiss me. My skin tingled at the thought of having his hands roam over my body. But he did not move any closer. He did not touch me, apart from where his finger still burned under my chin.

Hesitantly, his gaze slipped to my lips and I inched forward, not enough to touch, but enough so we were breathing each other. He left me wanting, his mouth only moments from mine and, just before I wilted and closed the gap between us, the edges of his mouth tugged into a smile as if he could sense my need, sense how much I wanted him as if he had won.

He moved quickly then, and pressed against me, groaning when our lips finally met. I gripped the door handle pressing into my back for support.

I longed to melt under him. His kiss was urgent and sensual, his tongue connecting with mine, his teeth grazing my lips. Unable to stand the feelings welling up within me, I tore myself away and ducked from under him to gain my escape.

I felt mortified at what I'd done, embarrassed that I let my desire get the better of me. But at the same time, as I watched him tip his forehead and bang it against the door a few times, I knew I had just tasted something I wouldn't be able to stay away from.

It was just the start of my addiction.

"Denied again," Gabe said finally, drawing in a deep breath.

"I… It's just…"

"You're older than me, we work together, yeah, I know. But just so you know, you're the only person it bothers, Lauren."

"I'm sorry."

"You don't ever have to say sorry."

"I should go."

"You shouldn't drive. Stay with me." He walked over and placed his hands on my shoulders, ducking his head until I returned his gaze. "I promise I'll behave."

"This is ridiculous," I said, shaking my head and looking around the room for my jacket, before remembering I wasn't wearing one. I rubbed my arms, suddenly feeling cold. "Look, I don't know what I'm doing here." I gave a half-hearted laugh. "This isn't me, this isn't who I am. I don't go to the beach, I don't eat pizza from cardboard boxes and drink beer, and I certainly don't smoke pot."

Gabe crossed his arms and grinned, watching as I wandered around the room, looking for nothing.

I stopped. "What?" I demanded angrily.

"You're all flustered."

"Of course I'm flustered. You kissed me."

"So?" Gabe shrugged. "I rather liked it. You didn't?"

I took a deep breath and found myself smiling. "Yes. It was fine," I conceded.

"Fine?" Gabe blinked.

"Okay, it was nice."

"Oh." Gabe uncrossed his arms and walked over to me. "Nice. Thank goodness. I was a little worried there, but if it was nice and not just fine, well that's dandy."

I laughed. "Dandy?"

Gabe sat on the bed and nodded. "Yep. 'Twas a fine and dandy old time." He stretched out his hand. "Please, Lauren. Stay?"

9

LAUREN

I didn't stay. Not because I was afraid he wouldn't stick to his word to keep his hands to himself, but because I was afraid of how much I didn't want him to. I made a mental note to self, don't mix alcohol or drugs with Gabe. The sensible, grown up part of me got messed up when I did.

I got a taxi home and fell into bed. My mind raced with the thought of him. Having someone like Gabe desire me, left me feeling like I was floating on clouds. But still, there was that nagging fear that kept me from him. I couldn't imagine any reason for him to want me.

I was scarred. I was broken. I was used.

He was perfect. He was young. He could have the world.

I had the next day off. It was a national holiday and the café was going to be busy, so I was rather glad to be missing the chaos. It was a relief, really, as I didn't want to see Gabe. I didn't know what to say to him, or how to act. Derek was the only man I had been with. I didn't know how things worked. I didn't know if taking things further with Gabe would actually mean anything to him. But it would to me, so there was no way I could allow myself to get close to him again.

What I needed was a good download session with Peta, a chance to debrief and let it all out. I picked up the phone but it went straight to voicemail. I considered calling the café, but I didn't want to run the risk of Gabe answering. The way I was feeling, the sound of his voice alone could undo all the internal scolding sessions I had been giving myself.

Smudge climbed up onto the bed and reminded me I needed to get up and feed him. He sat on my chest and stared at me, blinking slowly and meowing painfully every few seconds.

"Alright, alright," I said, pushing him off and getting out of bed. He scampered down the hall, towards the kitchen and his food bowl. I tipped in a pile of cat biscuits which he sniffed and turned up his nose. I opened a packet of jelly meat and dumped it in front of him. He took one bite then meowed again. You almost couldn't call it a meow. It was more of a howl. Giving up, I walked away and wondered what I could do to keep myself occupied, and my thoughts off Gabe. I considered doing housework, but since it was just me, there really wasn't any to do. I used to nag Derek about the way he dropped his clothes on the floor or left his shoes in the lounge, but now, I wished I had something, anything, to pick up. Out the window, the sunshine streaked across the wipe marks from my last attempt at window washing. I could wash my windows, or I could grab my running shoes and hit a trail. I decided on the latter.

It had been years since I ran, and after only a few metres, my body reminded me of that. Instantly, I turned red and sweaty and started sucking in long breaths that never seemed to be enough. My jogging pants kept slipping down with every bounce and I had to keep hoisting them up. I really needed a better sports bra too.

Running used to invigorate me. Now, it was just depressing. After probably no more than a few hundred meters, I decided to walk until I eased back into things. I couldn't very well not exercise in years and then expect everything to be the same. I needed to start out slow. The problem with walking, though, was that it gave my mind nothing to concentrate on. Without my chest heaving for air and my thighs crying out for me to stop, my mind filled with thoughts of Gabe. And they weren't innocent thoughts. They were thoughts of him pressed against me, thoughts of running my hands over his muscled shoulders, and him sucking in breath as I ran my fingertips over his chest and followed the slight trail of hair that ran from his belly button and down to…

I had to stop. This was nonsense. I wasn't some twenty-something who had just discovered the gorgeous boy next door liked her. I was a mature, recently single woman who knew better.

I stopped walking long enough to grab my phone out of the small pouch in my pants and plug in the headphones. The little ear buds were annoying, but the deafening sound of music would keep my mind in check.

I was just beginning to enjoy the damp scent of the forest and the sound of music in my ears when my phone started ringing.

"You called?" Peta said in a sing-song voice.

"I need a wine session," I replied with no preamble.

"Tonight? Oh, please let it be tonight. We're supposed to go to the in-laws for dinner and I need an excuse to get out of it. I'm in no mood for them today. I would far rather your company and a good bottle of wine. White. No, red. No. You can choose. I don't care as long as it's alcoholic. Shrek won't say no if I say you need me. It's an emergency, isn't it? Please say it's an emergency."

"Oh, it's an emergency, alright."

"It is? Really? Or are you just saying that because I need it to be an emergency?"

I laughed and a passing runner looked at me, annoyed. Clearly, this trail was not meant for casual phone conversations.

"Either way, it doesn't matter," Peta said.

I could hear the gurgle of the milk steamer in the background and wondered if it was Gabe operating it.

I was in desperate need of help.

"The usual place?" I asked, referring to the little place Peta and I used to like visiting. It was the perfect combination of rowdy and quiet. Half the room was a restaurant and the other half reserved strictly for drinking only. No pool tables, no loud music, no dance floor. Good food and drink only.

"Can we still call it our usual place? We haven't been there in years."

"It will always be our usual," I replied.

"It's a date. I'll meet you at Mana at six o'clock. That way Shrek can drop me off on the way to his parents' and I won't even have to face them. They'll be thrilled. They'll get Dylan dearest and the kiddies all to themselves. Goodness knows what the kids will be like afterwards, they'll probably be all hopped up on sugar and bouncing off the walls. Not that I'll care, because I won't be there!" She sang the last part triumphantly. "Where are you, anyway? It sounds weird."

"I'm out for a walk. Thought it was time I dusted off the old running shoes and took a jog. I think I lasted about two minutes before resorting to walking."

"My, my, I am impressed. I hope you're not going all healthy though. We are having dinner tonight, aren't we? You know how much you love their pasta."

Pasta was somewhat of a treat for me. Certain noises were like a form of torture; chewing too loudly, zips jiggling when people moved, people clicking pens, fingers rapping on hard surfaces, taps dripping, clocks ticking, small noises that somehow managed to overwhelm all my other senses until I felt like screaming. But the worst noise of all was the sound of sauce being mixed through pasta. The squelching sound assaulted my senses, made me shudder and grit my teeth. That was why I never cooked pasta at home. And that was why I just about always ordered it at restaurants. It was a treat, and the pasta at Mana was the best of them all.

* * *

Peta was on to her third glass of red and I lagged behind, still on my first by the time we finished the main course. We looked over the dessert menu enviously, but as neither of us could claim to be at our most slender, we refused the offer when the waiter came back, claiming we were way too full to even consider it. Liars, the both of us.

It was a lot busier than expected for a Monday night, as most people had the day off work. There were no seats left in the bar area so we just stayed at the little table in a darkened corner.

"What's the date?" Peta asked suddenly.

"Twenty-seventh," I replied, looking for a watch I no longer wore.

She grinned. She was wearing makeup tonight, something which she normally didn't do. She said it felt like paint on her skin and even at the age of thirty she still couldn't get used to it. Her hair, streaked with blonde and reddish-brown, hung around her face, shiny and smooth. Her cheeks were flushed with wine. "It's almost one month until your birthday."

"Don't remind me."

"We'll be the same age again. The big three zero." She took a mouthful of wine, tossing her head back and swallowing in a rather unladylike fashion. "Are you heading home?"

I shook my head guiltily. "I told them I couldn't get the time off work."

"Tough boss." She laughed. "You know you can go, if you want."

It was tradition for me to go home for my birthday. My parents, as well as my sister and her family, lived a four-hour drive away. I usually went up to visit four times a year. Christmas and birthdays. Fortunately, my parents' birthdays were a day apart. But the latter part of this year had been all about breaking traditions. The tradition of promised marriage, broken. The tradition of working a desk job, broken. And the tradition of not getting completely wasted while drinking was about to be broken for the second time in a matter of weeks. What was one more tradition?

"I'd rather not. I can just imagine the jibes Mother would work into the conversation. I just don't want to deal with her crap."

"Your dad will be disappointed."

I shrugged and emptied the contents of my glass. "I'll see him at Christmas."

We were onto our second bottle of wine before I began to realise just how much it had affected us. Peta's voice was rather loud as she described Shrek's increased appetite, entertaining our fellow diners with her stories.

"I just don't know what's gotten into him," she slurred. "He wants it, like, every night, and sometimes I just can't be bothered, you know? I just feel like lying there and saying climb on and do your thing. Let me know when you're done."

I laughed and it came out as a snort. A little wine shot into my nose, and it stung and tingled painfully, leaving me light headed. "Why don't you?" I yelled back, because she was yelling.

She rolled her eyes. "Because he's not happy with that. He wants me to enjoy it too," she whined in a deep voice, mocking her husband. She shook her head and took another sip, studying the wine as she rolled it about the edges of the glass. "Considerate arsehole." She dumped the glass on the table before continuing, "But sometimes, I just can't. I mean, I try, but I just lie there while he does his thing, trying to concentrate, and the whole time I'm thinking about the coffee order or if changing suppliers will mean I can get cheaper milk." She picked up the glass again and drained the contents. "The poor guy. He's at home with the little snots all day. Three of them." She held up four fingers, then lowered one. "Three, Lauren. How the fuck did I end up with three?" She shook her hand, dismissing her comment. "Anyway, all he needs is to feel wanted and I can't even muster that. I'm a rotten wife."

"No, you're not. I used to feel the same way with Derek sometimes. Especially while trying to get pregnant again. It became so…" I thought for a moment, struggling to find the right word. "So forced. And then, afterwards, it just never really returned to the way it used to be. It wasn't anyone's fault, it was just different. Sometimes it was good again. You don't feel like that all the time, do you?"

Peta lifted her glass. "A little more of this and I certainly won't be feeling like that tonight!"

The waiter saw her lift her glass and we fell silent as he came over with the bottle. I quickly took the last gulp of mine and he refilled both glasses.

"I saw Derek again the other day," Peta said while staring at her now full glass. "I'm not sure I should drink this. He's looking good."

"He's on a health kick or something, Mother said. Must be the thought of being a parent." I looked down at the band of white around my finger which had faded somewhat.

"I'm sorry." Peta covered my hand with her own. "I shouldn't have brought him up."

"Do you know what gets to me the most about him and that man-stealing-bitch?"

"That he cheated on you? Arsehole."

"Smudge," I said, and we both laughed. "Well, yes, that gets to me, of course, but it's not even really the fact that he cheated. Well, it is, but it upset me more that I didn't even suspect. I feel so stupid.

"You are far from stupid, Lauren Lees." She hiccupped, as was her custom as soon as more than one glass of wine had been consumed. "I'm sorry, Lauren Greer."

"Looking back it was so damn obvious, but at the time I had no fucking idea," I said.

Peta sat up and tilted her head. "Did you just say fucking?" She blinked. "Well, well, look at you, little-miss-good-girl, finally swearing like a trouper. Feels good, doesn't it?"

I threw my head back and laughed a lot louder than I intended to. Some people at the bar turned and looked at me, so I pulled my chair in closer to the table and leaned towards Peta, talking softly. "There was this one time when we were both working late trying to negotiate some contract deal, and the man-stealing-bitch comes in and literally asked if she could 'steal him' for a moment. She needed help with something, and I, innocent and dumb me, was only too happy to oblige. I can just imagine them screwing on her desk in the next office, laughing at my foolishness. I hate feeling stupid."

"He's the stupid one, Ren. He'll realise that soon enough. But by then, you'll be madly in love with someone who sweeps you off your feet and you'll never think of coffee beans while making love."

"Coffee beans are good though. Coffee beans make good husbands."

Peta nodded, and her whole body swayed with the movement. "Coffee beans are good," she said firmly.

I fell silent, thinking of Gabe. The whole reason I wanted to come out with Peta was to tell her of my stupid mistake in kissing Gabe, but I didn't even know how to broach the subject. I'd been avoiding it all night. Finally, I took a deep breath and decided to just blurt it out. "I kissed Gabe."

It was Peta's turn to snort wine. She wiped her hand across her nose. "Excuse me? It sounded like you just said you kissed Gabe. As in the young man—and I emphasise young—that works for me?"

I covered my face with my hands. "I did," I mumbled through my fingers.

"Oh, Ren, you've really got to stay away from him. Nothing good can come of it, unless you're into casual fucking, and I know you're not a casual fucker."

"I know!" I wailed. "I know I'm not a casual fucker, and I'm trying, but he's rather persistent, and just oh so yummy." I sighed.

Peta patted my hand. "Sure, he's yummy, as you put it, but as soon as he's had you, he'll move on and you'll be left feeling like the fool. Again. Remember? You don't like feeling stupid."

"But couldn't I just do it for fun? People do it all the time. One night stand, a tumble in-between the sheets and then it's all over, back to friends, like it never happened."

"Sure," Peta said, raising her eyebrows while taking another sip. "From what I've heard, Gabe would be able to do that no problem, but would you?"

My shoulders slumped and I started to pick the wax off the candle in the middle of the table. "No," I said finally.

"You're a good girl through and through, Ren. You could try to have a casual fling, but we both know you wouldn't like it."

"But I don't really want him as a boyfriend, I mean, he's so young. Maybe I could—"

"Speak of the devil." Peta nodded behind me and my heart started to pound. I pulled myself up straight and looked wide-eyed at Peta. "Or rather, his henchman," she amended. "Hey, Stefan." She pushed back her chair and stood, wobbling slightly and Stefan reached out to steady her.

"Easy there, boss." He turned and noticed me. "Oh, hey, Lauren."

"Hi," I replied brightly. Too brightly. I stood and the room swayed a little. Steadying myself against the table, I turned to face him, sticking out my hand.

He raised one eyebrow, grinned, and shook it, while still steadying Peta. He was with Elise again and she looked at me, not registering. She didn't have a clue who I was.

"Having a good night, ladies?" He gently let go of Peta's arm. She swayed again and he reached out to guide her to the seat. "Very good night, I take it."

I could have chosen a million things to say, from, 'Nice day, isn't it?' to, 'How's Jordan?' But instead, the only words that came out were to ask where Gabe was.

Stefan shrugged. "Stayed at home tonight. Pussy. Something's made him sore and he's sulking in his room."

Elise looked at Stefan sharply and pulled out her phone. "Maybe I should let Haleigh know." She started tapping her phone but Stefan stopped her, glancing at me as he did.

"Don't think that would be a good idea right now." He looked between Peta and me and smiled awkwardly. "We better get going." Then he leaned in towards me. "You alright with getting her home?"

Peta's complexion had suddenly gone pale and she bolted from the table.

"We'll be fine," I said to Stefan, flashing a smile that I wasn't convinced of. "Nothing I haven't dealt with before." I tried to brush it off, embarrassed that we were the drunk ones. It was supposed to be the other way around.

I followed Peta into the bathroom and could hear her retching into the toilet bowl. "You alright in there?" I asked when the heaving stopped. She slumped down the wall and her feet stuck out from under the door.

"When are we going to feel grown up, Lauren? You know what I mean?" She vomited again and the sound of it splashing in the toilet bowl set my own stomach turning. The smell didn't help either. "When are we going to be mature and sensible and not vomiting in public toilets and shit like that?"

"To be fair," I said, opening the door to her stall. "We haven't vomited in public toilets for a while now, well, until tonight."

She laughed and heaved again. "I keep waiting for it to kick in, you know? I keep thinking that one day I'll wake up and be, like, ta-da!" She flung her hands out wide and hit the wall. "Ouch." She tried again and managed to do it without hitting the wall. "Ta-da.

I'm a grown up," she said with far less enthusiasm than the first time.

"Maybe when we're in our thirties?" I suggested.

"I already am and you will be soon," Peta scoffed.

I pulled myself up on the vanity and leaned against the mirror. My stomach kept turning and I hoped it wouldn't be my turn to hug the toilet bowl next.

"I've got three freaking kids, Ren. How on earth did that happen? Three."

"If I need to tell you that, we're in more trouble than I thought."

"Ha, ha." She was quiet for some time before continuing. "Sometimes I wake up, and I'm like—" She stopped talking long enough to concentrate on standing. "How on earth did I end up here?" The door creaked and Peta frowned, leaning heavily against the wall.

"Via a wine bottle, I'm guessing," a voice behind me said.

Peta looked up. "Hey," she said. "You're not supposed to be in here. You're not a girl."

My heart started racing when I registered who the voice belonged to. "Gabe?" I said, peering around the wall that blocked him from my view.

"Stefan called," he said as a way of explanation. He stepped in through the doorway, only to reel back. "My god! What have you been doing in here, boss?"

"Don't talk to me about what I've done. Let's talk about what you did." She wagged her finger at him then clutched onto the door. "I think I need to go home." She turned back to the toilet for a few moments before pulling herself up straight and holding the back of her hand to her mouth. "False alarm," she said and held out her hand to cover Gabe like he was a bright light. "Don't look," she said. "Oh god, this is mortifying."

Gabe cautiously walked over and took her arm. "It's all good, boss. It's nothing I haven't seen before."

"Not from me, it's not!" she said indignantly. She pulled herself away from Gabe but just ended up swaying before clutching for him again.

Gabe chuckled. "Your chariot awaits, boss lady."

With Gabe on one side and me on the other, we managed to get Peta outside and into the front seat of Gabe's jeep. I clambered into the back, and couldn't help the rush of alcohol-fuelled pleasure that rippled through me when I caught Gabe checking out my backside. Then I remembered my earlier mental note to self, do not engage with Gabe while drunk. Then I decided to add another mental note. Don't get a rush just because someone checks you out.

Shrek came out of the house as soon as we pulled up. "Thanks, man," he said to Gabe as they dragged Peta inside. "Looks like you had a big night, my love." They lowered Peta onto the couch.

Peta nodded pitifully. "Just can't handle the jandal no more," she muttered. She smiled at me but the corners of her mouth slanted downwards instead of upwards. "No coffee beans tonight."

10

LAUREN

"You okay?" Gabe asked when we were back in the car.

I nodded. "Just need to sleep it off. I'll be right as rain in the morning." Well, I hoped I would be. I had work the next day. My stomach started to turn and I felt an alcohol-induced wave of sickness wash over me. "Pull over," I said while reaching for the door handle.

Gabe pulled to the side of the road and I got out just in time to empty the contents of my stomach all over the sidewalk. I wanted the ground to open up and swallow me. I waved Gabe away when he stood behind me.

"Don't look," I muttered and heaved again.

Gabe simply drew my hair away from my face and gently rubbed my back. "Believe me," he said. "I've been here countless times before. It's all good."

I managed to slowly stand as the turning in my stomach quelled.

"Feel better?" Gabe asked.

"Just take me home."

Gabe shook his head. "No way, not when you're like this. My house is closer. You're coming home with me."

"No," I said vehemently.

"Don't worry, there is no way I would make a move on you while you're like this." He laughed. "What do you think I am?"

"That's not what I meant. It's just—"

"It's not up for debate. It would be irresponsible of me to leave you alone like this, so the only choice you get is your place or mine?"

My stomach lurched again and I ran over to the small strip of grass near the pathway. I heaved, but nothing came up. Fortunately, I managed to keep it under control for the drive back. Gabe's house was dark and he led me to the bathroom, turned on the shower, and held his hand under the water until the temperature was right.

"You'll feel better once you're cleaned up."

He walked out the door and closed it behind him as I undressed and gingerly climbed into the shower. It was bliss. The water ran over my face as I tipped it back and leaned against the cold tiles. The thoughts in my mind were heavy and thick. I picked up the soap and pressed it between my hands, lathering enough bubbles to run over my skin. When my hands passed over the scar, sadness welled up and the tears started to form. I knew many women had that same scar. But at least for them, it was a reminder of what they had, not of what they could never have.

Damn that alcohol.

When the door creaked open, Gabe informed me there was a t-shirt and a towel waiting. Under the curtain, I saw him pick up my clothes and take them away. I'm not sure how long I stood there, but the water had turned cold when I finally twisted the faucets off. Already, I was feeling a little better. I guess that was the only benefit of vomiting on the side of the road. All the alcohol had been dumped from my body.

I towel-dried my hair and slipped into Gabe's t-shirt. It smelled like him. I lifted up the hem and inhaled deeply.

Whenever women wore men's t-shirts in the movies, they were too big and their bodies sexily slipped into them. That is not how it happened. The t-shirt barely covered my butt cheeks and it clung tightly to my hips and chest. Gabe had broad shoulders and a well-developed chest, but it was still not as well developed as mine.

Pulling the edge of the t-shirt down, I tiptoed down the hall and slipped into Gabe's bedroom. He was already lying in bed, hands propped behind his head. He grinned and let his eyes wander over me unabashed. I tried to stand so my thighs didn't look quite so wide but there was really no point. There was no hiding. Noticing my discomfort, he rummaged in the drawer of his bedside cabinet and tossed me a pair of boxers. "Sorry, didn't think about underwear."

I pulled them on hastily and tossed back the covers so I could climb into bed. Turning onto my side, I curled myself up tightly and gathered the sheets under my chin, trying not to let the nauseating waves of the waterbed get to me.

"Sorry I'm such a mess," I said into the darkness when he turned off the light.

He didn't reply. Instead, he moved closer and snuggled in behind me, wrapping his arm around my waist and holding me tight.

"Night, buddy," he said and I could hear the smile on his lips.

"Night," I echoed, and promptly fell into a drunken sleep.

* * *

Gabe wasn't in bed when I woke the next morning but I could hear noises outside the door, people talking and pots clanging. I poked my head out and managed to slip unnoticed down to the bathroom. Even though I had showered the night before, I still felt grimy. Fortunately, my stomach felt fine. No alcohol left in my system meant no hangover. I was horrified when I looked in the mirror and saw my messed up hair and the lines of smudged mascara that stained my cheeks. Hastily, I jumped through the shower, pulled Gabe's t-shirt and boxers back on, and wrapped the towel around my wet hair.

"Morning," Gabe called as soon as I stepped into the lounge. He and the flatmates were in the kitchen. Drew was cooking bacon and eggs.

"Hungry?" he asked.

My wet clothes were hanging on one of the clothes racks. I had no choice but to walk into the kitchen wearing nothing but Gabe's t-shirt and boxers. Gabe's eyes instantly lit up as they roamed over my body and I was mortified when my nipples hardened, whether, from his gaze or the cold, I wasn't sure. I willed them away but failed. Gabe's eyes were stuck on my chest, his pupils wide and dark, but when he noticed the others doing the same, he yelled, "Eyes off," and the boys obeyed. Gabe pulled out one of the stools at the breakfast bar and Drew produced a plate full of bacon and eggs. It smelled divine, but after a little taste, I decided that was all I needed. Best not to push things.

Gabe disappeared into the shower and Stefan took the opportunity to harass me about the state I was in the night before.

"Gabe's got a hairdryer in his room," Drew said, nodding to my towel-covered wet hair.

I excused myself and walked into Gabe's room to find him stark naked, pulling on a pair of boxers. Mortified, I turned away and covered my eyes. "I'm so sorry! I thought you were still in the shower." The colour rose up my cheeks and I knew that it was the kind when I turned beet red.

Gabe didn't say anything and wrestled with his jeans until I heard him walk the few steps over to me. I stayed facing the door, covering my eyes with my hands, until the pressure of his touch turned me to face him. His eyes were dark. He reached up and pulled at the towel, releasing my damp hair. My breath hitched and I stood frozen as he brushed it back. He stepped closer and I backed into the door as he placed his hands either side of my face. Replaying the last time I found myself in this position, he didn't do anything but stare. His blue eyes burned into mine, waiting for me to pull myself off the door and inch closer to him. I didn't. I held his gaze and lifted my chin a little. If he wanted me, he could damn well make the first move. We were so close, I only needed to move a fraction and I knew I could have his lips on mine. But again, I didn't.

And then, in one smooth movement, Gabe's eyes fell to my lips, his hand snaked around my waist, up my back, and jerked me close until I was pressed against him. I could feel his heat, feel his breath as it came out hot and heavy. He waited for me again, still looking longingly at my lips. My breathing quickened and I could see the hunger in his eyes, but I still didn't move.

Finally, after a few moments where I wrestled with myself and almost gave in, he crushed his mouth against mine. The force slammed my body back against the door and, unable to contain myself any longer, I ran my hands over his shoulders and around his neck, threading them through his hair, pulling him harder against me. His hand fell to my breast and I groaned as my nipples hardened under his touch. His other hand skimmed up the back of my neck and twisted my hair, tugging it against my scalp. My hands remained tangled in his blond locks as he held my head back with his grasp and lowered his head to my breast, sucking on my nipple through the soft material of his own shirt. I melted. My knees buckled and I came undone.

Until I heard the sound of muffled laughter on the other side of the door. I stiffened and Gabe groaned with denied pleasure. He moved back up my body and placed his lips on my ear.

"I need you," he whispered, hushed and breathless. "Please say I can come over tonight."

"Yes." The word escaped before I could catch it.

11

LAUREN

Work was torture. I got three coffee orders wrong and burned the milk twice. Gabe wasn't scheduled on and Jordan, Mark and I completed the close.

"You alright, love?" Mark asked as I wiped the glass in the cabinet for the fourth time. I looked at him, not understanding, and he nodded to the cabinet. "I'm pretty sure that's clean now."

I looked at the way the glass sparkled and laughed nervously. "You're probably right."

"It's quarter to ten. We would like to go home, if that's okay with you?" Mark said, picking up his jacket and shrugging it over his shoulders. It was one of those fake leather ones he had obviously had for years and the elbows and shoulders were scuffed. Jordan was leaning against the counter, tapping on her phone.

"Sorry, I'm just distracted." I stood and wiped my hands down my apron. "Just let me grab my stuff and then we can lock up."

I was desperate, yet terrified, to get home. Gabe knew we closed up at nine and were usually out of there before nine thirty, so, no doubt, he would be waiting for me. I picked up my bag and sighed. I had almost talked myself out of going through with it. I hadn't slept with anyone other than Derek. Ever. What if I didn't do it right? What if he took one look at the stretch marks or my scar and went running for the hills? He wouldn't be used to bodies like mine. I couldn't stand the thought of it.

I drove the long way home and even slowed down at orange lights rather than racing through them. But Gabe wasn't waiting when I got there so I had the chance to take a quick shower, make sure I was groomed and smooth. What to change into was a problem. Usually, I would get straight into pyjamas, but I didn't want to greet him wearing something that had fluffy pink pigs on it. In the end, I blindly pulled a loose flowing sun dress over my head. I had chosen underwear that was neither flashy nor too casual. I didn't want him to think I had dressed up especially, but I also didn't want him to see me in the underwear I usually chose to wear. There was never this pressure when I slept with Derek.

Smudge became the most affectionate cat in the world and wrapped himself around my legs, smooching against me and purring loudly. I shoved him away but he persisted until I sat on the bed and pulled him into my lap. "What am I doing?" I asked him. He only purred in response. Fat lot of good he was.

I was in the middle of tidying up my bedroom and wondering if he had chickened out, or if he had only ever wanted me to say yes so he could then reject me, when the doorbell rang. My heart leapt to my throat. I looked at my reflection in the mirror and took a few deep breaths to calm myself.

"Hey," I said, pulling open the door and smiling brightly. Too brightly, probably. I toned it down a little and then just stood there awkwardly staring and holding the door open.

"Hey, yourself." Gabe kissed me on the cheek then walked past into the lounge. Placing a bottle of wine on the coffee table, he leaned back on the couch. "Hope you haven't been waiting too long. I didn't want to appear too eager."

I laughed and it came out high pitched and unnatural. "Shall we?" I said, reaching for the bottle and holding it up.

I had moved to the kitchen and reached for the wine glasses at the top of the cupboard when I felt the warmth of him behind me. I held my breath as his hands fluttered on my waist. A rush of excitement rippled in my chest. Slowly, I lowered the glasses to the bench as he placed his lips against my neck, kissing it softly. I closed my eyes, silently cursing as I literally quivered with desire. He ran the tip of his nose along the curve of my neck and nibbled on my earlobe.

"Which way to the bedroom?" he whispered.

I could do nothing but nod in the direction of my room. He took my hand and led me down the hall, stopping occasionally to push me against the wall and kiss me urgently. I wanted him. I needed him. But as he pushed against me, I couldn't help the terror that ran through me at the thought of him seeing me naked.

He pulled me into the bedroom and shut the door on a curious Smudge. I stood helpless and unsure of myself as he approached. Pulling his shirt off, I inwardly gasped at the sight of him. He was splendid. Tanned skin, mussed up hair and glorious smooth muscles that flexed as he moved.

But he gave me very little time to admire him as he drew me close, took my face in his hands and crushed his mouth to mine. His kiss was so sensual and I felt sick with nervousness as my desire for him increased. My hands hung limply at my side, unsure where to touch. Gingerly, I ran them softly up the skin of his back. The harder I pressed into him the louder he groaned. And it was a glorious groan, almost enough to make me forget myself, but not quite. When his hands ran down my sides and grabbed for the hem of my dress, I held them in place.

"Don't," I whispered.

"I want to see you," he said between kisses on my neck.

"I… I…" I stammered. "I don't—"

He pulled away from me and sat down on the bed, tugging me with him as he held onto the hem of my dress. Releasing his grip on the material, he undid the buttons on his jeans and then stood, letting them fall to the ground and I saw his fullness, hard and ready, under the thin material of his boxers. I swallowed and let my eyes drink him in as he stood before me, holding himself on display. I had never seen anyone so perfect, which only confused me all the more as to why he would want me. I ran my eyes back up his body to find him staring at me, just a hint of a smile playing at the corners of his mouth. He tucked his hair behind his ears and took my hands.

"I want you," he said huskily. He looked down at his erection and then back up at me. "I really want you. Every part of me wants you. Isn't that all that matters?"

I took a hesitant step forward and in one quick movement, he ripped my dress off. He barely glanced at me before nuzzling into my neck, kissing, licking and sucking on the flesh around my breasts. Reaching behind, he fumbled with my bra and, within moments, my breasts were bare and exposed.

"I want you," he said again.

Then he took me in his arms and we fell together on top of the bed. Running his hands along my sides, he took my breast in his mouth, swirling his tongue over my nipple again and again. My breathing quickened and I moaned as he teased my flesh, grazing his teeth over my skin and nibbling at will. I felt the moisture seep between my legs and knew my underwear was soaked. I ran my hands over his shoulders, taking in the firm smoothness of his muscles as he reached down and tugged at my underwear.

"My god, you're wet," he said as he pulled them down my legs and flung them to the floor. Bending over the side of the bed, he reached for his jeans, searching the pocket and removing a foil wrapper. He ripped it with his teeth, dropped his boxers and stepped out of them. He was hard. And large. But again, he barely gave me the chance to look, as he expertly covered himself, climbing over me and plunging inside. I gasped as he filled me and he groaned loudly. Propping himself up on his elbows, he withdrew slowly until he was almost out but not completely. He looked at me and kissed the tip of my nose. "Okay?" he asked.

I couldn't speak, I couldn't utter a word, so instead, I nodded and he slowly thrust back inside. I had never felt someone so hard, so virile, and it turned me on no end. He filled every part of me, causing me to moan in wonder. He kept his eyes on mine as he moved in and out. His rhythmic motion and the way the base of him pressed against me as he rose with each thrust, built inside. I bit my lip, trying to contain my growing desire. I had never come solely from penetration before but the urge was there, and it throbbed until I wasn't sure I could contain it any longer. The sight of me struggling caused him to start moving more urgently. His thrusts became harder and faster, and I arched back on the bed, twisting the sheets between my fingers.

"Come," he pleaded, and with an urgent thrust he grunted and stayed deep inside, as my body obeyed his request and I shuddered. His eyes stayed glued to my face, his body rigid as wave after wave of pleasure rippled through me and I clenched against him. When I finally began to breathe again, his release came quickly. He cried out with one final thrust and his hardness pulsated inside. He stayed still, eyes closed until the last ounce of him was done.

Slowly, he pulled out and flopped down beside me, his arm flung over my chest.

He grinned lazily, and the side of his mouth twitched. "That wasn't so bad now, was it?"

I couldn't help but laugh and slid out from under his arm, standing to reach into my drawers and pull out a night shirt to slip over my head. Gabe reached for his boxers and pulled them on, having discarded the used rubber. I tried to read the tattooed ink running down his left side but his arm was in the way.

"Want that glass of wine now?" he asked.

I moved toward the doorway but he stopped me, grabbing my arm and planting a soft kiss on my shoulder. "I'll get it. You stay here."

I flicked back the covers on the bed and hopped in. Moments later, Gabe returned, bottle in hand.

"Do we really need the glasses?" he asked as he moved to the other side of the bed and climbed in. I watched him, coveting every inch as he pressed close to my side. Even though I had just had him, I wanted him again. He lifted the bottle and took a large gulp before handing it to me.

"Cheers," I said and tipped the bottle back.

"Easy there, tiger. We don't want a repeat of last night."

"Hey! I'll have you know that was after numerous bottles of wine, not one sip."

"I wouldn't call that a sip." He took the bottle and brought it to his lips, tilting it slightly. "That was a sip."

"That's what I did."

Gabe rolled his eyes. "Sure it was." He took another swig of the bottle and winked at me.

"What does it say?" I took the bottle from him and took a polite sip.

"What?"

I nodded to his side. "Your tattoo."

He rolled over and tossed the covers off, exposing the flesh under his arm. I put the bottle down on the bedside cabinet and studied the words. They were in a thick, old fashioned calligraphy and a little hard to decipher.

"Don't die wondering," Gabe said. "It was Clark's favourite saying."

"So Clark, the one that helped out after the earthquake, he was the one that died?"

Gabe nodded. "He had just come home from university and he and Dad got into this big argument. It was really late at night, and despite the fact that he had not long arrived, he took off and drove back. He never made it though."

"So the last thing he did was fight with your dad? That's got to be tough on him."

"On Dad? He's a prick. He probably blames Clark. Clark wanted to quit studying law and go overseas to help with some charity thing. You know, save the kids, clean the water, build a house, something goody-good like that. He hadn't told Dad yet, but when he got home, Dad had already opened some letter saying he had been accepted into the programme. Dad blew his lid and Clark took off."

I reached over and traced over the ink with the tip of my finger. The skin beneath was raised and it tightened under my touch. Goose bumps dotted his skin. Gabe reached out and pulled me to him.

"Must have been horrible," I said as he wrapped his arms around my waist and I buried my head into his chest. His smell was heavenly.

"I haven't lived at home since. I pretty much spent the next six months drunk and living on people's couches. Then one day I woke up and remembered Clark saying to me, 'don't die wondering'. It was like one of those things in movies where people suddenly realise something they should have known all along."

"An epiphany?"

"Yeah, that's the one. Anyway, I got the tattoo, took off overseas and the rest is history."

"Are things okay with your dad now?"

The stubble on his chin rubbed against my scalp as he shook his head. Within minutes, his heavy breathing told me he was asleep.

12

LAUREN

I woke entangled in Gabe's embrace. I stirred and found him watching me, his eyes dark and burning. Gently, I ran my finger over the swell of his chest, tracing each ridge of his stomach and along the line of his boxers. Gabe sucked in his breath as I explored before letting it out with a low groan.

His groans were glorious. I had never heard such a delightful sound. And, when I ran my hands over the tops of his thighs, he moaned so quietly I strained to hear it. Pulling the covers back, I marvelled at his body. It was so tight, so firm, but at the same time so soft and smooth. I wanted to touch every inch.

Lifting myself off the bed, I rose and hooked my leg over him until I was sitting above him, feeling the pressure of him rise against the nakedness beneath my shirt. He locked eyes with me, his gaze scorched with desire, and I bent down to kiss him. He rose to meet me, urgent to embrace, but I pushed him back down onto the bed. I wanted to relish the moment, take time discovering his body. It was too new, too foreign not to explore.

I kissed him fully and he responded passionately and deeply, straining against where I had his hands pinned against his sides.

Placing a trail of kisses across his skin from his jaw line down his neck and over his chest, he leaned his head back into the pillow and sighed loudly. I kissed each nipple and he rose up on his elbows to watch. But I pushed him back down and continued to kiss him, ignoring his desperate groans of frustration. They turned more urgent when I kissed the soft flesh between the band of his boxers and his belly button. Slowly, I ran my tongue all the way up his torso, to the little dip between his collarbone. He reached up and gripped my arms, digging his fingers into my flesh.

"Want me to stop?" I asked.

"No." It came out a guttural whimper.

I pressed my breasts, hidden beneath the thin material of my shirt, to the naked flesh of his chest and kissed him fully on the mouth again. Cupping my face, he kissed me fervently, and clung to me as I pulled away.

"My god, let me have you," he hissed between breaths.

I shook my head and grinned seductively as I kissed my way down his chest and over the ridges of his hard stomach. His skin quivered when I slid lower down and kissed the line of the muscle that led to his pelvis and dipped under his boxers. Lifting his head off the pillow, he propped himself up on his elbows, eyes burning with hunger as he watched. I tugged on his boxers and pulled them down until they popped over his erection. As I kissed the soft flesh of his inner thigh, drawing closer and closer but never satisfying, he closed his eyes and rolled his head back, letting out a tortured and ragged breath.

When I took the tip of him in my mouth he tensed. I pushed deeper, feeling bold and daring, something I hadn't felt in years.

"Careful," he said. "I won't be able to handle that and I need to be inside you."

I climbed my way back up his body and couldn't help smiling at the way he watched me. His pupils were wide, his expression dark. His desire was extremely obvious. And I drowned in it.

"Let me get a rubber." Frantically, he searched through the pockets of his jeans lying on the floor and slipped on the protection. I sunk onto him and he let out something guttural, almost animalistic. He grabbed for the hem of my shirt but I shook my head and held his wrists in place so he couldn't lift my top.

"I want to see you," he groaned.

I moved slowly, distracting him by grinding back and forth and feeling every inch of him inside me. His hands moved up and over my hips until they found the soft flesh of my breasts. He started to take control of our movements, his hands falling to my hips as he dug in his fingers. I held onto his shoulders as he rolled us over and hovered over me.

"God, you're sexy," he breathed.

Then he was inside me again. Slower this time, rocking back and forth, sucking on my neck and nuzzling into my breasts under the shirt. We came together and he slumped over me.

"Wow," he breathed in my ear. He stayed pressed heavily on me until I nudged him with my shoulder. "Sorry," he rolled over onto his back. "Wow," he said again.

I climbed out from beneath the covers and walked into the ensuite. When I came back Gabe had rolled onto his stomach, his arms spread wide over the bed. He looked glorious. He grinned and lifted the covers back, patting the space beside him. Once I climbed in, he snuggled against me, sighing deeply.

I looked over at the clock. It was late and I was due in at work in a couple of hours. I sighed. Work seemed like another world from where I was.

"What's the matter?" he mumbled, his words slurred with relaxation.

"Work."

"Do you have to go in soon?"

"Yeah."

Gabe untangled himself from me and hopped out of the bed. "Guess that's my cue."

"You don't have to leave now. You can stay a little longer if you like."

Gabe shook his head as he pulled on his jeans. I watched him from the cover of the bed, once again marvelling at the design of him. He smiled but there was something awkward about it.

"You coming into work later?" I asked, suddenly feeling nervous and pulling the covers close to my chest.

Gabe shook his head as he pulled on his t-shirt. "Day off." He bent over the bed and placed a chaste kiss on my cheek. "Thanks for last night."

I smiled. What was I supposed to say? 'You're welcome?' 'Thank you, too?'

"And this morning," Gabe added. He hovered at the door. "Catch you later?"

"Later," I replied and then he was gone.

* * *

I didn't hear from Gabe for the rest of the day. That was normal though, wasn't it? I considered calling him but I didn't want to seem needy or desperate or too keen.

When Peta said he called in sick for his shift the following day, I began to worry. I had that dread in the pit of my stomach again. I began to replay our time together over and over in my head but each time I did, it seemed less and less romantic and more like I

115

was too eager. I could just imagine him retelling the tale to his friends, laughing and making fun. 'You should have seen her. She was all over me.'

I barely slept, not being able to get rid of the weight on my chest and the sickness in the pit of my stomach. I felt so foolish, so dumb. Again. Everything I had worried about had come true.

Peta noticed something was wrong at work but I just lied and said I was coming down with something. "Perhaps it's the same thing Gabe has," I offered.

She shook her head. "Something strange is going on with him. He came in this morning and said he needed a couple of days off to, 'sort some shit', as he put it. And then he asked for an advance on his pay. Strange boy."

I swallowed the lump at the back of my throat. He was avoiding me, plain and simple. I guess he was hoping that if he gave me enough space, I would see our time for what it was. Nothing but a tumble in the sheets. Nothing more than one of the many. Nothing more than an amusement.

He was a challenge which I had failed miserably.

13

GABE

I was an arsehole.

I was every name I had ever been called and worse. I didn't expect to feel so guilty. The lead up was a game, a challenge, but when it was all said and done, I felt guilty as hell. She didn't deserve to be treated that way.

It didn't hit me until I woke the next morning. It took me a few moments to figure out where I was, as I usually always woke up in my own bed. Regardless if I had shared a bed, a couch, or the backseat of a car with someone earlier, I always dusted myself off and returned home. I don't know what was different that made me stay. I didn't even decide to spend the night, I just woke up there. There was something so satisfying, so rewarding about having sex with Lauren, that I must have fallen asleep.

When I woke, her body was entangled in mine and the feel of her breasts, so soft, so full, pressed against my skin, meant I instantly got a hard on. I didn't realise she was awake until she started running her fingers over my chest. I couldn't ever remember being so hard. It didn't normally work like this. Usually, I woke with a hangover and alone, having had a drunken and sloppy fuck the night before, well, at least on my end. I'd never had this. I tried to stay still, tried to force myself to resist as she ran the tips of her fingers over my flesh, but in the end, it was simply too much and the urge to fuck her won.

As I said, I was an arsehole. I should have never taken that stupid bet. I should have never gone near her.

I couldn't face her. One look at me and what I had done would be written all over my face. Instead, being the coward that I was, I called in sick and then begged for an advance on my wages. Technically, I had won the bet. I just wished I hadn't. Mark was surprised when I handed him the money. I didn't offer any explanation, just shoved it in his hand and walked off.

Three days later and I still hadn't faced her. I spent my time playing x-box in my room and beating the shit out of the boxing bag. I had callouses on my knuckles to prove it.

She called once. I cursed myself for not answering but she deserved so much better than a jerk like me. The message she left was casual but forced. She had heard I was sick and was just checking to make sure I was okay. I never called her back. And she never tried again.

My flatmates assumed I was pissed because I didn't score, but I knew Drew, at least, suspected there was more to it. He usually did.

Sleeping with her had changed things for me. I couldn't think about that night, or rather, the next morning, without getting aroused. Maybe it had something to do with the fact that she was the first person in recent history I could remember making love to when I wasn't shit-faced.

Or, maybe it was the fact that I had just referred to it as making love.

Whatever it was, I needed to stay away. I knew how these things worked. Even if I ignored the guilt I felt, she would find out eventually. Mark would open his trap or Drew or Stefan would blurt it out one drunken night. And then she would look at me with those lonely eyes and I wouldn't be able to stand it. Of course, I would have to face her eventually, but I would prefer it if she thought of me as a general arsehole rather than a specific one.

Pulling myself up from my bed, I walked into the lounge. Drew was there, watching some crap on TV.

"Hey man," he said as I passed.

I grunted and reached for the bottle of bourbon on the bench. The one in my room was empty, not that it had done its job. Getting drunk was supposed to make me forget what a jerk I was, not make me think about it more.

"So, everything's good?" Drew turned down the volume a couple of notches. He obviously thought we were going to talk.

"Yep," I replied gruffly and flopped down on the bean bag. I lifted the bottle and took a long drink.

"Nothing you want to talk about?"

I glared at him and took another swig. "Nope."

"Fine." Drew nodded and turned the volume back up. We sat and watched the investigation of some dude who chopped up people for fun. I couldn't understand why people watched that shit. Zombies, sure, but not real stuff. Not reality. Then, the volume turned back down and I looked over to Drew, preparing for another question.

"What?" I asked when he said nothing.

"So you lost?"

"Lost what?" Then, it dawned on me. "The bet? Yeah, I lost."

"And you're dark about it."

"I'm not dark because I lost the fucking bet." I lifted the bottle to my mouth. "Seriously? You think I'd be sore about that?"

"Well, something's eating at you. What did you expect me to think?"

"I'd expect you not to assume I was so fucking shallow." I was highly pissed off. Blood pulsed through my veins. I needed to use the boxing bag again.

"Sorry, man. Just thought you might want to talk about it."

I ran my hand through my hair and looked at him. The volume went down some more. "It didn't go down how you think."

Drew didn't say anything. He just lifted his beer and drank.

"I won," I snapped.

"You fucked her?"

"I wooed her."

"You're really going with that?"

"Whatever. The point is, I won the bet. I just didn't want Mark knowing."

Drew shook his head. "I don't get it."

"I won and it made me feel like shit. I just don't want her to find out and hate me, okay?"

"So you're planning on 'wooing' her again?"

"No," I scoffed. Why couldn't he understand? I just needed to not be hated by her. I wanted her to smile when she saw me, not scowl. "I just feel guilty or something. I shouldn't have done it. It was stupid."

"You like her," Drew said, smirking.

I took another swig of bourbon. I guess I liked being around her. It felt good. I liked watching her as she talked. Her face was so expressive, so animated and when she laughed she threw her head back and laughed properly, not all fake and giggly or hiding behind her hair. And it wasn't just when she was doing the talking, either. When I spoke, she looked at me as though I was the only person that mattered. When I was around her, I felt like she saw me in a different way than other people did.

"Shit," I said and stared at Drew. "I think I do." Somewhere along the line, things had changed. I was just too fucking stupid to see it. Now I just had to hope she would forgive my stupidity.

14

LAUREN

On my day off I lay in bed and watched TV, trying to block the memory of sleeping with Gabe out of my mind. Everything was twisted in there and I didn't know which images to trust. The ones where it felt like heaven? Or the ones where I literally threw myself at him the next morning like some strange sex-craved cougar?

I didn't know how casual sex worked. Were there certain things you did or didn't do? Had I crossed some imaginary line that meant he couldn't even face me for days after?

My phone had been ringing since nine in the morning. Mother called, Morgan called, and then Peta called, twice. I let them all go to voicemail, and Smudge watched on in disgust. Even though no one knew what had happened between Gabe and me, I still felt foolish. I just wanted to press the undo button. But there was none.

When Peta called the third time, I caved to Smudge's indignant glare and answered.

"Hey," she said.

"Hey, yourself." I tried to sound lively.

"Are you okay? I've been trying to call and so has your sister."

"Morgan called you?"

"Your mother called her," Peta said.

"I'm fine," I lied. "Just feeling a little under the weather and I couldn't be bothered picking up."

"Okay, well just let me know if you need tomorrow off. I might be able to get Gabe to come in early to cover you."

My heart pounded a little harder. "Is he coming back to work tomorrow?"

"He's here now," she said. "Must have sorted whatever he needed to. He's rather quiet though." She laughed. "Well, quiet for Gabe, anyway."

I swallowed. "Okay. Well, I'll text you if I'm still not feeling well tomorrow. But I'm sure I'll be fine. I just need a good night's sleep."

Gabe was back at work.

Tomorrow, I would see him.

I should probably get out of bed and practise my, 'I'm-perfectly-fine-it-didn't-mean-anything-to-me-either-I-sleep-with-guys-almost-a-decade-younger-than-me-all-the-time,' face in the mirror. Pulling the covers up closer to my chin, I closed my eyes.

It could wait.

* * *

I watched the clock all day. The closer it got to four o'clock the more nervous I got. I told myself to do everything within my power to act normal, as if I threw myself at men all the time. So when someone cleared their throat behind me, I mustered all the strength I could and turned around with a blank, but strong, expression.

It was soon replaced with shock.

Derek was kneeling on the ground, a bunch of flowers in his hands, the entire café silent and watching.

I lowered myself down to his ear. "What are you doing?" I hissed.

"Please," he said quietly. "Just go with me." He cleared his throat again. "Lauren Lees," he began, giving me a hesitant grin at the use of my former nickname. "I've been a complete idiot and I know I have no right to ask you to forgive me. So, I'm not going to. I'm not going to ask for your forgiveness, not yet. What I want to ask you is, will you give me a chance to earn the right to ask for that forgiveness?"

"Derek," I half whispered, half hissed. "Don't do this. Not here."

The café was deadly silent. The customers looked at me expectantly, some with hopeful expressions on their faces, others with expressions that simply read, hurry up. A gust of wind flowed in as the door swung open and Gabe burst inside. He saw Derek on his knees and looked to me.

"Lauren?" His eyes flicked between Derek and me.

Derek, having recovered from the interruption and completely oblivious to who Gabe was, turned back to face me, and lifted the flowers higher. "Lauren Lees, would you please go out to dinner with me?"

My heart was in my throat. I looked from Derek back up to Gabe, whose eyes were wide and studying mine questioningly. But then his gaze dropped to the ground and I caught a glimpse of the guilt held behind them. I knew I meant nothing to him.

Derek cleared his throat again. "An answer would be nice." Some of the customers laughed. I looked around at all the people staring, waiting for my answer and smiled hesitantly.

Gabe looked up again and I couldn't help but look back at him. But the guilt was still there and I knew he was just gauging my reaction to him, attempting to ascertain what level of hatred was in my eyes. I let them glaze over and turned all my attention to Derek. Even though everything in me felt like screaming at him for putting me in this situation, I couldn't bear to see him embarrassed.

"Yes," I replied and the café broke into applause. Derek got to his feet and handed me the bunch of yellow daisies. He kissed me on the cheek and murmured thank you in my ear.

"You don't know how nervous I was," Derek said.

"There was no need to be nervous," I replied sharply. "You should have known there was no way I would have refused you in front of all these people."

He caught the anger in my tone. "I'm sorry, Lauren. I just thought a grand gesture would tell you how serious I was, how much I want you back and might show I know I've been a complete idiot." He dropped his head under my harsh glare. "You don't have to come to dinner if you don't want."

"I'm working tonight, anyway."

"What about tomorrow night?"

"I'll have to check with Peta as I'm scheduled to work." I folded my arms. "What happened to the man-stealing-bitch?"

"Tracey?"

I nodded. "That's what I said."

"She…" Derek dropped his gaze. "Well, it's a long story but she isn't in my life anymore." He looked back up and rested his hand on my folded arms. "Look, I don't want to go into it here, in front of all these people."

"Well, perhaps you should have thought about that before barging into my workplace and making a scene."

He took a step back. "I promise, I'll explain everything tomorrow. Just give me a chance. One dinner is all I'm asking."

It took all my will power not to look around for Gabe, even as my former fiancé was standing in front of me, begging for a second chance. I knew this man. I knew what to expect of him. I knew what he expected of me. I softened a little but still kept my arms firmly crossed over my chest.

"I said I'd go to dinner as long as Peta doesn't mind me taking the time off. I'll text you tomorrow, but, as for now, I really need to get back to work."

Derek smiled and it was a familiar smile, one that I knew how to read. He was genuinely happy and I couldn't help returning it, just a little.

"You won't regret it, Lauren," he said.

I turned away without saying a word and walked into the staff room. I needed to be alone. I needed to breathe. I sat down on a bag of beans and took a deep but shaky breath. Peta popped her head around the corner moments later.

"Well?" she said and took a seat on the bag next to mine.

I rolled my eyes and took another deep breath.

"Were you expecting that?"

I shook my head. I hadn't even heard from Derek since that day he came into the café.

"You okay with it?" she asked quietly, rubbing my back.

I shrugged, unable to trust myself to speak. The events of the last few days had left me feeling exhausted and this last encounter with Derek was a weighted pressure that was proving to be a little too heavy.

Peta patted my back. "You know I'm with you whatever, right?"

I nodded and pushed back the tears that were threatening. "I suppose one meal won't hurt me," I said finally, trying not to let my voice crack. "Can I have tomorrow evening off work? Maybe Gabe could cover." I wiped away the tears from under my eyes that had escaped.

"Something strange is going on with him. Have you noticed?" Peta said, no doubt thinking that directing the conversation his way would distract me from my current woes. Little did she know.

"What do you mean?" I grabbed the corner of my shirt sleeve and used it to wipe under my eyes, removing any mascara smudged by tears.

"Lazy bugger didn't even start his shift. He just walked out. Not sure what's going on with him but he better sort it soon. Good looks can only get him so far."

I was actually grateful that I wouldn't be working with him that night and breathed a little easier. "Goodness knows with that one." I tried to sound light hearted but failed miserably.

"Oh, Ren," Peta said, wrapping her arm around my shoulder and pulling me into her. "Why don't you just work the eight to five shift for the next week or so? It will give you the chance to sort things out with Derek. Or not."

"You sure?" I sniffed. Working that shift would mean I would only have to spend an hour or so around Gabe. "Would you mind terribly if I just went home now, though? I still don't think I'm feeling all that great." I hated lying to my best friend but I just couldn't face telling her the truth right now.

I was crying over a one night stand.

* * *

Once home, I hopped into my pyjamas and flopped onto the couch. I didn't eat. I didn't drink. I just sat and let the wonders of reality TV numb me from my own life. Around nine o'clock, I began to feel a little hungry so I pulled out the ice cream from the freezer and ate it straight out of the tub. The doorbell rang and I sighed, knowing it would be Derek. That man never had any patience. If you ever said yes to anything, he expected it right away.

"I said tomorrow," I started to say as I pulled the door open. But it was Gabe standing there. A flush of heat ran over me and I pulled myself up a little straighter and wiped at the smear of ice cream on the front of my t-shirt. "Sorry, I thought you were Derek."

Gabe stood with his hands stuffed into the pockets of his overly baggy jeans and stared at me hesitantly from under a backwards facing cap. It made him look even younger. "Can I come in?" he asked quietly, not yet meeting my gaze fully.

"It's late." I leaned against the door frame and folded my arms, trying to still the butterflies that were floating through every part of me.

He chewed on his lip and I momentarily got lost remembering the way his mouth felt on my skin.

Finally, he spoke. "So you're getting back with the soy-loving-ex?"

"I'm going to dinner with him. It's not the same thing." I waited for him to say more but he just kept looking between me and the ground, chewing on his lip. "Look," I said finally. "It's late. Is there something you want, Gabe?"

"I just want to make sure you don't hate me."

"Why would I hate you?"

Gabe looked down to the ground. "Because I was a jerk. I should have called or something."

"It's fine, Gabe. I'm not some little girl who expects you to marry her now that you've slept with her. I know what it was."

"You do?"

I looked back up, and his eyes were hooded with guilt. "Just go home, Gabe. I'll see you at work."

"So we're still friends?"

"That's all we've ever been, isn't it?"

He swallowed. "Right."

"Goodnight, Gabe," I said and began to shut the door.

"Lauren?" His voice was thick and his eyes desperate. "Don't go back to him."

"Why not?"

"Because..." He sighed deeply. "Because you deserve better." He turned and left me standing with the door open.

15

LAUREN

My alarm went off at seven o'clock the next morning and I felt like I had barely got a wink of sleep. I had become accustomed to lazy mornings, not normally starting work until eleven, and my body was not ready for the change.

Smudge nudged at my door and jumped onto the bed. He sat on my chest and purred loudly, close enough so I could feel his breath on my face.

"Morning," I muttered. He only purred in response. "Do we want Derek back, kitty cat?" He started to drool and I pushed him off. "Traitor." He just blinked and started to lick his paw.

My day at work dragged. Mark was in an unusually happy mood and Peta was treating me as though I would break at any moment. She didn't mention anything about my dinner date with Derek, though I knew she was dying to. She would open her mouth to say something, then shut it again and smile. Unfortunately, the topic she turned to as a way of distraction was Gabe.

"Hey, Mark?" she called through to the kitchen.

Mark came and leaned against the doorway. "You called, boss?"

She threw a tea towel in his direction but it landed on the bench beside him. "Do you have any idea what's going on with Don Juan at the moment? He never came back in for his shift yesterday and he wouldn't answer my calls. He better bloody turn up today or I'll be giving him a formal warning."

Mark's eyes sparkled and he picked up the tea towel and flicked it back over his shoulder with a smirk. "Oh, he's just a little sore at the moment. Can't handle losing."

Peta frowned and sighed. "Is this something I should know about, Mark?"

He laughed and looked over the café to make sure no one was listening. "I suppose it won't hurt to tell you now." He walked over and pulled himself up to sit on the counter.

Peta yanked him down. "The counter is for glasses not arses," she admonished firmly. "I got that one from your mother." Peta winked at me.

"Gabe and I had a little bet going on," Mark said. "And thanks to this beautiful lady here," he nodded at me, "I'm now five hundred dollars richer. But unfortunately, we now know that our Gabe is a rather poor loser and perhaps not the Don Juan he thought he was."

"Me?" I asked. "What did I have to do with it?"

"I bet Gabe that he couldn't get you to sleep with him within a month, well actually it was a week but I extended it, fairly confident in my bet. Anyway, I'm guessing from the money he tossed at me the other day and his recent downward spiral in mood, you, my little vixen, did not succumb to his charms. See, I know a sensible woman when I see one."

"You what?" Peta said angrily. Glancing at the customers, she lowered her voice. "You what?"

"Oh, don't get your panties in a bunch. It was just a little harmless fun."

My stomach dropped and nausea welled. He slept with me as a bet? The humiliation was far worse than I had even imagined and I thought I had done a pretty good job of running through all the shameful scenarios in my mind.

"Harmless?" Peta was saying. "What on earth possessed you?" She shook her head. "I don't even know what to say! And to think he asked for an advance on his wages just to pay you over a disgusting bet. Did you know about this, Lauren?"

"No," I said weakly.

"What if she had slept with him, huh?" She stood inches from Mark's face. "What then? You were quietly happy for my best friend to be nothing but a plaything caught between the whims of two idiots?"

Mark held his hands up in protest and took a step back. "But she didn't. I knew she wouldn't. She's far too sensible to fall for someone like him, weren't you, Lauren? No harm done."

Bile rose at the back of my throat. I needed to escape but there was nowhere to go. There was one thing that didn't make sense though. "He paid you?" I asked.

"Of course he did. He may be a sore loser but that man doesn't renege on his bets."

"You need to get out of my sight right now, Mark Hofstadter," Peta growled. Mark smirked and returned to the kitchen. Peta looked at me apologetically. "Well, I guess we know why Casanova was so persistent."

"Yeah," I replied, but my mind was still spinning. I couldn't let Peta see how much the conversation had upset me. At least Gabe had given me the decency of not having to face the others after winning the bet, but I wasn't sure why he did. He had won, after all.

"Where are you going tonight?" Peta asked.

It took me a while to register what she was asking. And then my promise to Derek came flooding back. "Mana's."

"Yay for pasta," Peta said.

I grinned and hoped I didn't look too distracted. There was still an hour and half of work left but the place was quiet and I really didn't feel like facing Gabe. Peta was fine with me leaving early, so after spending most of the afternoon on the couch and with only minutes left before I was due at the restaurant, I stood staring at the clothes in my closet and trying not to think about Gabe. Derek and I were together for thirteen years, high school sweethearts, he deserved a second chance. I clearly was not fit for the single world, having already been conned by one man. What would happen if I was left to my own devices again? Still, I couldn't get Gabe, or the bet, out of my head. In the end, I pulled out my phone and sent him a text, convincing myself that the only way I was going to move past this was if I confronted him.

Me: Why didn't you claim your winnings?

The reply was instant.

Gabe: I can explain.
Me: Nothing to explain.
Gabe: Can I come over?

I didn't answer and my phone beeped again.

Gabe: I'm coming over.

I was meeting Derek at the restaurant in a few minutes so I wouldn't be home, anyway. Gabe Thornton could do whatever the hell he wanted as far as I was concerned. I was done with him.

* * *

Derek stood nervously in the middle of the restaurant and pulled out my chair. "You look nice," he said before sitting back down.

I had gone for a simple black dress. It wasn't overly sexy, it wasn't overly business like, it was neutral and just what I needed. He leaned in for a kiss but I turned my cheek.

He didn't miss a beat. "Did you have a good day?"

"Enough of the chit chat, Derek." I couldn't be bothered pretending to be polite. If Derek wanted me back he better start explaining. I didn't want to talk about my day. I didn't want to hear about his. I just wanted to know why I was sitting at a table about to have dinner with him while another woman was pregnant with his child. "Just tell me what's going on."

He cleared his throat. "Right, okay." He smiled a tight, nervous smile and dabbed at his lips with a napkin. "I don't really know where to start, Lauren."

"How about with the man-stealing-bitch and your unborn child? That sounds like a reasonable starting point to me," I said bitterly.

Derek laughed nervously as the waiter came and took our drink orders. I hadn't stopped talking when the waiter approached and he had given Derek an odd look. I was sure Derek was going to scold me, that's what he would have done before, but instead, he just cleared his throat and started talking again.

"I was stupid. I know this now, but at the time I was lonely. You were so wrapped up in—"

"Let me stop you there, Derek." I spat out his name. "You had an affair, you left. None of this happened because of me, despite what excuses you might want to dream up."

Derek nodded and smoothed his black hair back from his face. "Fair call. I was just trying to explain the 'why' of it all."

"The 'why' is because you couldn't keep your cock in your pants." The waiter placed our drinks on the table. He was having a hard time keeping his face straight.

"Lauren, please," Derek begged, glancing at the waiter. "Do you have to embarrass me like this?"

I took a large drink of my wine. "I'm embarrassing you? Perhaps you should see how it feels to be left for another woman after thirteen years together. And not even a young woman, or a pretty woman, a man-stealing-bitch of a woman." She was both young and pretty, but I wasn't about to let that stop me. "Did you know I walked in on you? Later that night, after you so sweetly broke up with me, I drove to the office to see if I could get you to reconsider."

"Oh." Derek swallowed deeply.

"Oh," I repeated.

Closing his eyes, Derek breathed deeply. "I know you're angry, and you have every right to be, but I'm trying here, Lauren. I want you back."

"Fine." I took another gulp of wine and picked up my phone.

"Fine, you'll have me back?" he asked hopefully.

There were three unread text messages flashing on my phone. I glanced up and shook my head. "Fine, you can keep talking."

Gabe: Where are you?
Gabe: I need to see you.
Gabe: I need to explain.

Me: I'm having dinner with Derek.

I put the phone on the table and looked up. "You were saying?" He couldn't hide the annoyance in his eyes but I smiled and ignored it.

"She was never pregnant," he said finally.

I almost spat out my drink. I managed to swallow and then I threw my head back and laughed. "She was never pregnant?"

"No. She lied to get me to leave you."

"Oh, you've got to be kidding me." I snorted. "Original. What was she expecting would happen when she didn't produce a baby?"

"Well she tried to tell me she miscarried but she had forgotten I had experience in that area. She didn't expect me to be so…" He paused a moment. "So knowledgeable."

"And so now that your bit on the side turned out to be the lying bitch I knew she was, you come crawling back to me?"

"I know it seems that way," he started.

"It doesn't seem that way, Derek. It is that way."

The waiter came over with our orders. Pasta for me and steamed fished for Derek. My phone vibrated again and Derek glanced at it, annoyed.

Gabe: Please don't hate me.

"Steamed fish?" I asked, ignoring Derek's questioning look at my phone.

He patted his belly. "Trying to get rid of those last few pounds before the big fight."

I took another sip of wine. "You look good."

Derek smiled at that. He winked. "Just wait until you see me naked."

"That's rather presumptuous."

"Sorry," he muttered. "It's hard, you know. I keep forgetting that we're not who we were anymore. We're not us."

It was almost fun seeing him so off guard and unsure. I carefully pulled a strand of pasta and wrapped it around my fork careful not to make any squelching sounds. "Fight?" I asked before popping the pasta into my mouth.

"I thought Clem told you?"

"My mother tells me lots of things. Doesn't mean I always listen."

"I signed up for the charity boxing match. Hofstadter and I are going head to head. The fat blob won't have a chance."

Simon Hofstadter was Derek's nemesis. He worked for a rival company and they often went head to head trying to secure exclusive contracts on fancy houses that only the super-rich could afford. "Should be interesting. Still, I didn't pick you for a boxer."

My phone sounded again and I turned it off without reading the message. I couldn't even imagine Derek in a fight. He had only ever been aggressive in business.

"Everything okay?" Derek asked.

"It's just Peta," I said quickly, ready with my lie. "You know how she is, wanting to know how things are going. You were saying about the fight?"

"It's for charity, so hopefully I'll pick up some decent leads on the night. Lots of people go to those sorts of events. Maybe you'll come with me?"

"I think we should just take things slow, Derek. I can't just forget what's happened, even if I wanted to."

He reached across and covered my hand, even though it was clasped around my fork. "I know I don't deserve another chance, but we have so much history together, we've been through so much, it would be a shame to throw it all away. Thirteen years. It's a lot."

I bit my tongue at the responses that flooded my head. I had come here, almost convinced to give Derek another chance, but he wasn't making it easy on himself. Derek was the one that threw it away. Derek was the one who cheated.

But he was trying, and that was what I wanted, wasn't it?

We chatted for the rest of the night, catching up on friends, Derek relaying that my mother called him every second day since we separated.

"I suppose I should call her and let her know that we're going to give it another go," I said at the end of the meal.

Derek looked at me hopefully. "We are?"

I shrugged, amazed at the fact that I really didn't seem to care. "As you said, we've got history. We owe it to ourselves, even if one of us doesn't deserve it."

"You won't regret it, Lauren." He stood up and came across to kiss my cheek. "I realise what I had now and I never want to lose it again."

"Slow, though, okay? You were the one that rushed things when you left, selling the house and everything. If we are going to do this, we are doing it on my terms."

Derek nodded and grinned enthusiastically. "Anything you say. You hold the reins. I'm just grateful that you are at least giving me the chance to win you back. I love you, Lauren. I always have. I always will."

"Woah," I said, holding my hand up and attempting to lighten the mood. "Let's just take things one day at a time."

"Movie on Thursday night?" Derek asked, slipping his hand into mine as we left the restaurant.

16

LAUREN

The goodbye kiss Derek and I shared was strange. He was so familiar, yet in the matter of a few short months, he had become so foreign. I was used to hardening myself against him, not caving into the safety and familiarity we shared. But as he stood there and leaned in for a kiss, all the familiarity vanished and we were just two people unsure of what the other was thinking. He pecked my cheek and both of us laughed. It seemed so chaste, after what we were, but I certainly wasn't going to rush things.

"See you Thursday?" he asked.

"If you're lucky."

If the kiss was strange, seeing him walk away was even stranger. Part of me wanted to call out and invite him in, immediately return to that place where I was safe and comfortable. But then I thought of everything that had happened, and the fact that we had both been with other people since he left, and I let him go. Turning to the door, I fumbled in the dark to find the right key.

"Don't be scared."

I jumped and held my hand over my heart as a figure emerged from the darkness. "Gabe," I scolded.

"Sorry. I just didn't know how to approach without scaring you."

"Well, lurking in the dark like some stalker sure wasn't a great way to start." My heart was still pounding as I turned to insert the key into the lock.

"Sorry," he said again, dejectedly. "I just really needed to see you. I need to explain."

With the door now open, I turned to face him. "You could have called."

"I did. You turned off your phone."

He stood in the shadows with his hands deep in his pockets and a beanie pulled down over his head. Blond strands stuck out against his shoulders and his blue eyes looked forlorn in the dim light. He looked so sad that, for an instant, I forgot why I was mad at him. But then I remembered and stood taller.

"Mark told me about the bet, I don't see what there is to explain. The only part I don't understand is why you didn't claim your winnings. You did win, after all." I crossed my arms and did my best to be unaffected by his pleading eyes.

Gabe took a deep breath. "I didn't claim my winnings, as you put it, because I realised how stupid and cruel it was. I should have never agreed to it in the first place. I just didn't think. I didn't realise that I would feel this way. You've got to believe me, Lauren. I've been beating myself up over this. I know I fucked up."

"I don't see why you're so worried," I replied as nonchalantly as I could. "Just tell them you won, if it will make you feel better. I really don't care."

I did care. I didn't want everyone knowing that I had so easily succumbed, that after years of exclusivity, I jumped into bed with someone I barely knew after nothing but a seductive smile and a few nicely placed words.

"That's not what I mean. I don't give a shit about what anyone thinks. I care what you think though." He looked down at the ground and then back up at me. The intensity of his eyes made my heart swell. "I just don't want you to hate me. I couldn't stand it."

I sighed and reached out to brush his shoulder, drawing my hand back as soon as I did, scolding myself for touching him. "I don't think I could ever hate you," I said.

And once more that hopeful gaze stared back at me. "You don't?" He took a step forward, his slumped shoulders rising and his mouth showing a ghost of a smile.

I took a step back, not trusting myself that close to him. "I don't hate you. But that doesn't mean I forgive you, either." I took a deep breath. "It took a lot to let myself trust you, Gabe. That's what it was when we… well… when we, you know."

"Had sex?" he offered, his smile back in full force.

"Yes, had sex. You're the only person I've ever done that with other than Derek."

"Really?" He reached out and took the tips of my fingers in his, playing with them before lifting them to his mouth and brushing them with his lips. The sensation that tingled through my body at that slight touch was concerning. I couldn't afford to stay around him any longer.

"You have no idea how much I want you right now," he murmured.

I closed my eyes and willed myself to resist him. All the memories from the night we spent together came surging back and I thanked my lucky stars I had not consumed enough wine to dull my common sense.

"I thought that night was something more than a bet," I said, trying not to look too closely at him, scared I would get trapped. "I know that's stupid. I know that's not what people like you do, but I allowed myself to think that perhaps you even cared for me, despite our obvious differences."

"But I do," he started.

I pulled my hands from his, breaking the physical connection that had me transfixed. "It doesn't change what happened, Gabe. It doesn't change the fact that if you hadn't made that bet, there would be no way you'd be standing on my doorstep right now."

Gabe took my hands again and tugged me closer so I was only inches away from him. His eyes burned with desire. "But I am here. Please," he begged as my heart pounded with the closeness of his body to mine. "Give me another chance."

I pulled my hand away and turned to push open the door, ignoring the parts of me that were begging to lose myself in him. "A chance for what? I'm not the girl for you, Gabe. And I believe the only reason you want me now is because you can't have me."

"I can't?"

I shook my head with my back to him and stepped inside. "I'm giving Derek another chance."

"Lauren, please." He reached out and grabbed my arm. "I know I was stupid. I know I right royally fucked up. But everything I said to you, every moment of attraction, it was all real. It was all me, I swear. I just didn't realise it at the time."

I pulled away from him. "Go home, Gabe."

I closed the door and waited until his footsteps sounded down the driveway. Oh, how I wished what he said was true. My heart was soaring with hopeful desire but I knew I needed to quell it. Gabe was a boy. Admittedly, a devastatingly good looking, well built, Adonis of a boy, but still a boy. He didn't know what it was to commit to a relationship, but Derek did. Derek knew me and I knew Derek. He was the man I needed back in my life, and as much as my heart ached—or maybe it was something else—I knew

I had to forget him and acknowledge that what happened was simply nothing but the result of a challenge. He would have never even looked my way otherwise.

* * *

I tried to forget Gabe after that. I tried, but I didn't succeed. Even with my changed shifts, I still saw him for at least an hour each day before I went home. He was quieter than he used to be, but I still caught him staring at me and, when I did, he would grin wickedly, knowing the only reason I caught him was because I was looking too. But other than those silent exchanges he kept to himself.

On Thursday night Derek took me to the movies. On Friday night I sat alone and watched two episodes of Blood Too Sweet. After work on Saturday, Derek had a work dinner that he begged me to attend, but I couldn't face them. Not yet. Not knowing that all of them knew exactly what had transpired between us, and especially not with people who were all friends with the man-stealing-bitch.

I watched three episodes that night.

On Sunday we went for a walk. He laughed at me puffing and panting my way up the steep hill and dragged me the last few steps. When we reached the top and looked out over the ocean below, he reached into the pocket of his shirt and pulled out my engagement ring.

"This isn't a marriage proposal," he said, getting down on one knee. "This is just a promise that my heart belongs to you and no other."

I held out my hand and he slipped it over the barely visible pale band of skin. I felt nothing. I wanted to feel something but it simply wasn't there. The only thing that was there was familiarity and safety.

He kissed me then. And, as the wind whipped about us, tossing my hair into the air, I did everything I could not to think of Gabe. I tried not to compare Derek's lips to Gabe's. I tried not to compare the sudden thrill that surged through me at the mere thought of Gabe, and the complete lack of anything when Derek's mouth pressed against mine.

I tried but I failed.

* * *

On Monday night we shared an uncomfortable dinner with Peta and Shrek. Peta wanted us to be together, but she also couldn't easily forgive Derek, and she let him know. Shrek filled the evening in with crass jokes and stupid impressions but the awkwardness never quite left.

"Lauren?" Peta called out as we were getting into the car. "Sorry, but I need you to return to your old shifts tomorrow."

My heart leaped at her words, only, I didn't know if it was from nervousness or excitement. My old shifts meant spending time with Gabe.

"Sure thing," I said a little too brightly.

Derek shot me a scowl over the roof of the vehicle.

"Is that okay with you?" Peta asked, her hands on her hips and glaring at him.

"It's not up to me," Derek replied quickly, removing the scowl.

He was very quiet as he drove me home. He would look at me like he was going to say something, and then think the better of it and return his eyes to the road.

"What?" I asked him, frustrated.

"What?" he said back, feigning ignorance.

"Don't what me. You're annoyed about something."

"I'm hardly going to see you if you go back to working evenings."

I shrugged. "We'll figure something out."

He was silent for a good long while, staring at the road and driving very slowly. "I think you should quit," he said finally.

"Quit? Why would I quit?"

"You should come back and work for me again. We made a great team."

I sat, tossing replies back and forth in my mind. But this one I just couldn't let slide. He couldn't expect to upturn my entire life by leaving, and then think I would be willing to turn it all around the moment he decided otherwise.

"We did," I said sharply. "Until you decided to fuck it all up." My voice was cold and Derek looked up, a little shock registering on his expression when I swore.

"You swore," he said.

"I've done a lot worse too," I shot back.

"What do you mean by that?" He gripped the wheel tightly, his knuckles white.

The fact that I had slept with Gabe was burning at the back of my mind. I wanted to tell him, give him a little taste of his own medicine and see the hurt in his eyes for a change. But I knew to do that I would have to admit to it. It would also give him more reason to want me to quit, and if I had learned anything by Derek leaving, it was that I never wanted my life to depend solely on someone else again. It gave me nothing to cling to when they left.

"You left me, Derek. Do you understand that? You. Left. Me. Not the other way round, not by some mutual agreement. You left me for another woman. I had to change everything about my life. Everything," I emphasised. "And now you're back, and you simply expect me to give up everything I've built because you want me to?"

"Everything you've built?" He snorted and I glared at him. Pulling himself together, he looked at me apologetically, lowering his tone to continue. "Not because I want you to. But because I thought you would want to. Didn't you enjoy working for me?"

"Until I found out you were fucking the slut in the next office."

"Lauren!" he exclaimed. "Enough! This is not you, speaking like this."

"And you would know this, how?" I yelled.

"Because you've been mine for the last thirteen years!" Unable to control his anger, his voice rose in volume until it matched my own. "Not that you would know, based on the way you've given me the cold shoulder since we got back together. Barely a kiss, not one single cuddle."

"Cuddle?" I scoffed. "Are you serious?" My blood was boiling. "You're seriously going to have a go at me for not having sex with you when you've been off fucking, yes I said fucking, another woman?"

"I can't talk to you when you're like this, Lauren." Derek kept his eyes glued straight ahead, his nostrils flared and eyes flashing in anger.

"Let me out," I said, reaching for the door handle.

"Don't be stupid. We're just about there. Why are you getting so upset, anyway? It's hardly like pouring coffee for other people has been your lifelong dream."

"Let me out of this car now, Derek Lees!"

He pulled over and I climbed out and slammed the door. He followed me for a while, telling me through the open window how stupid I was being and how I should get back into the car. I walked all the way home without acknowledging him, flopped down on the couch and cried. Then I dragged myself off the couch long enough to change into my pyjamas, shove some food in Smudge's bowl and grab a bottle of wine. I drunk it straight from the bottle while watching another episode of Blood Too Sweet, and I cried some more. I fell asleep on the couch and woke up the next morning with a parched throat and smudged and blurry eyes.

Derek hadn't texted or called.

17

LAUREN

"Hey buddy," Gabe greeted me when he walked in that afternoon.

Butterflies flitted across my chest at the sound of his voice, but I mentally squashed them, breaking the wings that hovered against my heart. "Hey, yourself," I replied.

He grinned and I couldn't help smiling back, even though my head ached and my eyelids felt like they had been exchanged for sandpaper.

Stepping closer, he put his face in front of mine. "Ouch," he said, reeling back from me. "You look like shit."

"Why thank you," I replied sarcastically. "It's partially your fault, actually."

Gabe's eyebrows shot up. "Taking in the fact that you look like you barely got a wink of sleep, I'm wishing it was." He laughed and then held up his hands under my hard glare. "Lighten up, buddy." He winked and pulled himself up onto the counter, ignoring Mark's hypocritical look of disapproval.

"Peta will shoot you if she hears you were sitting on that damn counter again," Mark said, folding his arms and standing in the doorway.

"Well, let's hope nobody tells her then." Gabe turned back to me. "So, do tell me, how is this," he circled his hands in my direction, "my fault?"

"Stupid zombie programme."

"You watched it?"

"I had to go to the video store for the second season."

"I told you you'd like it if you just gave it a go."

Gabe kept chatting away for most of the night as the customers rolled through the door. Tuesday nights were always quiet and by eight o'clock the café was empty. Mark was in the kitchen, cursing, and cleaning the oven while Gabe and I restocked the flavour shots. He kept up his chatty demeanour until we were alone.

"I've missed you," he said, stepping close and lowering his voice. His scent was intoxicating and I had to physically stop myself from leaning over and inhaling him. "It hasn't been the same here without you." His eyes flicked over to where Mark's backside was visible, poking out of the oven. He reached out and tucked a strand of hair behind my ear.

"Gabe," I said, gently scolding him but at the same time wishing he would reach out and do it again. My cheek burned where his finger had brushed it.

He stayed close but didn't touch me again. "How is it going, anyway? Are you, Derek, and the man-stealing-bitch happy?"

I rolled my eyes and tried to hide the fact that after a week together, things were not going well. It was just a temporary glitch though. Derek and I would make it back to where we had been. Maybe.

I decided the best way to handle the Gabe situation was to pretend that nothing had ever happened, so I plastered on a smile. "You mean the lying-man-stealing-bitch?"

Gabe's eyes widened. "One extra word?" And then it dawned on him, the meaning of the first. "No way!"

I nodded and couldn't help the thrill that passed over me when sharing the gossip. "Yep, all a total lie."

"So he comes crawling back to you and you accept that?"

"It's not like that," I said quietly.

Gabe's eyes moved over to Mark again and he stepped even closer. He took the flavour shot bottle out of my hand, laid it on the counter, and then tipped my chin so I was looking up at him. "I want you back," he said.

I closed my eyes, certain that if I looked into his for much longer my resolve would melt and I would sink into his embrace. "You never had me, Gabe."

"Yes, I did. I don't care if I ruin your chance at fixing your relationship. I don't care if people call me the devil. I will have you again."

"Please don't, Gabe." I was begging him to stand back, let me go, because I didn't think I had the strength to do it myself.

"Look at me," he said and my eyes rose, despite my resistance. His gaze was scorched with lust and I longed to satisfy it. But instead, I pulled myself away and held my hand to his chest to keep him from following.

Gabe's eyes slipped down to where my hand lay planted against him and pain flickered across his expression. My ring stood out prominently against his black t-shirt. He swallowed and his chest rose and fell. "You've got his ring back on," he stated quietly.

I nodded and withdrew my hand. My heart pounded in my chest. I wanted to rip off the ring and toss it away, but for what? A boy who slept with me over a bet? A boy who only wanted me now because I was the forbidden fruit?

"I told you I was back with him."

"You told me that you were giving him a chance. I just didn't think you would really go back to him. I thought I was still in with a chance too."

"Gabe, you know we can't actually be together."

His brows formed a frown. "Well, why were you so upset then? Why did you talk about trust and hurt if you never thought we could be together?"

I sighed and leaned against the counter. "I guess I just got caught up in the fantasy. You're so…" I raised my eyebrows, trying to think of the right word. "Well, look at you, Gabe. You're gorgeous. And I guess I kind of got drunk on all the attention you were giving me. It wasn't until I found out why that I realised it was nothing but a fantasy."

"But it doesn't have to be, we could be together now. Just say the word. Kick the lowlife lying-man-stealing-bitch-believer to the kerb and be with me."

"I'm years older than you."

His gaze was direct and he took a step closer. "I don't care."

I sighed and struggled to find the right words. "It just wouldn't work. What would people say about me?"

"So, you're saying you would be embarrassed to be with me?" The hurt in his eyes cut at my heart.

"No." I shook my head. "No, I didn't mean it like that."

Gabe took a step away, his eyes clouding over. "So you only slept with me because you were physically attracted to me, nothing more," he said. "I thought you were different, Lauren. I thought you saw more of me than that. All my life that's the only thing people have said about me. I guess the tables have turned now."

He walked backwards a few steps, his eyes burning holes in mine. "Tell Mark I had to leave early." And he walked out the door.

18

LAUREN

The next night Derek appeared at work. He pulled me aside and apologised, saying it was difficult for him knowing how much he had hurt me and also knowing there was no way he could ever make up for it. Gabe walked past and glared at us talking in the storeroom. He looked much like I did the day before. Red, tired eyes, glazed from too much alcohol and not enough sleep. For the rest of the night he wouldn't meet my eye. In fact, he barely acknowledged me at all.

* * *

Thursday night Derek took me to the movies again and afterwards, he walked me to the door. Only this time, when he leaned in for a kiss, it wasn't a chaste peck on the cheek. He crushed his mouth against mine and held me against the door, pawing at my breast. "How long are you going to make me wait?" he breathed roughly in my ear.

I pushed him away. "It hasn't even been two weeks, Derek."

"It's been months," he moaned.

I couldn't understand why he kept saying things like that. All it did was remind me of why it had been a few months. It never seemed to occur to him though.

"I miss you," he whispered, stepping closer and bringing his mouth to my neck, gently peppering it with kisses.

I willed myself not to think about Gabe kissing the same spot but it was hard not to. The difference in the way I felt was poles apart, but I reminded myself it was only because Gabe was daring and tempting and forbidden. Had I been with him for as long as I was with Derek, my body's response would have been different. Still, I couldn't get him out of my mind. Every time I closed my eyes, it was his face I saw. The way he smiled and how one side of his mouth twitched higher than the other. The gleam in his eyes. The feel of his skin under my fingers.

I shook my head to clear the thoughts. "Not tonight, Derek. It's just too soon."

Derek stopped his attempt at seducing me and wrapped his arms around my shoulders, pulling me in for a warm embrace. "I'm so sorry, babe. I should have never put you through what I did, especially after…" He looked at me and stopped talking.

Tears welled in my eyes, and I pulled back from him, trying to brush them away.

"It was never my intention to hurt you. You believe me, don't you?"

I sniffed the tears away. "I just need to take things slowly, Derek. I'm still trying to come to terms with everything in my head."

"But you know I love you? You believe me when I say it, don't you?"

I was torn. Part of me wished to yell and scream at him but the other part just simply couldn't be bothered. And that was the part that scared me. The part that just wanted to forget the hurt, forget the last few months and just go back to the way things were before. It would be so tempting to run into Derek's arms, fall into bed and forget all the pain of the last few months. But I knew it would still be there. I didn't want to talk, I didn't want to go over the horrid details out loud. I just needed to process them within myself and come to terms with them in my own way.

Derek sighed deeply when I didn't answer. "What about the weekend?"

"What about it?" I asked, suddenly feeling tired and worn and ready to be done with this conversation. I wanted to crawl into bed. Alone. I couldn't help smiling inwardly at that. Wasn't it typical? For nights, I had longed to share the bed with Derek again, and now, faced with the chance, all I wanted was to be alone.

"Could I stay the weekend? I'd bring an overnight bag and we could just give things a go. See how it feels to be properly together again. A sleepover. And I wouldn't pressure you into anything you didn't want to do." On seeing my hesitation, Derek kept talking, "I know you want to wait, to give things time, but I don't know what we are waiting for. Tracey is gone. She is out of my life for good. I swear. You took my ring back. Why not give it everything we've got? What have we got to lose?"

I told Derek I would think about it. I knew I should just say yes. Everyone would be happy if I said yes. Mother, Peta, Shrek. But a certain man with blond hair tucked behind his ears kept appearing in my thoughts. It didn't seem fair to Derek if I was still plagued with thoughts of him. Still, there was a part of me that knew Gabe would just stay there unless I did say yes to Derek.

* * *

Peta sighed, put her hands on her hips and looked around the café. "You would think it was a week night or something."

The café was unusually quiet for a Friday night. It was just Peta and I left, as she had sent Jordan home early. It may have had something to do with the fact that Gabe had requested the night off. There were a few groups of girls that walked in and promptly left again when they saw he wasn't on. The clock seemed to tick louder than usual and I was having a difficult time blocking out the noise in the silence of the café.

"Guess we may as well start cleaning now," Peta said. "We'll leave the coffee machine until last." There was a moment of silence as I stood and glared at the clock. "You alright?" Peta asked. "You've been awfully quiet the past couple of days."

"I think we should take down the clock, or remove its batteries or something," I muttered.

Peta just raised her eyebrows.

"It's too loud," I insisted.

She folded her arms and leaned against the counter.

I sighed and slumped my shoulders. "Fine," I groaned. "Derek wants to stay the weekend."

"And?" Peta asked.

"And I'm not sure if I want him to."

She looked surprised and pulled herself up to sit on the counter. "I'm going to clean it later, anyway," she said, brushing aside my look of feigned shock. "Have you not, you know." She pumped her fists together and wiggled her eyebrows suggestively.

I shook my head. "Not yet."

"Hmmm," Peta said.

"Hmmm, what?"

She held up her hand innocently. "Nothing, just hmmm. And why do you think that is, Miss Greer? Or, is it Mrs Lees again? I noticed the ring."

My ring shone brightly and I twisted it around my finger. It was a pretty ring, not your usual engagement style. It was rose gold, set with rubies. It was Derek's grandmother's and meant a lot to his family.

"I thought having him back is what you wanted?" she said when I didn't reply.

"It was. It is." It was hard to explain how I was feeling. I loved Derek, I really did, despite everything he had done. It would be so easy to simply fall back into the way things were before, but there was that constant nagging in my mind, reminding me of what he had done. Who he had done. And then there was Gabe. Despite my efforts, I couldn't shake him from my mind even though I knew it was foolishness. "I'm just really confused."

Peta slipped off the counter and wrapped her arms around me. "It's okay," she said. "You're allowed to take your time. You're allowed to make him wait. You're allowed to refuse, if you want. You just make sure you do what you want to do and not listen to what anyone else wants." She pulled back and held me at arm's length. "I will always be on your side, no matter what. Okay?"

I smiled. "Okay."

"Much better." Peta straightened her apron. "Looks like we've got customers." She nodded to where a group of drunken young people were staring in the window. My heart leapt into my throat when I saw one of them was Gabe with his arm wrapped around Haleigh, the bikini-clad girl from the beach. Drew's ex.

Gabe pressed his forehead against the glass. "You still open?" he yelled.

"Not for the likes of you, Gabe Thornton." Peta laughed. "And take your sticky head off my clean windows!"

Gabe jerked his head off the window and stumbled backwards so Drew had to steady both him and Haleigh.

"Oh great," Peta said, shaking her head. "He's off his face. This should be interesting."

Gabe and his entourage spilled through the door. "Hey buddy," he said, looking over at me. "Having a good night?" I ignored him and turned away. Gabe clapped and rubbed his hands together. "What shall we have, people? My shout."

Peta keyed the orders and I began making the drinks. Gabe stood, his arm slung around Haleigh, watching me. "Not too hot, remember," he said, leaning over the counter. "I don't want a burned tongue. I've got to put it to good use later." He drew Haleigh close to him and kissed her. I stared at the milk frothing about the jug and tried not to let the jealousy that rose from the pit of my stomach show on my expression. He was playing games that I didn't want to play. "I'll bring them over," I said, without looking up.

"Sorry." Drew stood in front of me. "I tried to stop him coming here, but there's no reasoning with him when he gets like this."

I shrugged and plastered on a smile. "It's none of my concern."

Drew's expression told me he knew otherwise.

"But how do you feel about it all?" I nodded to where Haleigh was sitting on Gabe's knee.

"Over it." He shrugged. "Gabe's rather persistent when he wants something, even if his methods are a little off."

I just raised an eyebrow and finished making the orders. I wasn't sure if he was referring to Haleigh or me. Drew helped to take the drinks over to the table. Haleigh was still on Gabe's knee, which he jiggled violently, causing her over-exposed breasts to wobble. She wrapped her arm around his neck and looked up at me, blinking not so innocently.

"You alright there, buddy? Gabe asked. "You look almost pissed off. Is something bothering you?"

I smiled tightly. "No, nothing at all."

Dumping the remaining drinks on the table, I walked out to the storeroom. I needed to get away. I needed to breathe. I knew what he was doing, but I was annoyed that despite that knowledge, I was still insanely jealous. I wanted to walk out there and slap that girl. I also wanted to sit on Gabe's lap and devour him, even though he was acting impossibly stupid and immature.

"Everything okay in here?" Gabe said as he poked his head around the corner and leaned on the doorway.

"Fine." I grabbed a bag of coffee beans and held them up. "I just needed more beans."

"At the end of a shift?" Gabe grinned wickedly and stepped further into the doorway, blocking my exit.

"Yes, at the end of a shift." I pushed against him. "Move, Gabe."

Even though he was stumbling before, now he stood tall and solid, without a hint of drunkenness apart from the glaze to his eyes. I pushed against his chest but it didn't move him an inch. I'd never been considered a small girl, but standing there, trapped by him, I felt a little helpless. It grew hot and I became overwhelmed, feeling confined, yet exposed.

"Move, Gabe," I said again, this time more gently. "Please."

He slid out of the way and I felt his gaze burn into me as I walked back out into the café.

"Everything okay back there?" Peta asked when I reappeared.

"He's drunk," I replied.

"No kidding."

Gabe sauntered back to the table and Haleigh walked up behind him, wrapping her arms around his waist before snaking them up his chest. Gabe's eyes never left mine, and even when I tried to look away, I couldn't. He grabbed at Haleigh's arm and pulled her around to face him, lowering his head and kissing her deeply, watching for my reaction.

I felt sick.

"Yuck," Peta said beside me. "That's not an image I wanted to be burned in my mind. And just think." She patted my leg. "That could have been you." She laughed and I did my best to laugh too. Reaching into my pocket, I pulled out my phone and texted Derek.

Me: See you tonight.

19

LAUREN

Derek was waiting on the doorstep with his overnight bag when I arrived home. It was the same bag that was packed and ready to go when he left. We easily fell back into the old routine. While I cooked a simple dinner, he watched TV. I joined him on the couch after I had done the dishes, and he slipped his arm around me. It felt right. And wrong. His arm felt like it had always been there, but it just didn't fit anymore.

I managed to keep my thoughts from Gabe, but in the process, they wound up thinking of the lying-man-stealing-bitch and wondering just how much he had shared with her. Did they talk about me? Did he sit, just like this, with his arm around her while they watched TV in their apartment? What was she doing now? Did she know he had come back to me? And then I started thinking of Gabe, and Haleigh's hands all over him. I imagined ripping her hands away and replacing them with mine.

The programme ended and I looked up to find Derek staring at me. "Where were you?" he asked.

"What to do mean?"

"It looked as though you were miles away."

He smiled softly and I leaned into him a little more. "I wasn't anywhere other than right here."

Leaning over, he planted a kiss on my head, inhaling my scent. "I missed this smell."

I squeezed my eyes shut and pushed away the sharp questions that kept blistering on my tongue. "It's just shampoo."

The DVD cover left on the table caught his attention. "Zombies?" he asked. "I didn't pick you for a zombie lover."

I laughed nervously and pushed the cover away. "Someone at work suggested it."

"Did she not know that you only watch reality shows?"

I laughed again but didn't correct him.

After a few awkward moments of silence when we both pretended to be interested in the ads flashing across the screen, Derek spoke. "Shall we go to bed?"

I looked at the clock. It was nine thirty. "It's a little early, isn't it?"

Derek stood up and held his hands out. "I'm at the gym early six days a week." He pulled me to my feet. "You should come with me sometime."

I laughed. "Yeah, good luck with that."

"It would do you good to get some exercise back in your life."

"Oh, so a few gym sessions and you're Mr Well-Life? Don't forget I knew you back in the day when walking from the couch to the fridge was all the exercise you got."

"Not anymore, my dear," he called as he walked down the hall.

We undressed, smiling awkwardly at each other. He stepped out of his clothes and left them where they lay while I folded each clean item and put it away, before tossing the dirty ones into the clothing bin. Derek stripped down and I noticed he was wearing jockeys instead of boxers like he used to. He looked good. His shoulders were broader, his stomach smaller and tighter. And then I wondered if the jockeys were the lying-man-stealing-bitch's preference.

I blocked out all thoughts and pulled my night shirt out of the drawers.

"Don't," Derek said, climbing into bed. "Please?"

Shyly, I put the shirt away and lay in bed beside him with only my bra and underpants on. We weren't touching, but somehow, I was nervous. Would things be different? Would he be different?

Derek moved closer and reached out to stroke my breast. "I've missed these too." His fingers dug into my flesh and I squirmed. "Sorry," he chuckled. "I guess I'm just a little eager. It's been a while."

There it was again. It's been a while. A while since he had slept with anyone, or simply a while since he had slept with me? He pawed at me again, and I resisted the urge to crawl away. I needed to relax. I needed to get all other thoughts out of my mind and concentrate on Derek.

Propping himself up on his elbow, he leaned in for a kiss. "I've missed your lips," he whispered.

Shut up! Shut up! Shut up! The words echoed around my head. Did it not occur to him that there was only one reason why he had missed all these things?

He sucked on my neck and I tried to melt into it. Moving so he was on top of me, he pressed his erection against my stomach. "Something else missed you too," he said, grinning.

Really? Wasn't it otherwise occupied?

Derek reached over to grab a condom from the pocket of his jeans and I wondered how long he had carried condoms in his pocket.

I needed to get out of my head. I thought about getting up and grabbing a bottle of wine, but it probably would have been a little rude. Sorry honey, I need to be drunk to fuck you.

Derek was clearly ready to go. I just wished I was. I tried kissing him. I let my tongue slip into his mouth as he tugged at my underwear. I helped him pull them down and he sank into me, only I wasn't ready and it took a little adjustment before he could move easily. I gripped onto his shoulders and he smiled softly as he moved in and out.

Thoughts of coffee beans ran through my head and I hooked my legs around his, pulling him closer to me and causing him to grunt with each thrust. Removing himself he started to slide down my body, positioning his mouth between my legs but I pulled him back up. "Not tonight," I said as alluringly as I could muster. "Tonight it's just about you."

As his movements grew quicker, I grabbed his backside and dug my fingernails in with full knowledge of what it did to him. Crying out, he shuddered as he came.

* * *

Derek's alarm sounded at five in the morning. Rolling over, he kissed my cheek. "Morning." I grunted and turned away but he pulled me back. "Come to the gym with me," he said, tapping my nose repeatedly.

I swatted his hand and tried to pull away. Reaching out, he turned on the light and I buried my head under the covers. "It's not morning," I groaned.

He ripped the sheets off, letting the cool air flow over my skin which immediately prickled with goose bumps. "Come to the gym with me," he said again and started jiggling the bed.

"It's still night." I squeezed my eyes shut to block out the bright light but he was insistent. "Fine," I finally growled.

He smiled and pecked a kiss on the tip of my nose. "It's a new day," he said.

"Since when did you become so peppy?" Crawling out of bed, I made my way to the ensuite. I tried to wake myself with a shower but the water did nothing but lull me back to a warm place, and all too soon, Derek poked his head onto the bathroom.

"Come on," he urged. "Let's go."

I stumbled out of the shower, pulled on my jogging pants and an old hoodie and followed him out to the car. He slapped my backside as I climbed into the Beemer.

"You're wearing those?" he asked.

"We're going to a gym, aren't we?"

"Hmmm," he said getting in the driver's side and turning over the engine.

"Hmmm, what?" I asked, glaring at him.

He laughed at my stern expression. "Hmmm, nothing. I didn't say a word."

The gym was basically a garage behind someone's house. It was dirty and cold. Derek introduced me to his trainer, Evan, and started warming up by skipping.

"Going to join in today, love?" Evan asked.

I looked over to where Derek was jumping up and down repeatedly, his shirt flapping with the movement, and shook my head. I could only imagine what my jiggle would look like while doing that. "Think I'll sit this one out and just watch."

I wrapped my arms around myself and rubbed vigorously, trying to get rid of the coldness that had seeped into my bones.

"A week today!" Evan shouted in Derek's ear as he skipped. "Are you ready?"

"Hell yeah!" Derek growled. I laughed as he looked over and winked at me. This was definitely a new side to Derek.

By the time they had finished, Derek was drenched with sweat. Even though they were only training, Evan insisted he wear full protection to get a feel for how he would need to move on the night, and his dark hair was plastered to his head from being trapped under it. Derek spat his mouth guard onto the ground when Evan slapped him on the back, congratulating him on the effort he had put in. I was impressed. I had never seen Derek fight and his punches seem strong and sure. Maybe not as strong and sure as Gabe's had been the time I saw him at a punching bag, but still good. Evan left him standing in the ring, leaning on the ropes and panting, telling him he would see him bright and early Monday morning.

"That fat prick Hofstadter doesn't stand a chance," Derek said, rubbing a towel over the back of his neck and head, wiping away the dripping sweat. "Just you wait, lugging all that extra weight around means he'll be slow. I'll knock him out flat, just you wait and see."

"Fat doesn't always mean slow," I said, still smarting from his non-remark concerning my jogging pants.

"Really," he smirked. "Do tell me what it means then, my dearest." He pulled up the ropes and slipped under them to join me back down on the cold concrete.

"Fat could mean strong," I suggested. Derek picked me up and whirled me around. "Put me down! You're all sweaty."

He laughed and pulled me tighter, planting a sloppy kiss on my mouth. "It's going to be great seeing that smirk wiped off his face." He placed me back on my feet but still held onto me, grabbing my behind and jerking me close. He ground against me a few times until I felt him harden. "You just wait and see," he growled in my ear, rubbing his mouth over my skin.

"Derek," I said warily, trying to pull away. But he held me tight. "Not here," I said, tugging at his arms and looking around for any sign of Evan.

"Why not? Evan's gone now and I'm rather worked up."

I slapped his shoulder. "What's gotten into you?" Derek never used to be this adventurous. He was strictly a bedroom only man. A ripple of excitement tingled down deep, but it was quickly followed by the cold sensation of realising what would have made him that way.

Releasing me, Derek walked over to where Evan had left the door open behind him, shutting it and pulling the lock across.

"Are you sure he's left," I asked.

"There's no one here but you and me."

Pulling me close, he assaulted me with his lips. He tasted of salt and sweat. Reaching down, he slipped his hand into my pants and his fingers rubbed against me as we kissed. The thrill of the unknown meant, despite my hesitation, I was ready. Hastily, Derek turned me around and guided my hands to the rope of the ring. Roughly tugging down my pants, he entered me. He was rough and fast and reached a climax quickly, pulling up my pants, and slapping my butt, in what seemed like a matter of seconds.

"Maybe I like those pants after all," he said.

20

LAUREN

The gym was the last time Derek touched me for a week, telling me he needed to reserve his energy for the fight. We spent every night together, but we didn't even kiss as he said his resolve would waver and he needed all the help he could get.

Entering Derek's apartment for the first time unsettled me. There was artwork on the walls and vases filled with fake flowers which I knew he hadn't chosen. Even the colour scheme, bold and bright, reminded me another woman had been here.

It was the night of the fight and I was waiting on Derek as he anxiously fluffed his hair. "I don't even know why I'm worried, it's just going to get all sweaty and flat under the headgear anyway," he said.

I leaned against the white tiles in the bathroom. "You'll be great." I smiled at his reflection in the mirror.

He turned to face me, giving up on fixing whatever he thought was wrong with his hair. He was dressed in a matching tracksuit, his dinner suit hanging in a bag over the bathroom door. "Did I tell you Hofstadter pulled out?"

"He did?"

Derek grabbed the suit and walked out the door. "Yep. Couldn't handle the thought of losing to me. Whimp."

"So who are you fighting now?"

Derek shrugged. "Does it matter?" He bounced on his feet a few times and threw quick, short jabs into the air. "Whoever it is, is going to suffer."

"You've remembered it's for charity, haven't you?"

"You know that even charity fights are real, don't you?" He swung me around and pulled me close. "I can't wait until after the fight either," he said, kissing me firmly before pulling away. "Oh yeah. You and me after the fight." He let out a whoop and pumped the air.

I looked in the hallway mirror, ignoring the ornate gold-plated frame that Derek would have never chosen, and studied my reflection. I had bought a tight, silver dress for the occasion that hugged all the right curves and hid all the wrong ones. Derek had insisted on paying for me to get my hair and makeup done and my hair fell in thick loose curls around my face. Even I thought I looked pretty.

I had tried to get Peta and Shrek tickets but they were all sold out, so I was resigned to sitting with a group of Derek's workmates. My old workmates. I imagined the entire night smiling stiffly while they all internally commented on the state of my relationship. I would have refused to go if Derek hadn't been so desperate to have me there.

We pulled up in the taxi and Derek kissed me before heading off to where the fighters waited to be called to the ring. I scanned the crowded room, looking for Derek's workmates who waved me over. Doing my best to make small talk, I chatted politely. I had worked with these people but I barely knew them. I mainly stayed trapped inside Derek's office and chose not to attend many of the numerous work functions and dinners they had. In hindsight, maybe I should have.

"Do you think it's real?" Preston, the second best real estate agent in the company, leaned over and asked. Derek, of course, was the best. He managed to walk that fine line between pushy and charming and non-threatening. I looked where he nodded and saw Simon Hofstadter sitting at a table, his leg awkwardly poking out at a straight angle and wrapped in a cast.

"I don't see why he would be faking," I replied, not willing to be dragged into the rivalry between the two companies.

"Derek's got to face some little—"

I didn't listen to the rest of what he had to say as I spotted Mark sitting across the table from Simon. It wasn't until then it occurred to me that they had the same last name. "Excuse me for a moment," I said, patting Preston's arm absently and walking over to Mark.

"Well, well, if it isn't the wife of your would-be opponent," Mark said to his brother as he stood to embrace me. "Do you know Simon?"

"We've met once or twice." I held out my hand and smiled. Derek was right, Simon was a big man and looked nothing like his brother. Only fat wouldn't have been the word I would have used to describe him. Bulky would have suited better. If I was Derek, I would be pleased he had pulled out.

"Lovely to meet you again, my dear," Simon said and kissed the hand I held out.

I laughed at his display. "I never knew you two were brothers." Simon looked a little confused. "I work with Mark," I said, nodding to Mark.

"You don't work with your husband anymore?"

I shook my head. "He was my fiancé. Sorry," I corrected, "is my fiancé." I stalled, knowing that wasn't right either. "We haven't worked together for a few months now."

"Well if you're ever looking to move on, I know of someone who would be only too grateful to nab a personal assistant with skills such as your own." He winked and said, "Me."

"That's very kind of you but I'm quite happy where I am for the moment."

Simon smiled and pulled out the chair beside him, indicating I should sit. "Well, I owe enough to your workplace as it is for getting me out of this pickle."

"I'm sorry?" I turned to Mark for an explanation but he wouldn't meet my eye.

"Oh, Mark here organised for one of your workmates to take my place in the fight. Some young whippersnapper that's sure to knock the stuffing out of your fiancé there. No offence," he said, patting my knee.

I felt the colour drain from my face. "Mark?"

Mark shrugged his shoulders and took a swig at the bottle of beer in front of him. "Gabe was only too happy to oblige. He literally jumped at the chance, in fact. It was just handy that he was already approved to step in, having a membership to the training gym and all." He raised his eyebrows. "Is there a problem, Lauren?"

I thought back to Gabe, fists flying into the boxing bag time and time again. There was no way Derek could face him. He would kill Derek.

"Excuse me," I said, glaring at Mark. "I need to go and try to convince Derek to pull out of the fight."

I ran out the doors in search of Derek and found him skipping in the hallway, his trainer beside him.

"May I speak to Derek alone for a moment?" I asked, and Evan walked away, pulling his phone out of his pocket.

"What's wrong?" Derek bounced on the spot, looking at me, concerned.

I held my hand out. "Can you stop that for a minute?" He stopped skipping and I took a step closer. "I don't want you to fight."

Derek laughed and started skipping again. "It's a little late for that now, Lauren. It's sweet you're worried about me though." He smacked his lips together in a kiss.

"I heard the guy you're fighting is young and probably a lot fitter than you. I just don't want you to get hurt."

Derek stopped skipping again and pulled me close, kissing the top of my head. "I'll be fine. And you know what young means, don't you?"

"Fast?" I offered.

Derek shook his head. "Inexperienced."

"But not always," I insisted, thinking once again of Gabe's fists and the way his feet quickly danced across the floor.

"I'll be fine. Now off you go." He turned me away and slapped my backside.

Rounding the corner, I ran straight into Gabe. He had barely talked to me since that night at the café, and had called in sick a lot. It had almost got to the point where Peta was considering giving him a formal warning. That was saying a lot for Peta. As strict as she sometimes appeared, she hated confrontation.

"Lauren?" He seemed as surprised to see me as I was him.

"What do you think you're doing?" I hissed at him.

He smirked and leaned back against the wall, folding his arms, those beautiful arms, across his chest. "I'm just helping out at a charity gig."

"Helping out? You knew you would be fighting Derek."

"That was just an added bonus," he replied. "Really, I'm just doing it out of the goodness of my heart."

"You'll hurt him." I stepped closer and put my hand on his arm.

He stared down at my fingers splayed across his skin and then back up at me. "That's the point. And aren't you afraid that I'll get hurt?" He looked at me so intently my pulse rose with each moment that passed. "Break up with him and I'll pull out of the fight," he said suddenly.

"You would stoop to that?" I replied, jerking my hand back.

"I would," he said. "And much, much more." His voice was dark and filled with gravel. "You're all I can think about."

"Even while kissing Haleigh?" I shot back at him and then scolded myself for getting pulled into his game.

"Especially while kissing Haleigh."

My god, he was sexy, even with another woman's name on his lips. What was wrong with me? My heart hammered in my throat and he smirked, knowing the effect he had on me. I wanted to walk away but my legs wouldn't move. In the end, he was the one that left.

"Let me know if you change your mind," he called behind him.

I couldn't eat the meal when it was set before me. I couldn't hold even the smallest of conversations. Derek's workmates teased me about being nervous for him. They called me sweet. If only they knew the truth.

I almost left. My insides felt like they were being torn in two. And then 'Killing in the Name' blared across the sound system and Gabe walked down the line of carpet to the boxing ring. The crowd cheered and whooped as he removed his shirt and strutted around the ring, lifting his arms and egging the crowd on. He met my eyes and lifted an eyebrow in an unasked question. I looked away.

Derek's entrance paled in comparison and my heart sank for him. Even though no one else would be able to tell from his demeanour, I knew he was freaking out. He blew me a kiss across room and I felt like crying.

"Am I too late?" a voice drawled behind me. The lying-man-stealing-bitch sat down on the chair beside mine. The entire table fell quiet.

"What?" she said and placed her handbag under her seat. "I paid for my ticket just like the rest of you."

"Tracey," Preston said. "We thought you weren't coming."

"Really?" She turned and smiled at me. "I told Derek last night I was."

Without a word, I rose from the table and walked over to Mark who pulled out the seat beside him. "Is that who I think it is?" he asked.

I nodded and breathed deeply, trying to calm the seething anger bubbling beneath the surface. Suddenly, I didn't care so much if Derek got hurt.

He patted my hand. "Sometimes this town is entirely too small."

The bell sounded and Derek threw the first punch but Gabe ducked away easily and grinned at the crowd. He was toying with Derek.

Mark reached across and filled my glass to the brim. Leaning over, I slurped enough so I could lift it, and then held it in salute to Mark. He picked his glass up, knocked it against mine and then we both downed the whole lot.

I tried to avoid looking at what was going on in the boxing ring, but there were large screens projecting the action everywhere.

Derek threw a few more punches which Gabe avoided easily. And when Gabe decided to hit back, it connected with Derek's jaw, knocking him sideways. The room went silent as he swayed on his feet and the crowd erupted into applause as he shook his head and stood firm. The hit had unsettled him though and his training went out the window. He lunged at Gabe, throwing his punches wide and leaving himself open for Gabe to work quick, short jabs into his side.

Even Simon winced as he watched. "Keep your defence up, you idiot!" he yelled out to Derek.

Derek stumbled on his feet and blood dripped from his nose but he refused to stop. Gabe, on the other hand, was bouncing on his toes, shifting his weight from foot to foot and taunting Derek to punch him. Derek's next swing was so wide Mark covered his eyes, knowing what was about to happen. Gabe's glove-covered fist hit Derek squarely on the jaw again and his face flew to the side, spit and blood flying into the air. He hit the floor and lay there, still. The referee started the countdown as Derek stumbled to his knees. He made it to one foot before the referee called it and the crowd broke into thunderous applause as Gabe lifted his arms, triumphant.

"Well," Mark said, lifting his refilled glass.

"Well," I repeated. Gabe looked over and met my eyes before offering his hand to Derek to help him back to his feet. Derek shook his head and struggled up without help. Gabe's song echoed across the room again and Derek stood and waited as they announced Gabe's win by technical knockout and lifted his hand high.

Derek's eye and nose were swollen when he appeared in front of me minutes later. He reached across and grabbed a bottle of beer, downing it in one go before slamming it back down. "What are you doing at this table?" he asked me, glaring at Simon.

"I didn't feel like sitting at yours." I nodded across to where Tracey was talking to Preston, leaning into him and playing with his hair. She glanced over at Derek and smiled.

"What the fuck?" Derek said. "I told her not to come."

"So you did talk to her?"

Derek looked around the table. "Let's not do this now." He walked to the bar, leaving me behind as the crowd roared for the next fighters to battle it out in the ring.

Across the room, I spotted Gabe being congratulated by his friends seated on the rows of chairs that surrounded the tables. They slapped him on the back and he laughed, downing a beer in one gulp, much like Derek had just done, only for different reasons. He looked across the room and raised his second bottle to me. Dressed in a purple shirt, tie, and a dark grey suit, I couldn't help but notice how good he looked. What was wrong with me?

When Derek finally came back to the table, his eyes were glazed and his words slurred. Goodness knew how many vodkas he had consumed at the bar.

"Fucking upstart," he said, nodding over to where Gabe stood. He swayed and held onto the back of my chair.

"Just how much did you drink over there?"

"Not enough," he said, still glaring at Gabe, his brows furrowing in confusion. "I know him," he growled.

Simon snorted. "Of course you know him, he's Hamish Thornton's kid."

We all knew who Hamish Thornton was. His name was well known within the real estate world, owning most of the upmarket properties and buildings in this town as well as many others, but most of his properties were in the city. I was surprised that it hadn't occurred to me that Gabe was his son. Clearly Gabe hadn't inherited any trust funds.

Derek swung around to face Simon. "You're fucking kidding."

"Nope. Hamish is here somewhere." He rose awkwardly, his broken leg still resting on the chair in front of him, and looked around the room, shrugging his shoulders and sitting back down when he couldn't find him.

"That little twerp is Hamish's son?"

"I swear." Simon held up his hands.

Even though Gabe was across the room, Derek lunged in his direction before stumbling and grabbing onto a chair.

I got up to steady him. "Maybe we should get going?" I suggested.

"Keen to get home, are we?" Derek smirked and tried to caress my cheek but ended up just mashing his hand against me.

"You're drunk."

"Not as drunk as I want to be."

I hooked my arm under his shoulders. "Come on, let's get you home." I dragged him across the floor but unfortunately, exiting meant passing by Gabe and his group of friends. When Tracey appeared in front of us, I was almost thankful. At least she would distract Derek from Gabe.

"Hey, it's Tracey," Derek said, raising his beer and drinking. He leaned forward and whispered loudly. "You shouldn't be here, my wife doesn't like it." He took another gulp of his beer and then turned to me. "Sorry, not wife, fiancée." He shook his head. "Nope, not even that. Girlfriend?"

I had never seen Derek so drunk. I wasn't even sure how he accomplished it in the time that had passed since he left the boxing ring. He leaned heavily on me and I was tempted to move away, let him fall in front of Tracey, let her clean up the mess.

"Lauren." Tracey nodded and sipped on a straw in her wine glass.

At that moment Gabe draped his arm over Tracey and poked his head into the triangle. "Well, well, what a nice reunion we have here."

"Not now, Gabe," I said, trying to drag Derek towards the door.

"You know him?" Derek slurred rather loudly in my ear. His breath reeked.

"Of course she knows him." Tracey wrapped one arm around Gabe's waist, her eyes sliding over him.

I had visions of punching her in the face. Was it not enough that she stole my fiancé? Now she wanted Gabe, too? I took a deep breath.

"She works with him," Tracey said.

Derek smiled, a light bulb going off in his head. "You're the fucker that burnt my tongue."

"The one and only," Gabe said, bowing low.

Derek's eyes narrowed. "You didn't tell me you knew him before the fight."

"I didn't think it was important." I tugged at his arm but he dug his feet in and stood firm, seeming a little less drunk than he was before.

Gabe clutched at his heart. "Ouch. That hurt, Lauren."

"Please Gabe," I pleaded. "Just leave me alone."

"You heard the woman," Derek slurred. "Leave her alone."

Gabe tutted under his breath, shook his head and leaned in close to Derek. "That's not what she said the other night." He grinned and turned his eyes to me knowingly.

My heart dropped to my feet.

"You little fucker!" Derek shouted and lunged towards Gabe, swinging madly. But Gabe was ready for him and his punch landed on Derek's jaw, knocking him to the ground. Gabe took a step back, panting with the adrenaline that was pumping through his veins and looked up at me. Tracey ran to Derek's side and helped him to his feet as he wiped the blood from the side of his mouth. The room stilled and all eyes turned to me, so I ran.

I didn't look to see if anyone followed. All I knew was I didn't want them to. I needed to be alone. I needed to clear my head. Running down the entrance of the stadium, I made my way out into the foyer, accidently running straight into the very firm chest of a man juggling multiple beer bottles in his hands.

"Sorry," I muttered, wincing as I saw the stains on his shirt.

"Watch where you're going, would you?" the man replied, dumping the now nearly empty bottles into the trash. He looked over at me, a frown pressed between his brows, but then his expression changed and a slow and seductive smile replaced his frown.

But all it did was remind me of Gabe's smile. Only, he wasn't Gabe. He wasn't Derek. It was some dark-haired, handsome, but random stranger.

"Sorry," I muttered again, moving around him and continuing out the door.

"Wait," he said, but whatever else he was about to say was cut off when the doors slid shut behind me.

21

LAUREN

I was in bed, not asleep, but in bed, when the banging started at my door. I ignored it but Derek wasn't giving up. Finally, afraid the neighbours would call the police, I stormed down the hallway and ripped open the door.

"Fuck off!" I yelled.

"I'm so sorry," Gabe said as he stumbled through the door. "Lauren, I'm so, so sorry. I didn't mean to. I never wanted—" He crumpled to the floor and sat with his back resting against the couch. "I'm just so sorry."

"I thought you would be Derek," I said, staring down at him, arms crossed and unimpressed.

He pulled himself to his feet and sat on the couch, holding his head between his hands. "Not Derek." He shook his head. "He took off with the lying-man-stealing-bitch after I knocked him down. He doesn't learn very quickly, does he?" His eyes were red and swollen. "He doesn't love you, Lauren. Not like I do."

His words cut me, but I had at least expected as much. Derek had been speaking to her without telling me. She thought it was okay to turn up at a function I was attending. Clearly, she wasn't out of his life like he had said. Surprisingly, I was not angry about it. In fact, right now I couldn't care less. I was done with the night. Done with drunk men. I just wanted the blissful oblivion of sleep.

"Go home, Gabe."

"Didn't you hear me, Lauren? I said I love you."

"And you thought beating the crap out of Derek would prove that to me? You're drunk. Go home."

Gabe stood, all previous drunkenness disappearing as he grasped my shoulders. "I'm not that drunk, Lauren. I know exactly what I'm doing. I know exactly what I want. And it's you."

His eyes searched my face and my resolve started to waver. What was it about him that so easily undid me? He cupped my face and slowly drew me close. His blue eyes were dark yet hopeful, the closer he got, and when his lips finally touched mine, they were so soft they felt like a feather.

"Please," he groaned. There it was again. That groan. "Please say you forgive me."

His kisses grew more urgent and I felt my body responding, even as I willed it not to. I wrapped my hands in his hair and pulled him closer until our bodies melded into one. His body pressed against every inch of me as he ran his mouth down my neck and nuzzled into the curve of my shoulder. His breathing became erratic and laboured and I pulled away from him.

"No," I breathed shakily.

Gabe stood at arm's length his eyes pleading. "Let me stay."

I started to shake my head.

"I won't touch you. I won't kiss you. I won't do anything. Just let me stay. And if you want me to leave in the morning, I promise I'll leave without a word."

I should have said no. I should have steeled myself against those pleading eyes.

But I didn't.

* * *

Gabe kept true to his word. Well, not exactly but close enough. I woke with him huddled against me, arms around my waist, cheek pressed against my back. As I tried to slide out from his embrace, his grip tightened.

"Not yet," he whispered.

I relaxed into him, relishing the feel of his skin against mine, his arms around me. "Good morning," I whispered.

His cheek crumpled against my back and his fine stubble grazed against me as he smiled. "Good morning," he whispered and sat up to kiss my cheek before lying back down. "Can I ask you something? Why are we whispering?"

I laughed and rolled over to face him, feeling happier than I had done in days. "I have no idea." Propping myself up on my elbows, I studied him. "How's the head?" And then I added, "And the body?"

"Surprisingly good, actually." He stretched into the air, testing his muscles for soreness. "Head's a little achy but other than that, pretty fucking great." He reached over and brushed a strand of hair away from my face. "So now that we're here in the cold light of day, am I leaving?"

There were two sides to me. Well, at least two sides. One was the sensible side that told me when something was bad, a stupid idea, or just plain dangerous, and the other side was the one that ached for fun.

In the past, the sensible side was responsible for telling me to save money, do the housework now instead of reading that novel, it told me not to eat that bar of chocolate, or drink that next glass/bottle of wine. It was the side that said hard work equals reward. That good things were worth waiting for. Be patient. Wait.

And then there was the flipside. The wilder side. The side that told me to enjoy life, eat the chocolate, drink the wine, and to hell with waiting. Grasp life with both hands and screw the consequences. Live for the now. Fuck the Adonis of a boy lying next to me.

And, as I lay there and watched Gabe anxiously wait for my response, one side was speaking a lot louder than the other.

"You can stay," I said.

Gabe leapt on top of me, pinning my hands to my sides and kissing me repeatedly, over my face, my neck, my shoulders, every inch that was exposed from the covers as I squirmed and laughed underneath him, revelling in his attention.

"You can't tell anyone, though," I said with mock severity.

Gabe shook his head and continued to kiss me. There was something so undeniably honest and open about him, so joyful and unabashed, I almost didn't want to insist that he keep whatever we had a secret. But I also couldn't bear the thought of wagging tongues.

"I'm serious, Gabe," I said, wriggling my hands free and grabbing his face. "I don't want people to know."

He grinned and tried to kiss me again but I held onto his face. "Fine. Whatever you want, Ren," he said and kissed my nose.

I shook my head and laughed as his feather-like kisses tickled me. "Don't call me that. Only Peta and Shrek call me that."

"Any other nicknames that I don't know about?" He cocked one eyebrow.

"My sister calls me L, but I don't really like that either. And Peta's kids call me Stimpy."

Gabe froze above me, looking confused. "Stimpy?"

"Yeah, like in the cartoon. Their eldest boy, Nicholas, has got this obsession with that old cartoon, Ren and Stimpy."

Gabe's forehead wrinkled. "Never heard of it."

I gently whacked his arm. "Of course you wouldn't. It was a ninety's show. You were barely even born when it was on."

"Well, what's a kid his age doing watching it?"

I shrugged. "You Tube."

Gabe grinned. "I know," he said. "I'll call you, Mrs Robinson."

"You will not!" I exclaimed.

"It suits us. An older woman, a younger man? You can just call me Dustin."

"He was called Benjamin in the movie and he wasn't as young as they made out when he played the part. In reality, there was only six years difference in their ages."

"Oh, was he? You seem to know an awful lot about this movie."

"I have a talent for retaining useless information." I squished his cheeks together and kissed his puckered lips. "And how come you know that movie but not Ren and Stimpy?"

"My mother is obsessed with old movies," he said, his words mumbled by his squished cheeks. "She refuses to watch anything made in this century." Pulling my hands away, he placed them around his neck. "Now," he said with a slow sexy smile. "How about what I want?"

His eyes turned from playful to burning in an instant. He brought his mouth down to mine and kissed me deeply, cradling my shoulders with his hands, drawing me down the bed, closer to him. His tongue explored my mouth and his teeth nipped my lips, tugging and pulling. A well of desire rose within me, and I pulled his head closer, trying to remove the last breath of distance between us.

The doorbell rang and Gabe froze, his mouth still on mine. I cocked my head to the side and listened. The doorbell rang again.

"Just ignore it," Gabe said.

"I can't just ignore it." I pulled myself from the bed and wrapped a dressing gown around me. "Wait here," I instructed.

Gabe lay back with his hands folded under his head. "As you wish." His eyes twinkled playfully. I shook my head and leaned over the bed to kiss him but he grabbed me and pulled me on top of him. Taking my face in his hands, he kissed me firmly before whacking my behind. "See? You just can't keep your hands off me, Mrs Robinson." He pushed me away playfully. "Go answer that damn doorbell, would you?"

I pursed my lips and left him laughing as I walked down the hallway, tightening my gown around my waist. I pulled open the door and found a battered and broken Derek on my doorstep.

The sensible side of me came rushing back in one fell swoop, and I felt ill after indulging on my Gabe-flavoured chocolate and wine. Gabe was in my bed and I hadn't even properly broken up with Derek. I was a horrible, horrible woman.

"Hi," Derek said, peering up at me anxiously. His left eye was swollen and beginning to darken at the edges. His lip was enlarged and there was a bruise spreading across his chin.

"Hi," I said back, tightening my gown again.

"Can I come in?" He didn't wait for an answer and instead, walked past me and into the lounge. I silently urged Gabe to stay hidden in the bedroom. I no longer felt angry at Derek. I no longer cared what he did, or didn't do with Tracey. I just didn't want him to find Gabe.

"I guess it's over?" Derek said. It was a question, not a statement, and I couldn't even look him in the eye as I nodded. "For what it's worth, I love you, Lauren, and I know this horrid mess is all my fault."

There was only one question I wanted to ask, as if, somehow, it would make my own transgressions feel a little less awful. "Did you stay with her the night?"

Derek swallowed. His Adam's apple bobbed up and down and he stared at the ground. "I was drunk."

"That's not what I asked."

He nodded, and visibly braced himself for the onslaught that never came. Twisting the ring from my finger, I held it out to him. "Thanks for being honest."

"I'm really sorry, Lauren." He stood before me, hesitant to take the ring back.

"I am too." I pushed the ring into his hand, opened the door and let Derek out of my life.

* * *

Gabe was waiting in the hallway, dressed in the same clothes from the night before. "You okay?" he asked. He took my hand and kissed the finger where Derek's ring had been only moments before.

I sighed and looked up at him. "I feel like shit."

"You shouldn't. He cheated on you, not the other way around."

"It's not that simple."

"It can be, if you want."

"I wish I could look at the world the way you do, Gabe." I sighed again and leaned against the wall. "But it really isn't that simple. I just broke up with my fiancé, again, while I had you, a man over ten years his junior, waiting in my bed. It's going to take me a while to come to terms with that."

"Tut, tut, Mrs Robinson." Gabe grinned and took my hands in his. "Tomorrow?" he said hopefully.

"Maybe it's too soon," I said, already regretting how quickly I let Gabe back into my bed.

"Please? I just want one day where we're not at work, a day with no ex-fiancé, or flatmates. Just you and me."

"Fine," I said, unable to resist his enthusiasm.

"I'll pick you up at four. Bring your camera."

"Where are we going?"

But all he did was tap his nose and plant a kiss on my cheek before walking out the door.

* * *

I felt strangely free wandering around my house that day. I didn't ache for Derek, I didn't long for Gabe. I turned the music up loud and started unpacking all the boxes that should have been unpacked long ago. Once that was done, I sat on the couch, feet curled under my legs and looked around the room triumphantly. It was still rather bare but with some books on the shelves and artwork on the walls, it looked a little more like someone loved it. I had three missed calls from Peta so I figured now was a good time to call her back. I needed to tell her about Derek but I wasn't yet ready to come clean concerning Gabe.

"Got time to talk?" I asked as soon as she picked up.

"You have to fill me in," she demanded. "I've been waiting for you to call all day. I've heard so much drama about last night and I don't know what's true and what isn't."

I squished down in the couch and settled in for a good old gossip session. I told Peta everything, well, almost everything. I told her about Derek and Tracey, about Simon pulling out of the fight and Mark organising Gabe to take his place. I told her it all, apart from the connection between Gabe and myself. I just couldn't face it. I knew when it came down to it, she wouldn't care, but I also knew she wouldn't be able to keep the shock out of her tone. I just didn't feel like being judged.

"I almost wish I was there," Peta exclaimed when I was finally done. "So, that's it for you and Derek?"

"Looks like it."

"You sound surprisingly okay with it," she said warily.

"I am. Today, anyway. Ask me again tomorrow and you might get a different answer."

"You want to come over? Shrek's cooking pasta for dinner."

"Think I'll just stay here tonight. Thanks though."

"I'm here if you need me, okay?"

22

LAUREN

I felt stupid doing it, but I went shopping before my date with Gabe. Of course, I told myself that I wasn't shopping because of him, I was merely shopping as I desperately needed some casual clothes that didn't consist of worn sweatpants and stained t-shirts. But still, if it hadn't been for Gabe, I would have been quite content lounging around the house dressed like a slob. I ended up buying several pairs of jeans and some printed tops and shirts, still casual, but a lot better than my usual comfortable clothes.

Gabe pulled up right on time. I felt that familiar flit of nervousness again, but as soon as I pulled open the car door and Gabe smiled at me, it vanished.

"Hey," he said over the blare of the music before turning down the volume.

"Hey, yourself." I settled into the seat and pulled on the seat belt. He reached out and ran his hand over my thigh and down to my knee, unable to contain his grin.

We drove out to the countryside and pulled up at the ruin of a dilapidated house standing proudly in the centre of a plantation of pine trees. Its desolate beauty hitched in my throat. I lifted my camera to my eye and began pressing the shutter, trying to capture the forlorn beauty. "It's so beautiful, Gabe," I exclaimed every time I came across a crumbled and rotten board, the new shoots of spring creeping over it.

"I hoped you would like it. It would be my dream to live somewhere like this."

"Like this?" I laughed and gazed over the building where entire chunks were missing. "Something like this would have to be torn down, wouldn't it?"

Gabe nudged the door and it groaned against the rotting floorboards before creaking open. "Not if I had anything to do with it. I'd love to somehow preserve its beauty and protect it from further decay, while making it livable again. Like somehow building a house around it with some of the walls made of glass so the old building was still visible."

"Is that even possible?"

Gabe walked ahead of me, gingerly avoiding the holes of exposed dirt in the floor. "Careful," he said, holding his hand out. I lifted my camera and took a photo of him, hand outstretched, the light streaming through an open doorway behind him, framed in ivy. "I'd like to think it's possible," Gabe continued once he had helped me over one particularly large hole. "That's why I want to become an architect."

"You do?" I asked.

He frowned. "You didn't think I wanted to pour coffee for the rest of my life, did you?"

I shrugged as he led me down the hallway a little and into another room. "Why not?"

The room had a broken window facing out of the porch and an old, overstuffed chair sitting in front of the fireplace. A blanket had been laid over the leaf-strewn floor and a picnic basket rested on it.

Gabe grinned at me shyly. "Too much?"

I blinked. "It's sweet," I assured him.

"Sweet?" He groaned, flopped down on the chair and swung his leg over the side. "I just wanted to do something… you know, nice, to let you know that I like you and stuff."

My mouth twitched and I bit my lip. "You like me and stuff?"

"You know what I mean," he said wryly.

I sat down on the blanket and pulled the basket over. "Sweet isn't a bad thing, Gabe."

"It's not?" He joined me on the blanket.

"Not at all. In fact, no one has ever made me a picnic before."

"Well, if I'm honest, Peta made the picnic," he said.

My eyes flew wide.

"I didn't tell her who it was for or anything," he said quickly. "I felt bad about pulling yet another sickie, so I went into work and explained that I needed the afternoon off so I could take this girl I was rather keen on out on a date. She was fine with it."

I narrowed my eyes. "She was fine with it?"

"Fine might not be the right word, but she assured me I'd still have a job tomorrow and she made me up this basket."

I opened the top flap of the basket and pulled out one of Mark's famous buttermilk scones. I lifted it to my nose and inhaled. "He really is the best at these, isn't he?"

Gabe stretched over and lifted one out of the basket. Leisurely, he lay on his side across the blanket, head propped on his hand and looked over at me. "I want to know about you," he said. "Tell me about your family."

I shrugged. "There's not a lot to tell."

"Well, I've told you about mine."

"You haven't told me much about your family at all," I protested.

Gabe lay back on the blanket and rested his hands under his head, staring up at the patch of sky visible through the ceiling.

"Ah, where to start? It's a bit of a complicated story. My mother was Dad's second wife, he's got two older children with his first wife, and then Clark and me."

We fell silent, thinking of the brother he no longer had. Gabe took a deep breath before continuing. "They split when we were young and Dad won custody, just like he did with his first two, though they had been sent to boarding school by that stage. I'm sure Hamish only won full custody because he had more money."

He looked down at the blanket and traced the floral pattern with his finger while he talked. "Dad moved on and married some ditzy thing." His eyes flicked back up to me. "I don't see them that much, not after..."

He fell silent and I ate my scone, breaking pieces off and popping them into my mouth one by one.

Gabe cleared his throat. "Sorry, talking about my family isn't exactly a happy affair. Your turn now."

I swallowed the last piece of scone. "Well, my family is rather boring, I guess. Mother and Dad have been married forever, and I've only got one sister, Morgan. There's a six year gap between us, I think that's how long it took Mother to agree to do the 'marriage act' again." I used imaginary quotation marks to emphasise my point and Gabe snorted.

"Marriage act?"

"That's what she calls it."

"You're kidding."

"I wish I was. Mother believes that coupling should only be committed for the God-given reason of creating children. Anything more than that would just be a sinful desire of the flesh."

"Your poor father." Gabe shook his head and snickered. "And do you always call her Mother?"

"Anything else would be too casual and she isn't a casual sort of person. Morgan calls her Mum, but they have a different relationship than Mother and I do. She's always been Mother to me."

I reached into the basket and pulled out a bunch of grapes. Gabe followed the grape with his eyes as I put it into my mouth.

"Morgan got married to a nice, sensible man and had a kid one year later. As for me, I was just a disappointment, the black sheep of the family. Well, sort of, I never really did anything to earn that title. It was more just that I didn't do what they wanted."

"So you're saying you're really a good girl and they have you pinned all wrong?" Gabe's eyes flashed teasingly.

"Well, not according to them, but in my mind, all I did was live with a man instead of marrying him immediately, and then I got pregnant out of wedlock which was a big no-no. When we lost the baby, Mother assured me it was because I was unmarried. It was also a huge failure on my part when he left." I let out a deep breath and rolled my eyes. "I've given up ever trying to please her."

Gabe bit into an apple and the crunch was loud in the stillness of the old house. "Your family doesn't sound boring. They sound a little crazy."

"Oh, if she knew about you, she would be convinced you came from the devil himself. And as for me, well, I'd be branded a harlot."

"Harlot?" Gabe questioned.

"The biblical term for a prostitute."

"That's ridiculous. I never paid you," he said with an impish grin. Then he laughed nervously when I raised an eyebrow. "Best not go there, huh?" He looked around the room nonchalantly before his gaze rested back on me, the shadow of a grin remaining. "What about your dad, what's he like?"

"Dad's just Dad." I reached out and plucked a stray leaf off the blanket, tossing it away. It got caught on a slight breeze and tripped over the doorway. "He just does his own thing while Mother rants and raves around him. Occasionally, she'll stop and ask him to agree with her, and he always does, but you can tell he's just keeping the peace."

"And Derek was your first boyfriend?"

I looked up at him and squinted. The sun was setting through the open window behind him and the rays of the sun were setting his hair alight. I held my hand up to shield the glare. "I met him at high school. I was into art and he was into music."

I thought of a young Derek sitting across from me on a bean bag in his room, his guitar propped across his legs, and strumming some god-awful sound. You couldn't call it a tune, it was a noise. A screech. He had a thick flop of black hair, an unlit cigarette hanging out his mouth, and wore only a long white singlet over his jeans. He was so exciting to me then, so forbidden. He would have been five years younger than what Gabe was now, but it seemed like a lifetime ago. So much had happened. So much had been lost.

I shook the memory from my head. Sitting up, Gabe reached out and took my hands between his. "I shouldn't have asked, sorry."

He brought my wrist to his lips and kissed the soft underside. The warmth of the pressure ran through my veins and flushed over my cheeks. I sat up a little straighter, but he didn't let go of my wrist. He continued to slowly work his way up my forearm, leaving warm kiss-prints on my flesh. I swallowed and tried to calm my racing heart.

"What about you?" I asked.

He looked up mid-kiss. "Girlfriends?"

"I'm guessing you've had a few."

He sat up straighter and looked me in the eye. "Well, no, I've never actually had a girlfriend, so to speak. In fact, apart from one other, you're the only person I've slept with more than once."

"So you only slept with all those women and never dated any of them?"

He dropped my hand and narrowed his eyes. "Just how many women do you think I've slept with?"

"Well let's just say that word on the street is that you've broken a few hearts."

"It's not that many, people just assume. And I've never given a girl the impression that it would ever lead to anything further. I'm straight up with shit like that." He scooted closer and picked up my wrist again, staring at me, while pressing his lips to my skin. "If I want something, I will make it known."

He worked his way up my arm and trailed kisses over my shoulder until his mouth rested in the curve of my neck. I did my best not to let his attention overwhelm me, but with each kiss, my pulse quickened just that little bit more. Slowly, he pushed me back until I was lying on the blanket, staring up at him, and he lowered his mouth to my lips. He kissed me gently, then lifted his head and concentrated on undoing the buttons on my shirt. He flicked the first one open and leaned down to kiss me again. With each button's release, his finger grazed against my bare flesh. When all the buttons were all undone, he sat back up and looked down at the narrow strip of exposed flesh. He reached to open my shirt, but I grabbed his wrists and held them firm. While looking at him hovering above me, there was nothing stopping me from thinking of the differences between us. His skin, so perfect, unmarked by scars, not bent out of shape by life. He had seen me naked before, of course, he had seen the scar that stretched across the base of my stomach, seen the loose flesh that remained, but not like this, not with me so exposed with nowhere to hide.

"Why?" he asked and cocked his eyebrow, while my hand held his away. "I want to see you. Don't hide from me."

I almost laughed at that. "Look at you, Gabe." I ran my hand under the hem of his t-shirt and rested it against his chest. "You look like you belong on the cover of a fitness magazine or something."

"Really?" he said with a devilish smile. "I was hoping for more along the lines of a romance novel." He bent down and kissed the dip between my collarbone and tugged to release my grip on his hands.

"Please?" he uttered.

Sensing my hesitation, he pulled me to my feet and over to where there were fragments of a mirror still left on the wall. Green mould stained the edges and large cracks ran up the broken panels. He stood behind me and began to lower my shirt over my shoulders, meeting my eye in the mirror. When my shirt fell to the floor, he unclasped the hooks of my bra and it also fell. Sliding his hands around my waist, he fumbled with the buttons on my jeans before slowly lowering them, his mouth so close to my skin, his breath ran hot across it. I closed my eyes as he lowered my underwear and I stepped out.

"Open your eyes," he said, his lips brushing against my neck.

I stood naked before the fragmented mirror.

"You are beautiful," he said, walking around to face me. He dropped to his knees and began to place soft kisses on the skin of my belly. I held my breath as his lips trailed over my scar, fighting back the memories it brought.

"Don't hide from me," he said again, before standing and kissing me deeply, gently reaffirming his words and begging for me to open to him. When he felt my hesitation melt away, he pulled back and took off his shirt, flicking open the buttons of his jeans while I watched him with hunger pooling in my depths.

Standing naked, he stared openly, his eyes trailing over every inch of me. When I began to fold in on myself, feeling exposed under his unabashed gaze, he shook his head and lowered me to the ground, running his hands along my sides before encasing my wrists, and pulling them up until they were stretched above my head.

"Stay," he instructed.

His hands glided over me, coming to rest on the soft mounds of my breasts. He massaged the flesh in his hand, clutching and moulding it to his will. With both hands, he trailed over every exposed inch of my skin, drinking me with his eyes before devouring me with his mouth. I moaned and twisted and he looked up, smiling with satisfaction before returning his attention to my body. As he worked his way down, I felt his breath brushing against the apex of my thighs. I tensed and he gripped my flesh, holding me in place. He moaned when he tasted me and I clenched in response. The noises he made were uttered with such longing, they reverberated through to my deepest parts and I reached down and twisted my hands in his hair. He moaned again and I writhed under him.

Just before it became too much, before I shattered into pieces, he raised his head, moved to cover himself and then lowered into me, heavy and hard. I took him eagerly and raised my hips to allow him to thrust into me again, our bodies slamming together as I exploded from within. He cried out, and it sent trembling shoots of contentment through me. I ran my fingers over his back when he slumped over me, happy, content and marvelling in the gorgeous man that lay over me.

"That wasn't supposed to happen like that," he said.

"What do you mean?"

"I had no intention of touching you. I didn't want it to be about that out here." He grinned apologetically. "Sorry, I just couldn't help myself."

I laughed loudly in his ear. "Believe me, no apology necessary."

"You are beautiful," he said while untangling himself.

I stretched out on the ground and he lay down, resting his head against my stomach.

"You shouldn't need someone else to tell you that."

"It's a little hard when you've been scarred and beaten by life," I replied dryly.

"But that's what makes you so beautiful." He tipped his head so he could look at me better. "Don't you see that? It's our blemishes that make us who we are, not our perfections."

"That's awfully wise and mature of you," I said, teasing him.

"No, I'm serious. Think about it, think about this house. A modern house, a house freshly built with its plain walls and straight lines, when you look at it all you see is a house. There is no character, no personality. But when you look around this house, you can imagine the people that used to live here, imagine what the house has seen over the years it sat abandoned and forgotten. Are we the first people to make love here in the last fifty years? Or have other people wandered across the fields and crept through its rooms?"

"So you're comparing me to a rotting old house?"

Gabe laughed and turned his head to press his lips into my belly, kissing it firmly. "You're impossible. All I'm saying is don't hide yourself from me. I want you. If I didn't, I wouldn't be here. Trust in that."

He twisted so he was lying on his side, eyes directed at the underside of my breasts. Walking his fingers up my torso, he gently brushed them over my nipples causing me to draw in breath as they hardened under his touch. He sighed contentedly and smiled as he stroked my breasts, massaging them gently under his palms, his fingers leaving imprints as he pressed into the soft flesh. "Is it normal to want you again so soon?"

I followed the line of his body down to where he hardened and swelled under my gaze. After slipping on protection again, he rose over top of me, his eyes dark. Without uttering a word, I opened for him and he sunk into me. I relished the look of pure gratification that came over him, knowing that it was me that had filled him with such desire.

He was slow and gentle, rocking above me, eyes locked on mine until our breathing quickened and we both dissolved.

23

LAUREN

That night, after Gabe had made love to me for the third time and was sleeping soundly, I watched him in the light of the moon that seeped in through the crack in the curtains. His jawline was covered in blond stubble, and a dark freckle sat in the crease of the smile line that ran from his nose to mouth. In the pale light, his skin looked close to perfection. The dips of his muscles were shrouded in shadow and the smooth surfaces exposed to the moonlight glistened as if they were illuminated from within.

He was beautiful.

My chest constricted at the thought of him being mine, that somehow, in this strange world, he had chosen me to lay beside. I brushed the hair back from his face. He stirred and reached out, sighing contentedly as he drew me close. I huddled in and rested my chin against the bare skin of his chest. Nudging at him with my knee, he opened his legs and I slid mine between his.

"Careful," he muttered, his voice drenched in sleep. "You'll start me off again."

I smiled against his chest. "You've got stamina, I'll give you that."

With his eyes still closed, he shook his head, the movement rustling the pillow. "Not stamina. I just recover quickly. I'll work on the stamina."

I stretched up so my mouth was close to his. "I like it when you tell me to be careful," I whispered. "It's almost a challenge."

He moved his lips against mine and I felt him stir against my belly. "I have great difficulty containing myself around you, Mrs Robinson."

As I pushed myself closer against him, he groaned. There wasn't a more seductive sound in the world. The effect it had on me was instant, and the urge to feel him fill me once again throbbed intensely. I pressed my mouth fully and openly onto his, and reached down to wrap my hand around his growing hardness.

"You're going to exhaust me," he groaned in my ear.

"I'm sure you'll manage somehow." I pushed him onto his back, reaching down to grab a condom from the beside cabinet and then rose over him, sinking onto him as he sat up and jostled me until my legs wrapped around his waist. Joined together, he dipped his head to my breast and wrapped his arms around me while I clung to his shoulders, pressing him deeper and removing the last whisper of distance.

* * *

I was scared walking into work, afraid that Peta would take one look at me and know my secret. She didn't though. She came over and hugged me, and for a while, I couldn't think of a reason for her affection before remembering that it was only two days ago that Derek and I broke things off. Two days I had spent in the arms of another man. Peta chatted easily and I tried to act as if everything was normal.

When Gabe arrived, the look he gave me had the blood rushing to my head. And other places.

"Hey," was all he said as he passed. But his eyes. My god, his eyes. They said the things left unspoken, and my heart skipped a few beats. Each time I looked up from my work, he was watching me, eyes alight, and a smile playing at the corners of his mouth.

"Stop it," I whispered as I walked past him.

"I'm sorry?" he said loudly. "Stop what?"

I looked over to Peta, but she was restocking the flavour shot bottles and paying no mind to me at all. "Stop looking at me like that."

He stepped closer and lowered his tone. "Like what, exactly?"

I moved away as Mark drifted through the doorway. "You know damn well, like what," I hissed.

"I'm afraid I don't." His eyes shone roguishly. "Would you care to enlighten me?"

Mark narrowed his gaze. "What are you two whispering about?"

"Nothing," I said quickly.

"Actually we were talking about the staff Christmas function," Gabe said with his gaze levelled on mine. He cocked his head to one side. "Weren't we, Lauren?"

I nodded and bent down to pick up some imaginary coffee beans off the floor.

"What's the plan, boss?" Gabe said, turning to Peta.

"My goodness, who knows? We've got another month to worry about such things. But speaking of functions…" She left it hanging and I stood up to find her staring directly at me, arms crossed.

"What?" I said.

"Are we doing something for your birthday, or are you hiding from that, too?"

I laughed nervously.

"It's her birthday?" Gabe asked, turning to Peta. "When?"

"Sunday," Peta replied and I inwardly cursed her for letting him know. "The big three-o." She grinned.

"Thirty?" Gabe sucked his breath in as a low whistle. "That's getting rather old there, Lauren. Climbing that hill fast, aren't we?"

I swatted him with the tea towel hanging over my shoulder and scowled.

"Since you're not going home this year, Ren, we need to do something," Peta said. "Why don't you come over to my place for dinner, I'm sure Gabe and Jordan can handle the close that night. Can't you, Gabe?"

Gabe cleared his throat. "Sure. No problem." He looked sadly over to me and mouthed 'your birthday?' sticking out his lip and feigning a pout. I shook my head and hoped no one caught the exchange.

"It's sorted then. Birthday dinner at my house. No excuses." Peta put her hands on her hips and glared at me.

"Sounds lovely." I smiled and stared hard at Gabe who was still pulling pleading faces.

Later, he cornered me in the storeroom when no one was around. "Birthday dinner?" he said, leaning against the doorframe as I tried to tug another sleeve of cups from a high box. "I want to come." He crossed his arms and watched as I struggled.

"You can't," I replied and pulled harder at the thin plastic material encasing the cups.

"Why not?" He walked over and easily tugged the cups down and handed them to me. I couldn't figure out how, with only being slightly taller than me, it was so much easier for him.

"Because no one knows about us," I explained.

"What if I want them to?" He stepped forward and tucked a strand of my hair behind my ear.

I reeled back from him and looked at the door. "Gabe," I warned. "You promised."

"I've changed my mind," he said and tugged me to him, kissing me urgently. I pulled away, knowing that being in such close proximity to him caused my thinking to become unhinged and he laughed, fully aware of the effect he had on me.

"No," I said firmly.

He smiled and chewed his bottom lip. "Do you know what I was thinking that first day I found you in here?"

I frowned. "That I wasn't tall enough to reach the top boxes?"

"What a glorious backside." He pulled me close before I could register what he was doing and gripped my cheeks. "That was the exact word. Glorious." He bent down to whisper in my ear. "I just want people to know that this backside belongs to me and no other. That isn't too much to ask, is it?"

I pushed away from him, petrified that someone would see, and he let out an irritated sigh.

"What about Peta, then? Surely you would be alright with telling your best friend?" He stood, eyebrows raised and arms crossed, waiting for my reply. "Let me come to dinner. Please?" He battered his eyelashes playfully and I had to laugh. "Just Peta and Shrek, that's all. I promise I won't ask for any more. I just want to be there with you on your birthday. Surely that's not too much?"

I couldn't resist him. "I'll see what I can do."

Gabe glanced out the door, checking no one was around and kissed the tip of my nose. "Then, I'll behave."

* * *

Later that evening, Gabe sat beside me on the couch, my feet resting on his lap while we watched another episode of Blood Too Sweet.

"Did you talk to her?" he asked.

I looked over at him, amused. "When would I have had the chance?"

"You will, though, won't you? I know you don't want to be the subject of gossip, but surely you can tell Peta." He hesitated a moment then said, "My flatmates know."

"They do?"

He squeezed my feet. "I hardly ever stay away from home, they knew something was up. Don't worry, they know you don't want anybody knowing anything. They'll keep their mouths shut."

"I'll talk to Peta tomorrow, I promise," I assured him.

Gabe tugged my feet so I fell down on the couch and he moved over me. "You won't regret it, Mrs Robinson." Then his mouth was on me and I forgot anything else existed.

* * *

I woke the next morning with Gabe sound asleep and breathing heavily beside me. I nudged him but he didn't move. "Gabe?" I asked and he grunted. "What time do you have to be at work?"

He sat bolt upright, throwing the blankets off and exposing us to the cool air. Goose bumps prickled over my skin. "Shit!" he said. "I'm late." He bounded out of bed and walked towards the ensuite, his backside pale compared to the tanned skin of his torso. "Okay if I shower?" he asked, sliding the door open. I smiled mischievously and ran my eyes down his body.

"Hey, Mrs Robinson," he said grinning. "Eyes up."

He left the door open and I lay back and watched as he stepped into the shower. He had his back to me and the glass walls gave me full access to watch him as he lathered the soap and rubbed it over himself.

"Shit, you've done it again," he cursed.

"What?" I called out.

He didn't answer and instead stepped out of the shower dripping wet, and fully erect. "Care to join me?"

I had lost count of the times we had made love, and if I was perfectly honest, I was beginning to feel a little tender. But at the same time, it seemed a waste to refuse him. I knitted my brows together.

"It won't take long." He raised one eyebrow and grinned suggestively as he walked over and stood in front of me. The sight of him glistening wet had me reaching out to him just as a droplet of water ran down his body and got caught by the fine trail of hair that ran down to his pelvis. He led me back to the shower and my skin tingled as the warm water ran over my skin. He grabbed me from behind and I felt his hardness press against my backside. The water ran over us as he kissed me urgently and groped at my body before pushing me against the wall. I sucked in my breath as he flattened me against the cold tiles and nudged me open with his knee. He entered me quickly and held my arms out wide as he moaned in pleasure. He was true to his word and came quickly, grunting with satisfaction and sucking the curve of my neck.

Pulling away from me, his eyes shone cheekily. "I promise to tend to you later." He washed quickly and stepped out of the shower while I stayed under the warm stream and watched as he dried himself and pulled on his jeans and his work t-shirt. "I really need to bring a fresh change over when I come," he muttered. "And a tooth brush." He looked up at me hesitantly. "That is if you don't mind."

I had become distracted watching him. His attention in the shower only served to awaken a part of me, not satisfy it. "You'd better leave."

He looked over, a little concern carried on his expression as he ran my hair brush through his hair. "Why?"

I let my eyes fall over him and, as realisation dawned, he grinned wickedly. "Oh, don't you worry. I won't forget I owe you one." He pulled open the door and leaned in to kiss me, but dropped his head when I tried to meet him and instead ran the width of his tongue across my breast. My nipple swelled immediately and I breathed in sharply.

"God bless you, Mrs Robinson," he muttered as he walked out the door and down the hallway.

"That song doesn't even mention anything about an older woman and a younger man!" I yelled after him.

"But I'm pretty sure the movie did!" he yelled back.

24

LAUREN

At work, I hovered around Peta. I knew I had to tell her, but I just couldn't force myself to bring up the subject. It didn't help that big-ears Mark kept popping his head around the corner, either.

"Your snots over their colds yet?" Mark asked. It was a slow day in the kitchen and Mark had been poking his head into the café whenever he felt bored, which turned out to be rather often.

Peta groaned. "Just as soon as one recovers the next one starts. By the time it makes its way around all three boys, the first one catches it again. It's horrible! Snot and tears everywhere!"

Mark screwed up his face. "Unwanted visual." He shuddered and walked back into the kitchen.

Placing her hands on her hips, Peta frowned, worry lines creasing her forehead. "I'm shipping them out to the in-laws for your birthday dinner."

I shook myself out of my Gabe-obsessed headspace and shrugged. "It wouldn't worry me, they don't have to go. Actually, I haven't seen them in a while and I'd love to."

"I've managed to ship them off for an entire night. You're not taking that away from me." She walked over and placed her hand on my shoulder. "But something's worrying you. You've had a permanent frown on your face since you walked in this morning."

"Have not," I insisted.

"Not to mention that rather suspicious looking bruise on your neck."

My hand flew to the left side of my neck where Gabe had attached himself rather forcefully in the shower. Blood flooded my cheeks and a wave of panic washed over me.

Peta looked at me sceptically, and a little curiously. "You may as well just tell me. You know I'll harass you until you do."

I sighed and swallowed the lump that had risen to the base of my throat. "Fine. But can we sit down for a bit? I don't want a certain someone overhearing."

Peta grinned. "Sounds juicy."

"You have no idea."

Mark manned the counter while Peta and I sat at the furthest away table. My hands were clammy and I wiped them against the legs of my pants. It was stupid to be so nervous about telling her. What was I afraid of? Peta had been my friend through thick and thin, it wasn't as if anything I told her would change that. I was more nervous about what she wouldn't say to me, the things she would go home and say to Shrek. She wouldn't think badly of me, but she would be surprised.

And probably a little shocked.

Even though to some people the age gap wasn't that big, the visual appearance of that age gap was. With his long hair, cheeky smile, and baggy pants, Gabe looked young. I, on the other hand, looked every one of my twenty-nine almost thirty years.

Peta groaned and laughed. "The suspense is killing me, spit it out. Who gave you the hickey? Did you make up with Derek? Is that what you're afraid to tell me?"

"Hell, no! Derek and I are done." I stretched my neck, trying to catch a glimpse of the bruise in the reflection of the window. "It's not that noticeable, is it?"

"Only when you tilt your head to the side," Peta snickered. "So if you didn't make up with Derek, did you have an unfortunate accident with the vacuum cleaner?" She burst out laughing, but I was having difficulty seeing the funny side. I was angry and suddenly flustered. I was doing my best not to show it, but the fact that he had marked me, somehow feeling that he could stake his claim even when he knew full well how I felt, had left my thoughts writhing in resentment.

"OMG," she laughed. "It's like we're sixteen again!" She saw my face and tried to contain her laughter. "I'm sorry, Ren. But you've got to admit…" She pressed her lips together but they trembled as her eyes welled with mirth. "I'm sorry, I'll stop now." Peta stretched her mouth wide, as if to rid it of the urge to twitch into a smile, and looked at me solemnly, only the faintest hint of a grin remaining. "So you're not back with Derek?"

I shook my head. It was worse telling her now. "It was Gabe."

Peta's eyebrows shot skywards. She blinked a couple of times but other than the eyebrows, her expression was blank. It was her 'panic-while-I-scramble-to-think-of-something-to-say' look, a look she would usually give other people then turn to me, her best friend, roll her eyes and smirk.

So I started from the beginning and told her everything. It just poured out of me, every little thing, even the stuff I was ashamed of, which, in the cold light of day, seemed like everything.

"Well," Peta said, lowering her eyebrows and sinking her head to her hand that was propped on the table. "Gabe?" she said. It wasn't really a question, it was more a request for a second confirmation. "Gabe gave you the hickey."

I nodded. "Are you disappointed in me?"

"In you?" She shook her head. "Never. I'm just a little shell shocked. More that you didn't tell me than that it happened."

A breath I hadn't realised I was holding exhaled out.

"And Derek doesn't know?" she asked.

I shook my head. "You're the only person I've told. Though Gabe said he told his flatmates."

"And the bet?" She frowned. "This was after the bet?"

I shook my head and Peta's frown deepened. "He paid up even though he hadn't lost? With the money I advanced to him?" She elongated the 'I'.

"I know it's weird, and a little strange, well, for me, anyway, but he's so sweet."

"He's sweet? Gabe is sweet?"

"He is. I know with the bet and all, it really doesn't sound good for him, but he does care about me. And, in my own way, I care about him too." I shrugged and looked up at her, hoping my eyes were weighted with enough honesty.

"So it's not about the..." Peta shielded her mouth from the rest of the café and the twinkle returned to her eyes. "The sex?" she mouthed while grinning wolfishly.

I couldn't help the smile that widened across my face. "Well, that certainly has its advantages, but honestly, he's sweet and nice. And he tells me I'm beautiful. Can't I just enjoy it without feeling guilty for a bit?"

Peta laughed and shook her head. "Lauren James Greer, you do astound me." She creased her expression into a frown. "It is going to take a little getting used to though." She snorted and shook her head again in disbelief. "You and Gabe."

"Well, that's why I wanted to talk."

"There's more?" she asked, her eyebrows tilting.

"No, nothing more like that, it's just, well, he wants to come to my birthday dinner on Sunday night."

Peta blinked once. "Sure," she said and smiled widely. "Sure. It will be fun. You'll have to give me more details later." She took the last sip of her coffee. "Or maybe I don't want to hear them." She tilted her head. "Do I want to hear them, or will I get jealous?"

I didn't say anything, but my smile may have curled up, just a little.

"Don't tell me." Peta stood and pushed her chair back from the table, and then she added, "Okay, do. But later. You can tell me later."

When Gabe arrived at work, Peta stood with her hands on her hips and looked between us. She didn't say anything, but just glared at Gabe for a moment, and returned back to the kitchen, only to come back a fraction later and glare at Gabe again.

"I hear you're coming to dinner on Sunday night?"

Gabe looked over at me quizzically, then back to Peta. "If you can find someone else to handle the close, I'd be grateful... boss." He scratched his nose and grinned wryly.

"Mark!" Peta yelled. "You're covering Gabe's close Sunday night."

Mark strode to the door. "Like f—" He looked around the café. "I don't do the weekends."

"Well it's Lauren's birthday and I'm having her over for dinner. Gabe has also requested some unexpected time off. What do you suggest I do?"

Mark held up his hands at her clipped tone. "Fine. I can close Sunday night."

Peta closed her eyes and breathed deeply before opening them again and looking at me. "I'll be fine by Friday."

That was why I never wanted to tell her. It wasn't the disapproving look or the amused look that I had feared, it was the look of utter shock. Like she honestly thought me never capable of such a thing, and it had momentarily disbanded her from knowing who I was. That was how Peta had looked at me.

Like I was a stranger.

"So you told her?" Gabe asked. It was a question yet somehow his expression held a nervous apology.

"She's fine. Just a little shocked. You're a little out of my normal, Gabe."

"Well, you're a little out of my normal too." He stepped close and chewed on his lip, releasing it slowly between his teeth as his mouth was overcome with a smile.

I pushed him away and laughed before controlling it into a faint smile. "You're an idiot," I said. Then his eyes fell to my neck and I remembered. "You're also an arsehole."

* * *

As soon as Gabe arrived at my place that night, I ripped into him. "A freaking hickey?" I said, tugging the collar of my uniform aside.

"Oops?" He offered an apologetic, but not really sorry, smile. "And I'd prefer it if you called it a love bite."

"You know I don't want anyone to know and yet you do this to me."

"I didn't mean to, I just sort of got carried away. Besides, no one will know it was me that gave it to you."

"If you hadn't noticed, no one my age walks around with hickeys or love bites on their necks!"

Gabe shrugged which infuriated me. "I hadn't done it before now, either. It just sort of happened."

"Well, it better bloody not happen again." I crossed my arms and glared at him.

He tilted his head to the side and grinned slightly. "Are you done?"

"Only if you know that I'm serious. You can't do that again. Ever. Okay?"

"Never ever?"

"Never," I said again. The closer he stood, the weaker my anger became. I sighed when there were only inches separating us. "Promise me."

"I promise you." Gabe kissed my forehead. "No, I solemnly swear to you," he kissed each cheek, "Lauren Greer," he kissed my nose and then stood so his lips touched mine when he spoke, "that I will never ever touch my lips to your neck again."

"Gabe... be serious," I said, though my resolve was wavering.

Gabe straightened. "I promise never to mark you like that again."

"Thank you."

"Unless, of course, you ask me to. Then I'll do it again quite willingly."

25

LAUREN

By the time my birthday arrived, the hickey had faded and was barely noticeable under a thin cover of concealer. Gabe was coming to pick me up and I was ready and waiting when the doorbell rang. He was perfectly on time. I swung the door open and was greeted by wide arms and a smiling face.

"Happy Birthday, Aunty L!"

"Madi!" I said, surprised as my sixteen year old niece wrapped her arms around me. Behind her, my mother, father, sister and brother-in-law stared back at me. Mother held a large box in her arms while Dad stood dutifully beside her, looking at the overgrown ivy climbing up the wall of my house. My sister and her husband, Alistair, stood arm in arm, Morgan smiling apologetically while Alistair stared down at the ground.

"You always come home for your birthday so, when you called us and said you couldn't, we knew we had to come. Happy Birthday, darling." Mother bustled past me and walked into the lounge, staring at every corner of the house and frowning. "Where's your kitchen? I need a cup of tea."

Madison, who still had her arms wrapped around my waist tightly, grinned. She was a pretty girl, with a wide, innocent smile. Her eyes were hazel, touching on the golden side, the same shade as her hair. Across her cheeks was just the lightest dusting of freckles. She looked like the pastel version of her mother. Water colour to Morgan's oil canvas. "Happy Birthday, Aunty L." She squeezed me tight before letting go.

Morgan strode past, her arms burdened with bags, while Alistair stood in the doorway. "Happy Birthday, L," she said wryly. "Surprise."

"Where's your kitchen, Lauren? All I can seem to find are hallways and living areas." Mother yelled from down the hall.

"This way, Mother," I yelled back to her while I ushered Morgan through to the kitchen and told Alistair to stop standing in the doorway and come in.

"Oh," Mother said when she found us again. She looked around the room disapprovingly. "Your kitchen is part of your second living area. How quaint."

"It's called open plan living," Morgan said, dumping her bags and collapsing onto the couch. "Al, come grab these and put them in a room somewhere." She turned to me. "Which room, L?"

"Must you do that, Morgan? Her name is Lauren, not L. And how do you not find it confusing to call both your husband and your sister by the same name?"

Morgan rolled her eyes. "They are not the same."

"L and Al?" My mother blinked and held her eyebrows high, waiting for Morgan's response.

Unfortunately, my mother and I looked undoubtedly similar. All my life, people told me I was the spitting image of her. Morgan took after Dad. Open face, dark eyes and deadly straight hair, only, Dad didn't have his anymore.

"It's perfectly clear in my mind," my sister replied.

"Well, we don't live in your mind, Morgan. We live out here in the world where L and Al sound exactly the same."

Morgan rolled her head in my direction. "Lauren," she said sarcastically sweetly. "Which room are we staying in?"

My mind went blank. I stared around the small room, now crowded with people and I couldn't think of one thing to say.

Then the doorbell rang.

Gabe opened the door before I could get to it, and walked in carrying a single, white lily. He grinned divinely when he saw me, and it wasn't until he was halfway across the room that he noticed the others. He stopped and held the flower out, clearing his throat. "Ah, Happy Birthday."

"Who is this, Lauren?" Mother said, coming up behind me and staring at Gabe and his outstretched lily.

I stepped forward and took it from him. "Thank you." I smiled and tried to express my panic in one desperate look before turning to my mother. "This is Gabe. I work with him and I was giving him a ride out to Peta's tonight. She invited us over for a sort of birthday-work thing."

"Does he know that a white lily is a symbol of death?"

Gabe looked at me, slightly panicked.

"I love it," I assured him.

"I thought we were going out for dinner?" My father said, walking through the door. He must have finished his inspection of the outside of my house. "You said we were going out, Clementine."

Gabe looked at me and mouthed, "Clementine? As in, 'Oh my darlin'?"

"Of course we're going out for dinner," Mother said. "You can just call Peta and tell her to meet us at the restaurant. What's that one you wanted to go to Morgan?"

During the conversation that ensued over which restaurant we should go to, Gabe sidled over to me. "A bit of a surprise, huh?"

Madison took the opportunity to stroll over to Gabe and smiled widely. "Hi. I'm Madison." She held out her hand and smiled shyly when Gabe shook it. "Do you work with Aunty L in real estate?" Her eyes skittered excitedly over him and I had to stop myself from scolding her.

I left Gabe fixated in her gaze and went to call Peta from behind closed doors. "My mother is here," I said as soon as she answered the phone. "No, correction. My mother, and father, sister, brother in law, and niece are here."

"Fuck," she muttered.

"Yes, f-word," I whispered.

"You can say it, you know."

"Not when my mother is within earshot, I can't. Gabe just arrived. They think we were going to have some work function slash birthday dinner at your house and they're insisting you come out to dinner with us at a restaurant instead. Please say you'll come."

"Of course we'll come," Peta said, almost annoyed, then she laughed. "I wouldn't miss this for the world."

"There are no sheets on any of the spare beds," I announced when I walked back in.

"We will worry about that later," my mother said. "Did you call Peta? Will she just meet us there? I'm starving. We should get going, don't you think?"

"It's only five thirty," Morgan said.

"People eat at five thirty," Mother replied.

"We haven't even booked," Morgan said.

"Nonsense. You don't need to book." Mother waved her hands in Morgan's direction. "We'll be fine." She twisted on her heels and looked at Gabe. "You needed a ride, didn't you, young man?"

Gabe stood up from where he was perched on the arm of the couch. "Yes, thank you. I do."

Mother narrowed her eyes at him a fraction and looked over to where Madi was gazing at him wide-eyed. "Why exactly are you here again?"

"He's a workmate," I said, stepping between them. "And a friend of mine." I touched my hands gently to her shoulders and steered her towards the door. "I'm starving too. Let's just go."

After Dad went to the bathroom, Morgan had to go. And then Madi wanted to change her outfit. Then Mother thought it best to put on her 'going out shoes' and finally we were ready to leave for the restaurant. The family all travelled down together and were able to fit into Dad's car, which left Gabe and I free to ride in my car. Madi insisted on going with us. Gabe's jeep sat parked on the side of the road as we left.

"Do you like working in the coffee shop, Aunty L?" Madi asked, sitting forward and poking her head through the gap in the seats.

"Yes, it's fine," I replied.

"Gabe said he likes it, didn't you, Gabe?" She rested her hand on his shoulder and Gabe couldn't help but grin at my expression.

"Yes, I like it fine, Madison." He tried to hold in his smile.

"Though you want to study architecture?"

"Yeah, hopefully, next year."

"I'll be done with high school in a couple of years. I'm not quite sure what I'm going to study after that yet though. Mum thinks I should get into early childhood education. She thinks I'd be good at it, but I'm not sure if I could handle the bratty ones. The cute ones would be fine, but looking after the ones that cried all the time, or had one of those little painfully high voices, nope. I just couldn't do it." She sat back and looked out the window for a few moments before leaning forward again. "So you don't have your license yet, or do you not have a car?" she asked Gabe.

Gabe looked confused.

"Why did you need a ride?" she clarified.

"Oh," he said. "No license, I guess."

"So you must live pretty close if you walked over to Aunty L's?"

"Not too far from Aunty L, no." His eyes slid over to me as he drew out the word aunty.

"I might come visit you. We're down for a few days."

"You are?" I asked, my heart dropping to my stomach.

"I've got time off school and all. Gran is worried about you, Aunty L. She says that you're not telling her everything and that you haven't called in ages. She said every time she gets you on the phone you're too busy to talk."

"Do you listen to Gran every time she wants to talk?" I asked her.

She laughed. "Fuck no."

"Madison! Language," I warned. "What would your mother say?"

"She isn't here." Grinning, she looked over to Gabe. "I'm sixteen. I'm old enough to swear. What about you? How old are you?"

Gabe swallowed before he answered and his smile dropped just a fraction. "Twenty-one."

Madison's eyes lit up. "There's only five years between us."

I learnt a lot about my niece in that short trip. Mainly, that she wasn't as innocent as she looked. And, although she still had a girlish appeal, she certainly didn't consider herself to be young anymore. Gabe had a difficult time controlling his amusement as she gushed over him. He didn't exactly encourage it, but he certainly found it entertaining watching me squirm as Madi recklessly flirted with him. I was grateful when we pulled up at the restaurant and exited the car.

Peta and Shrek were already waiting at the table. There were hugs and greetings, then, as we sat down, it fell silent. Gabe sat to my right, Madison next to him and Morgan on my left.

"So is Derek meeting us here?" Mother asked.

Colour rose to my cheeks. I never made the phone call to my mother, the one to tell her I was no longer with Derek. As far as she was concerned, Derek and I were still giving things another chance. I guess her phone calls to him must have stopped as I doubted Derek would have kept it a secret. Gabe ran his hand across my thigh and I tensed. "No, he won't. Derek and I are no longer together."

"You didn't give it very long," Mother scoffed as the waiter came over. She scowled at me as she ordered her sparkling water. "Did you even try?" she hissed in my direction.

"Of course I tried. It just didn't work out."

Mother folded her arms. "Marriage isn't something you just toss aside when it gets hard, Lauren. It was a vow you made before God, before your family and your friends. I hardly see what excuse you can give that warrants giving up on that."

"We weren't married, Mother."

"You were in the eyes of God."

"He was a fucking cheating bastard," Gabe growled. I reached over and gripped his thigh, urging him to be quiet.

Mother looked at Gabe and blinked slowly. "Mind your words, young man," she warned.

"Surely not." Dad spoke up for the first time since we got to the restaurant. "He didn't, did he, Lauren?"

"I'd really rather not talk about this here." I picked up my wine the waiter had just delivered and drunk deeply, meeting Peta's eyes over the rim of the glass.

"So, Morgan," Peta said loudly. "How are the music lessons going? You'll have quite the number of students now, I imagine?"

Morgan picked up on Peta's distraction techniques and happily chatted away, discussing her students and their talent, or in some cases, lack of talent.

"It's great that you've found something you love doing," Peta said.

"Well, someone needs to pay the bills." Morgan pointedly looked over at Alistair who stared down at his hands resting in his lap.

"Morgan dear, that is no way to speak about your husband," Mother admonished.

"Well, there's one simple way to stop me." She raised her eyebrows and glared at Alistair again, but he wouldn't meet her gaze, so she sighed loudly and took a sip of her lemonade.

"Is your name short for Gabriel?" Madi piped up, her attention to Gabe undeterred by her mother's glare.

Gabe swallowed the mouthful of beer he had taken. "Ah, no." He wiped his mouth with the back of his hand. "It's short for Gable."

"Gable?" Madison and I said at the same time. "As in, Anne of Green?" I added, trying to hide my laughter.

"Gable," Gabe repeated. He turned to me. "As in Clark. And yes, my brother's name was Clark. My mother had an addiction to Gone with the Wind."

"What's that?" Madison asked as I struggled to contain my smile.

"A movie you shouldn't be watching," Mother admonished.

"So," Gabe said, changing the subject. "Alistair, what do you do for a living?"

"Oh, he tinkers with computers all day, but as for making a living, that's up to me," Morgan answered for him.

Peta and Shrek shared a knowing look between them while Alistair ignored Morgan and looked over to Gabe. "I'm developing a new app. Hopefully it will revolutionise the need to carry around countless reward cards, but it's taking a while to sort out the glitches."

"A while? Try an entire year," Morgan said dryly.

"Sounds interesting," Gabe said as the waiter came to take our food orders.

"It is interesting, isn't it, Daddy?" Madison piped up once the waiter left. "He's just got to figure out how to process the cards, some work off a bar code, others work off a magnetic strip. Daddy just needs to figure out how to convey the correct information most efficiently and compatibly."

Alistair smiled at his daughter.

"Gabe is going to be an architect." Madison smiled her wide smile at Gabe.

"Is that right?" Alistair said, leaning over the table. Soon, all the men at the table were involved in a lively discussion regarding the building industry and the costs it took to construct a house.

I caught Peta staring at Gabe during the evening, a puzzled look on her face as if she really couldn't quite grasp what he was doing here.

"It's strange," she said when I followed her to the bathroom. "I'm trying, but I just can't see him with you."

"Well having my entire family here sure isn't helping matters any," I grumbled. "Mother keeps asking me if the rest of my workmates are going to turn up too. And Morgan, well she knows something's up because she keeps looking at me with this stupid grin on her face. I don't think she's clicked that it has anything to do with Gabe though. She's too busy scowling every time Madi talks to him."

Peta laughed and flattened herself against the wall to let a lady pass. "She's sure taken a shine to him. Jealous? She is far closer to his age than you."

The door opened again and Morgan walked in. "So?" she said. "What are we in here gossiping about?"

"Derek," Peta said quickly.

"So it's true? He really cheated on you?"

I nodded and she hugged me tightly. "Arsehole. Why didn't you tell me? You know Mum's not going to drop it, don't you? In her eyes, you're bound to that man for life."

"Why would she change now?" I asked wryly.

Morgan sighed. "That workmate of yours though."

"What about him?" I swallowed the nervous lump in the back of my throat.

"I'm afraid Madi is going to start dancing on the table in order to get him to notice her. Should I be worried? How old is he, anyway?"

"Twenty-one," I replied.

Peta snorted. "Sorry," she said, covering her smile. "I just didn't realise he was that young. I mean, I hired the guy, I knew he was that young, I had just forgotten for a moment. He's harmless enough though," she assured Morgan and smirked at me behind her back. "I've heard he's into older ladies." I shot her a death glare and she laughed. "He's probably more into you than your daughter."

"A woman can dream." Morgan sighed again.

"Morgan!" I exclaimed.

"What?" she said. "There's no harm in looking, or dreaming, or perhaps…" Her smile turned wicked and the temperature of my blood rose as I imagined the things she was thinking.

"I've heard enough," I said, pushing open the door.

"Oh come on, L. Where's your sense of humour? You can't tell me you hadn't noticed. I've seen the way you look at him!" she yelled at me as the door swung shut.

Madi and Gabe were the only ones to order dessert.

"Oh to be young again," Mother said and looked longingly at the cheesecake Madi was devouring.

Madi pushed the plate across the table. "You want some, Gran?"

Mother shook her head violently. "You know what they say, Madi. A moment on the lips, a lifetime on the hips. Isn't that right, dear?" She looked at me pointedly. "Maybe if you had spent a little less time enjoying those moments, Derek would still be here with us."

Gabe choked on his sticky date pudding. He shot me an incredulous look and reached down to squeeze the flesh of my thigh. Madi was watching him and her eyes narrowed before turning back to my mother.

"I think Aunty L looks fantastic and Uncle Derek must have been smoking something wacky to leave her."

Mother's eyebrows just about clean shot off her head. "And what would you know about such wacky stuff, Madison Grace Wright?"

She grinned. "Oh you know, just what I've overheard the kids saying at school. First hand, I wouldn't have the slightest clue."

Gabe's thigh was pressed against mine and I felt him tense up. His face went red, he pushed his dessert away and cleared his throat. "Maybe we best get going," he said.

Dad stood up. "Best suggestion I've heard all night."

26

LAUREN

"Can I drive, Aunty L?" Madi asked, skipping over to me.

I held the keys out and wrapped my jacket around myself tightly. It had grown cold while we were in the restaurant. Madi clambered into the driver's seat and slammed the door.

"You've got one forward niece there, Aunty L," Gabe whispered. "She literally grabbed me under the table. Not backwards at coming forward that one."

"Grabbed you where, exactly?" I frowned and looked through the window at Madi who was taking her time adjusting the seat and the mirrors.

"Well, let's just say she ran her hand fairly high up."

"The little hussy." I looked at my niece in a new light. One I didn't really want to see her in. "You be careful around her. You aren't—"

Gabe threw his head back and laughed heartily. "You're not jealous are you, Mrs Robinson? I assure you I've only got eyes for you."

I shook my head and smiled a little. "You're an idiot." I pulled open the car door. "You can hop in the back."

"Tell me where to go." Madi smiled at Gabe in the rear vision mirror. "I assume we're dropping you home?"

"Just take me back to Lauren's. I'll walk from there."

"You sure?" she asked. "We could come in for a night cap or something, couldn't we, Aunty L?"

"We will not be going anywhere for night caps, young lady."

"You used to be more fun." She sulked and her eyes flicked to the rear vision mirror once more.

"Eyes on the road," I instructed.

Gabe walked right past his jeep when he left, pretending he didn't have a vehicle. The rest of us walked inside and started to make the beds fit to sleep in. I didn't have enough room so Madi was assigned to the couch in the lounge. She complained for a bit before realising the only other option would be sharing a bed with her mother at which time she promptly shut up. Just before heading off to bed, I opened the presents they had brought. I got a pizza stone from Mother and Dad, and a subscription to a photography magazine from Morgan and family. I already had three pizza stones in the cupboard, and I had given one away. They were a popular gift at my and Derek's engagement party. I would be able to start my own collection soon.

Mother cornered me and made me give her all the sordid details concerning Derek. I could tell she still didn't really believe me, and she still insisted I hadn't tried hard enough.

"And what of the young man tonight?" she asked.

"What of him? I said, looking up from flicking through the glossy pages of the magazine.

"Don't give me that, Lauren. What was he doing there?"

"He's a friend and a workmate, that's all," I said, pretending to be distracted by one of the photos.

"The devil comes to tempt us in many forms," she said solemnly.

"Gabe is not the devil."

"You may think me naïve, Lauren, but I'm not as stupid as you'd like to think. That boy looks at you with a lustful glint in his eye. You would do well to stay away from him. Something like that could ruin your chances of ever getting Derek back."

"But I don't want Derek back," I replied through gritted teeth.

"Well, you should. He's your fiancé and it's your duty to stay by his side."

"My duty?" I could almost feel my hackles rising.

"Yes, your duty," Mother took a sip of her tea and looked at me pointedly.

I considered debating with her, telling her exactly what I thought of my duty, but I bit my tongue as I knew it was pointless. "I'm heading to bed," I told her. "I'll see you in the morning."

Mother stood and pulled me into an embrace. "Happy Birthday, Lauren." She squeezed tightly. "See you in the morning."

I fled down to my bedroom and shut the door a little harder than necessary. The conversation with Mother left me feeling so useless. I pulled at the zipper and let my dress drop to the floor. Staring at it, I considered picking it up and putting it away, but that act alone reminded me of my mother so I left it. For now, I just wanted to climb into bed and forget today ever existed. It was not a birthday I wanted to relive in a hurry. I reached behind and pulled off my bra. Something tapped on the window. Noticing the crack in my curtains, I pulled my nightshirt to my chest, covering myself, and cautiously approached the window to pull aside the curtain. In the darkness, I could only just make out Gabe's figure staring back at me. I opened the window a fraction.

"You really need to be more careful with your curtain placement," he whispered. "I was rather enjoying the show."

"What do you want?" I hissed back, glancing to the door, certain that someone would hear.

"Let me in?" He rubbed his hands over his arms, trying to warm himself.

"But my parents are in the next room."

"I'll be quiet." He pouted and leaned forward, eyes dropping to my chest. "You can't stand there exposed like that and expect me to leave."

I adjusted the shirt to cover myself better and opened the window wider. "Fine." Gabe pulled himself through the opening as I tugged on my shirt and hopped into bed. "You can't stay, though," I warned.

Pulling his shirt over his head and tugging his jeans off, Gabe just smiled and jumped into bed, shivering as he wriggled close to me.

"You're cold," I said quietly, scared that my mother would be able to hear the slightest whisper. I pressed the length of my body against him and he reached across to clutch me, taking all the warmth he could from my body.

"Well, that was an interesting night," he said, shivering. "Shit it was cold out there!"

"Shhh," I hushed him. "You should have just gone home." I rubbed his back, trying to coax some warmth into him.

"But I wanted to see you. I didn't even get the chance to wish you a proper happy birthday."

"What have you been doing out there?"

He shivered again. "Just walking around, waiting for you to go to bed. You took your time."

"You could have just driven home."

He huddled closer. "I was afraid I would get caught getting into the jeep and ruin your perfectly planned excuse." He pushed me away a little. "Can you roll over? I think I've drained all the warmth from this side." I shook my head a little and smiled as he squished even closer. "Your mother's just a lovely ray of sunshine, isn't she?" He chuckled. "Clementine. You look an awful lot like her. It's like getting a peek into your future."

I flicked his chest with my finger.

"Ouch!"

"Behave," I warned.

"It's true," he insisted, laughing softly.

"Quiet. They'll hear you," I pleaded.

He pressed cold lips to my ear. "Speaking of behaving, roll over." He tickled me and I squirmed as noiselessly as I could until I relented and turned over. Gabe nestled into me, pulling me tight, and when my backside pressed against him, he surged with awareness. "I guess not all of me is cold." He pressed his lips to the nape of my neck.

"We can't," I whispered back and looked pointedly at the wall which my parents would be sleeping next to.

"I'll be quiet," he whispered devilishly.

Gabe ran his hand down my side and gripped the flesh of my hip, massaging it as he worked his hand down my thigh. He nudged his way under my arm curled across my chest and stroked my breast gently until he took my nipple between his thumb and forefinger and twisted it gently. My breath caught in my throat, then escaped with a small moan.

"Shhh," Gabe whispered again. He kept gently teasing me until I was grinding against him, virtually begging. Running his hand over my stomach and then trailing further down, he plunged his fingers into me.

"My god, you're wet," he groaned. "I want to taste you."

"No," I breathed, though my body language was saying otherwise. Before I could stop him, Gabe dove under the covers and I struggled to contain the pleasure surging through me. It was too much. It needed somewhere to escape, to release, or else I would come undone. I moaned and gripped the sheets. Gabe slid up me and pressed his finger to his lips, grinning wickedly. Then he covered himself and entered me, thrusting with sharp, hard movements. I couldn't help the little yelps that escaped with each thrust, and Gabe covered my mouth with his hand, his eyes stuck on mine, dark and burning with the knowledge of the way he was making me feel. After tormenting me with ripples that reverberated through every inch of my being every time he moved, he plunged in deep and used his fingers to complete me. Afterwards, I turned limp beneath him, my body melting to liquid as Gabe bit his lip rather than cry out, and fell back to his side of the bed, spent.

"Now I'm warm," he said.

27

GABE

Climbing out of windows in the early hours of the morning was not something I ever aspired to, but that's exactly what I found myself doing. It wasn't easy. I was sort of stuck, one foot on the ground, the other caught by the window frame.

"I can't believe you're making me do this," I said, yanking my foot free until I was finally firm on the ground.

"What did you expect? It's how you came in." Lauren poked her tongue out and shut the window. She stood with her hair mussed up from our time in bed and wearing a pale nightshirt, looking at me. I could see the shape of her breasts and the curve of her hips outlined beneath the thin material. She looked so inviting. I wanted to crawl back through that window and pull her close, but she smiled slow and sexily, and shut the curtains to block me out. No more peeking for me.

I sighed and crept down the path. When I passed the spare bedroom, Alistair was standing at the window and saw me. Lauren was not going to be happy. He looked back to the bed with his sleeping wife in it and then back at me. Shaking his head just the slightest bit and without a hint of a smile, he winked. I sort of waved, or gave the thumbs up or something as I passed him, and jogged out to my car.

I knew what I saw in Lauren wasn't what everyone saw. She tried to hide herself. But when she gave herself completely, if you were there in those moments when she was lost, it was hard to look away. I just wished I was enough for her.

I didn't want to be the one climbing out windows.

* * *

Stefan froze when I walked in, a bowl of cereal in his hand. He grinned stupidly. "You do exist! We were beginning to wonder if you were a figment of our delusional minds. 'Remember our flatmate Gabe,' I would say to Drew. 'Gabe?' Drew would ponder for a bit, 'Why yes, there is something in the back of my mind.'" Stefan slapped me on the back, then reached down to grab at my crotch. I squirmed and ducked away. "Old codger a bit tender there, Gabe?" Stefan laughed and shovelled another spoonful of cereal into his mouth.

"Fuck off," I said, laughing, and flopped onto the couch. It was comfortable and I groaned loudly, feeling like the stress of pretending to only be Lauren's workmate in front of her parents could finally drain from me. "What are you doing up this time of night, anyway?"

"Morning shift," Stefan said with his mouth full. "We've got a shit load of work on at the moment." He jerked his head in my direction. "What are you doing here? Mrs Robinson kick you out?"

"Don't ever call her that when she's here, okay? I shouldn't have fucking told you."

"No, you shouldn't have." Stefan grinned and shovelled in another few mouthfuls. "So why'd she kick you out?"

"She didn't kick me out."

"What are you doing home then?"

"It's where I live, you arsehole. I don't need an excuse to come here."

"Did you not even get a birthday fuck?"

I fumbled behind me until I found a cushion and threw it at him. He ducked out of the way and it hit the wall behind him. "Her family arrived."

"So?" Stefan said.

"So, she hasn't exactly told them about us."

Stefan grinned as he chewed and for some reason, it annoyed me. I had to look away.

"You're her dirty little secret." He shoved in another mouthful but kept grinning so I could see the cereal mushed between his teeth.

"She's just worried about what people will say."

Stefan grinned wider. "Because she's a cougar and you're her little sex toy?" He laughed loudly.

"Fuck up."

"Hit a bit of a sore spot there, did I?" Stefan put his bowl onto the table and picked up the discarded cushion. He tossed it at me hard and it hit the back of my head. "Pussy whipped!"

I groaned into the couch. "Fuck off!"

Stefan bowed ceremoniously. "As you wish, princess." He went to walk out the door but, instead, turned around. "Pool Saturday night, or will Mrs Robinson's family be gone by then and you won't want to hang with your pathetic flatmates anymore?"

* * *

I called her the next day but she didn't want me to come around. Not even to climb through the window. I knew I shouldn't care. I knew I should just sit back and relax, enjoy the time to myself, hang with the boys, but I couldn't stop thinking about her. I think it was the fact that she didn't want me to come over. I wanted her to want me and when she didn't, it drove me a little insane. Over the next few days, I worked, I drank, and I beat the shit out of my boxing bag. I saw her most evenings at work, of course, but with her family in town, she became even more paranoid someone would see us. She hid herself again and I couldn't stand it. The sooner her family left the better. When her niece came into the café, which seemed to happen a lot, I was even tempted to flirt with her, just a little, to see if I could get something, some flash of emotion out of Lauren. Having her angry with me was better than ignoring me. I considered it, but I didn't do it. To be honest, the girl was so obvious and keen, it would have been hard to flirt with her without ending up somewhere I really didn't want to go.

* * *

It was five days before they left. When Lauren texted me to tell me, I was at the movies trying to distract myself with explosions and gunfire. I left in the middle, not caring what happened. Stefan gave me a sort of surprised glance, one eyebrow cocked, but then just shrugged and went back to stuffing his face with popcorn.

Lauren was still in her dressing gown when I rang the doorbell. I was going to just barge in, but there was that little something that stopped me. Just in case something had gone wrong and her psycho mother was still there. I didn't want to run into her.

"Hi." She smiled and I wrapped my arms around her, picking her up and inhaling her scent.

"I've missed you," I said into her hair.

She laughed. The laugh that was all her again, not hidden, not the one she had around her family, not the one she had around her ex-boyfriend, or even the one she had around Peta. This laugh was all mine.

"I've missed you too," she said and wove her hands around my neck.

I reached down and pulled her up so her legs wrapped around my waist, her backside snug in my hands, and I kissed her deeply. I moaned as I felt her melt into me. Slowly, I let her down. Must not get myself too excited.

"Thank goodness they're gone," she exclaimed. "Mother Dearest was driving me insane." She walked through into the kitchen. Since putting her down, the gap in her dressing gown had been mussed up, and I could see the swell of her breasts. "You want a cup of coffee?"

I shook my head. If I tilted my gaze, just a fraction, I could see the rise of her nipple.

"Do you know how many times she asked about Derek? Morgan told her to shut up in the end. It was actually the most fun I had the whole time they were here, watching Mother's mouth flap open as Morgan ripped into her." She reached for the coffee out of the cupboard and the hem of her gown rose to reveal the smooth rounds of her backside. As far as I could tell she was naked underneath.

I shifted and adjusted the fit of my jeans.

"And poor Alistair. Morgan berated him the entire time."

I didn't know what berated meant, but I didn't care.

"Nag, nag, nag, and the man never said a word. He didn't stick up for himself once." She had her back to me and the material of her gown got caught between her butt cheeks.

I couldn't stand it anymore. Approaching her slowly, I turned her to face me.

"Dad was fine though. Barely said a word, no surprises there, but he seemed happy enough."

I cupped her face and kissed her mouth softly. My cock strained against my jeans. My eyes were closed but I felt her smile against me.

"Didn't like doing nothing though. He fixed just about everything I needed to be fixed."

I groaned and kissed her again.

"Cleaned that little patch of mould I couldn't reach on the bathroom ceiling," she mumbled against my mouth. "Fixed the trellis."

I reluctantly pulled away from her and opened my eyes to find hers twinkling with mirth.

"You're killing me," I groaned. "Please, please let me fuck you."

With a slow and seductive smile, she dropped the gown and stood naked before me. My eyes fell to the swell of her breasts. They were so full. I wanted to take as much of them in my mouth as I could. I looked at her longingly and her smile vanished, to be replaced by a look I could only describe as need.

I needed her and she needed me.

The soft curve of her waist called out to me and I stroked my hand over it and brought it around to cup her backside. She trembled as I dug my fingers into her generous flesh, causing her to lift on her toes and push into me. Bending down, I took her breast in my mouth. Each time I flicked my tongue across her nipple, my cock twitched in response. Fumbling with my jeans, I stepped out of them, my mouth still at her breast, her hands tangled in my hair. Breaking away from her only long enough to rip my t-shirt off, I devoured her mouth, her breasts, her belly button, down and down until I reached the place I needed to be. She smelled divine. Parting her thighs, I licked her once. She sucked in her breath and my cock swelled. I took her by the hand and led her to the table where she lay down before me. Gently parting her legs, I lowered my mouth to her, holding her firm when she squirmed and pushing her back to the table when she rose off it. She began to pant.

I loved hearing her pant.

"Careful," she warned, but I intensified my efforts. "I want to feel you," she whimpered.

I lifted my mouth only long enough to answer. "You will," I assured her.

"I want to come with you inside me." She moaned and tried to push my head away.

"You will," I growled.

She cried out and I lapped at her, holding the base of my cock with one hand, willing myself not to share in her pleasure just yet.

28

LAUREN

I was undone. But Gabe wasn't.

My skin gripped against the wood as he pulled my limp body towards him. After covering himself, he gripped my thighs at the end of the table and entered me forcefully and repeatedly, staring at me in such a manner that I soon found myself quivering to maintain control again. And then I lost what control I had the same moment he lost his.

Gabe flopped down on the table beside me. He held one hand to his chest, ran the other through his hair, and laughed. Sitting up, he kissed me firmly. "Thank you."

"You're thanking me?"

He nodded slowly and ran his hand through his hair again. "Yep. I needed that."

I couldn't help the grin that spread over my lips. His was a smile of utter satisfaction. And I had put it there. "You're welcome?" I said and laughed a little. Sitting up, I gathered my robe. "Best I go shower. Again."

Gabe sat bolt upright. "I'm not done with you yet."

"Well, you're going to have to wait. I start work in half an hour."

He grabbed my hand. "Call in sick."

"Gabe," I scolded gently.

"I'll pack a picnic and we could go back to that house." He tugged me toward him. "Please?"

I pulled my hand away, but he gripped hard and peered at me with exaggerated sad eyes.

"Gabe," I warned again.

He jiggled my hand, dropped my fingers and grinned. "See you tonight?"

"You know how Peta has that awards dinner thing?"

He nodded slowly. Peta had been nominated in a local competition for the business woman of the year. Tonight was the night she found out if she won.

"Well, she needed a babysitter, so I offered and she swapped my close shift with Jordan."

"So you're not even going to be at work tonight?" He sighed and frowned. "I haven't seen you in days."

"You're seeing me now. In fact, you just saw quite a lot of me."

"That's not the same thing." He grinned. "That was just so I could calm down and actually concentrate on what you were saying."

"Well, it's all you're going to get today."

Gabe shrugged his t-shirt over his head. "Tomorrow?"

"After work tomorrow night, I'm all yours." I walked over and kissed his forehead.

He pulled me against him and dipped his head to my chest. "The boys want to play pool tomorrow night and I said I'd go with them." He looked back up.

"Oh, okay." I shrugged. "Maybe Sunday?"

"I want you to come with me."

I started to draw back but he held me tight.

"Not, you know, with me, with me. Just come hang out, like we did that other time. Just as friends. I'll keep my hands off you, I promise. I just want to do something with you, something other than this." He buried his head into my chest and found some exposed flesh to nuzzle into. Then he froze and looked back up warily. "Not that I want to stop doing this. I like this." He grinned again. "Very much."

He was hard to say no to. "Okay."

"Okay?"

I nodded and smiled a little. "Okay. Just as friends though."

Gabe held his hands up. "Strictly as friends." Then he placed them gently on each cheek of my backside. "Unless, of course," he said, with mock severity. "You turn up wearing something similar to the top you did last time. If you do that, Mrs Robinson, all promises are off."

* * *

Peta's house was chaotic when I arrived. The middle boy, Charlie, was tearing down the stairs shooting his Nerf gun.

Peta walked down the stairs, Henry on her hip. "Charlie! I told you to go have a shower and change into your pyjamas. Now, go do as you're told!"

Charlie ignored her and Shrek walked down the stairs, knotting his tie. "Do as your mother says. Scram!" He ordered and Charlie flew back up the stairs, laughing, but heading in the right direction at least.

"Ren." Shrek nodded and grinned at me. "Looking as young as you feel, I assume?" His head almost wobbled with his smile as he walked past me. I just narrowed my eyes and shook my head. "Speaking of young, how's Gabe these days? I hear he's proving to be rather useful to you."

"Enough," Peta said, walking over and dumping Henry in his arms. "He needs to be changed. You can do it before we leave." Turning to me, Peta sighed. "Sorry."

"You look pretty," I said, stepping back and admiring her dress. She was dressed all in black. "Understated but elegant," I offered.

"Who cares? It's all I've got," she said. "I had no idea of the state of my wardrobe until tonight. I had no idea how desperately I need to go shopping."

We walked into the large lounge where Nicholas was seated on the cream and gold striped couch, glued to his device. I was just about right in front of him before he looked up.

"Stimpy!" he said and grinned. He pulled the earplugs out of his ears and slapped my hand, returning my high-five.

"Hey, you." I sat beside him. "What are we going to do tonight?"

"Watch the 'Happy Happy Joy Joy' song!" He leapt from the couch and started dancing strangely, bopping up and down on the spot and singing the ridiculous lyrics.

Joining in, I looked over at Shrek who had walked back in with a freshly changed Henry. He rolled his eyes and poked his tongue out at our strange antics before joining in, lifting a chuckling Henry up and down in the air.

"You're an idiot, Dad." Nicholas flopped back down on the couch.

"You're all idiots," Peta said, shaking her head. She turned to me. "Will you be alright here?"

I looked to Nicholas. "What are we playing?"

"Skylanders," he said.

"Yep, we're good," I called out to Peta and picked up a controller.

Babysitting three boys, aged from one to nine may seem hard, but only if you cannot balance a baby on your hip while swaying and using a gaming controller. Thankfully, I was a master, and in no time at all, I was putting the youngest to bed.

Henry went down at seven. He was an easy baby during the day and an even easier baby to put to bed. He snuggled into the blankets and stuffed his thumb into his mouth, asleep within seconds.

Nick and Charlie weren't quite so easy. I had to read a story, and then I had to read another story because Nick got to choose the first story and Charlie didn't get to choose one. Then they remembered they hadn't brushed their teeth. Then they wanted a drink of water. When they came and tried to insist that they hadn't had breakfast that morning and should really eat now, I put on my stern face. "Bed!" I ordered.

"Yes, Stimpy." They giggled and ran back up the stairs.

Once in bed, I scrolled through my social media newsfeed on my phone which was mainly filled with friends from high-school gushing over their children, and selfies of Madison. I was one of the unseen people of social media. The ones that have a profile, a couple of pictures but you see no activity, apart from when they are tagged by other people, and instead, they hover in the background as a silent stalker.

"Did you win?" I asked as soon as Shrek and Peta walked in the door.

Peta pulled a face and hung her head. "No." She sighed and dumped her handbag onto the coffee table. "Everything okay here?"

"Good as gold. You should've won."

Peta nodded. "I should have."

* * *

I was a little nervous when I pulled up outside Gabe's house. I wasn't sure how his friends were going to greet me. And what if it wasn't just them that were there? What if I ran into that Elise? Or, heaven forbid, Haleigh? I almost didn't go in. I almost turned the wheel and pulled away from the curb. But I swallowed the urge and hopped out of the car. Gabe pulled the door open before I could even knock.

He leaned out the door, his hands gripping the frame and smiled so happily, I felt a little giddy. "You came."

"I did." I pulled a bag over my shoulder. "See? I even packed a bag."

Gabe's eyes twinkled and looked me up and down. "You've made me a very happy man, Mrs Robinson."

"Don't call me that here," I hissed.

He released his hold on the door frame and wandered out to cup my face in his hands and kiss me. I hesitated because we were standing outside and Gabe laughed. "Come on then."

I followed him inside. Drew and Stefan were sitting in the living room, drinking beer and watching TV. They raised their bottles in salute and nodded.

"Lauren," they said, one by one, both with a varying degree of amusement.

Gabe tugged my hand and pulled me into his room. "Don't worry, they won't be dicks for long. They'll get sick of it soon."

"Are you sure?" I asked when I heard the distant sound of guitar music coming through the walls.

Gabe listened and his shoulders slumped. "Arseholes," he muttered and shook his head. "I'm so sorry, Lauren."

There was really nothing to do other than laugh as the words of Simon and Garfunkel surrounded us. I yanked open the door and took a bow as they hooted and wolf whistled. Gabe laughed, encircled my waist and dragged me back into the room, shutting the door firmly behind him.

Cupping my face, he kissed me firmly. "Thank you," he said and pulled me onto the bed. "We should make them listen, just to teach them a lesson." I looked at him sternly, but he laughed. "I was kidding. Sort of."

* * *

"This is nice," Gabe said, standing beside me. He rested his head on his fingers wrapped around the tip of his pool cue and leaned towards me. "It's nice being here with you. In public."

"It's not bad." I smiled cheekily and leaned over the table to take my shot. The ball sank into the pocket so I moved around the other side to sight up the black. "Just so long as—" I paused, squinting with one eye to gain my line.

Gabe held his fingers out from the pool cue and said a little sourly, "No touching. I got it. I wouldn't want to ruin your reputation."

I frowned at him. What was he getting at?

"I'm here, aren't I? You should be happy." I made the shot but my calculations were off so the ball stopped just shy of its destination.

"Oh, I'm happy," Gabe whispered in my ear as he walked past.

Stefan had already deserted us for some girls at the bar, and Drew was playing someone else on the next table. Gabe sunk his ball and went for the black. He missed.

"So kind of you to give me another chance." I smiled and wandered around to take the shot again. This time I sunk it.

"That's two nil. One more game and you'll be walking around this table with your pants around your ankles."

"Is that what you're trying to do?" He walked over and stood in front of me. "Because all you needed to do was ask." He smiled, bit his lip and wiggled his eyebrows. Gabe jumped when someone called his name and I backed away and took a sip of my drink.

"Shame on you, Gabe Thornton." Haleigh ran her finger down his arm. "You never called."

Gabe winced and his eyes flicked nervously to mine. "Hey, Haleigh," he said, taking a swig from his beer bottle. "You remember Lauren?" He nodded to me.

Haleigh looked me up and down, dismissed me then turned her attention fully to Gabe. She leaned over him as he perched himself on the edge of the pool table and tried to look at the ceiling. "Are you having a good night?" She ran her finger down his neck. He gripped it tightly when she reached his collarbone and held her hand away from him.

"My night is fine, thank you," he said tersely.

My blood was boiling. I wanted to look away but my eyes stayed glued, which was pure torture if I wasn't going to allow myself to claim him in public.

Haleigh pressed against him and he awkwardly tried to slide away from her. "You're playing hard to get tonight, aren't you?" she cooed.

Gabe breathed deeply and shook his head. "Drew is just over there." He jerked his head to where Drew was glaring at them.

My heart was pounding. My hands, clammy, wrapped around the pool cue tightly as this girl basically rubbed herself over Gabe.

My Gabe.

I thought of that night that he kissed her in front of me. It looked like it didn't just stop there. It had crossed my mind but it wasn't something I wanted to dwell on. Until now.

"It didn't stop you last time," she breathed in his ear.

Gabe stood up abruptly and moved away from her, stuffing his hands into his pockets. "Leave," he said.

Haleigh cocked her hip to one side and pouted. "You know they all said you were like that. A one trick pony. Guess I should have listened."

She strode away and Gabe slowly lifted his eyes to meet mine. I stood still, thinking, and chewing on my lip. I had no right to be angry at him. I wasn't with him then. I was with Derek. But seeing her there with him, and the familiarities she took had my mind a little addled.

"You slept with her," I stated when he came close.

"I was drunk."

"And that makes it better?" I closed my eyes and tried to calm down. I really had no right to be angry. So why couldn't I stop it?

"How could you do that to Drew?" I asked, only because I had no right to say what I really wanted to.

"To Drew? You're worried about Drew?"

"Of course I'm worried about Drew. He loves that girl."

"Well, he shouldn't."

"That's hardly the point."

Gabe sighed. "Drew and I had it out. He knows I regret it. He understands that I was in a bad place."

"A bad place," I scoffed. "It didn't look like you thought it was that bad from where I was standing." I was being petty and whiny. I realised it, I just couldn't seem to stop.

"I was messed up over you."

"You mean after you had finished sleeping with me for a bet?"

248

Gabe narrowed his eyes. "I mean after I came to tell you how sorry I was and how I really felt, and I found you basically being proposed to by Derek. You know, that time you said yes?"

"He was my fiancé!" I looked around and lowered my voice. "Well, I hope you enjoyed fucking her," I threw at him, ashamed of my behaviour but strangely unable to stop.

"I thought of you the whole time," he said, his voice dissolving to a growl.

"And that's supposed to make me feel better? That you thought of me," I leaned over and whispered, "While you stuck your dick in another woman?"

Gabe's eyes turned to ice. "What about you? Did you think of me when you were letting your fiancé fuck you? Huh? Was it him you were crying out for when you came? Derek!" he mimicked, breathing deeply. "Or was he not able to make you come at all?" He grinned sadistically.

I flushed red then tossed, what turned out to be, a tiny splash of drink in his face.

Drew stopped his game to stare at us. Gabe simply glared at me with a cold hard stare, then wiped his hand down his face and stormed out the door.

I felt a little nauseated and turned to Drew who had come over to stand beside me. "Will he come back?"

He shook his head. "What happened?"

"Haleigh," I said.

Drew frowned. "He walked off because of Haleigh?"

I didn't want to tell him the truth. "Sort of."

Drew shrugged and walked back to the pool table, throwing over his shoulder, "Best to just leave him when he gets like this. We'll be done soon. I'll give you a ride home."

29

LAUREN

I didn't take Drew up on his offer for a ride home. The night air would help clear my head. I was annoyed at Gabe for walking off. How were we supposed to resolve our argument if his response was to simply walk away?

Fortunately, my house wasn't too far of a walk and I only managed to terrify myself into imagining two people were following me suspiciously. Turned out, neither of them were. When out at night, I usually left a light on at home, but since I wasn't expecting to stay at my place that night, the house was dark and cold. I stumbled down the hallway, tossing my clothes off angrily, and dove into bed, throwing the covers over my head.

I woke to someone pounding loudly on my door. "Lauren!" a drunken voice called out. "Lauren, please open the door. I'm sorry. I'm so so fucking sorry."

I opened my eyes and peered at the clock. It was four in the morning. Pressing my pillow over my head, I tried to ignore the incessant pounding but Gabe wouldn't stop. Finally, I threw the covers off and walked down the hall, ripping the door open.

"What?" I demanded, crossing my arms and glaring at him.

Relief flooded his face. "Lauren," he breathed and stumbled towards me. A wave of alcohol scented air hit before he reached me and I took a step back. He stopped and swayed slightly, looking at me through glazed eyes. "I'm sorry," he said again.

"Apparently so." I left the door open and walked into the lounge, taking a seat on the couch. Gabe followed and sat opposite me as Smudge walked over and plonked himself on his lap. Gabe stroked him absently, seemingly transfixed by the sight of his hand moving back and forth over the cat's black and white coat.

"Where did you go?" I asked finally when it seemed Gabe had nothing to say.

"Out," he replied.

"Where?"

Gabe shrugged and patted the cat again. "Just out."

"Well, I walked home. Alone."

Gabe gently pushed Smudge off his lap and came over to sit beside me. "I'm sorry," he said again, taking my hand in his. "I don't handle stuff like that very well. It's just, when Haleigh came over and we started arguing and then Derek came up, well—" He let his voice fall. "I couldn't stand the thought of you being with him and I kind of saw red. I knew I was just going to end up doing something I would regret so I walked away. Besides, you were the one who threw the drink in my face."

It was my turn to feel ashamed. I had never done that before. Never retaliated in that sort of way. I had wanted to, many times, but they were only fantasies that I kept well under control. But when I was around Gabe, I lost control. I tugged my hand away from him, but it only made him inch closer to me on the couch, this time taking both my hands and holding them firmly. "Lauren, listen. I'm just not sure how to act around you. I mean, I've never actually had someone ashamed of being with me before."

"I'm not ashamed," I protested.

Gabe nodded. "Right. And that's why you won't tell anyone. That's why I had to beg you to tell your best friend."

"But it's not you I'm ashamed of. It's me."

"You? I don't get it."

And then I realised what I wanted to say was that I was ashamed of myself for sleeping with him. I didn't want people looking at me. I didn't want people seeing Gabe, how young and carefree and gorgeous he was and making assumptions. But most of all, it was because those assumptions were true. Sensing my hesitation, Gabe leaned over and tried to kiss me.

"Not now," I said and turned my cheek.

Gabe pulled me closer and tried to nuzzle into my neck, groaning seductively, if not a little drunkenly.

"I think you should just go home," I said, tugging my hands from his and walking over to the door, holding it open.

He glared at me and walked out, slamming the door behind him.

* * *

He called in sick for work the next day, and he didn't call or text. Part of me wanted to reach out to him, assure him that everything was fine, but the other part was annoyed that he was avoiding me and slacking off at work, once again. If he wasn't careful, Peta would have no choice but to fire him.

After two days of no contact with Gabe, I drove over to his house after work and knocked on the door.

Drew answered, nodding to the garage. "He's in there," was all he said.

I walked over and pulled the side door open to find Gabe, shirtless and drenched in sweat. My eyes travelled over his body as he pounded the bag time and time again, drips of sweat trailing down his perfect skin. I took a deep breath and cleared the thoughts distracting me from my head. "Hi," I said when he didn't notice me.

Gabe glanced up but kept pounding his fists against the leather.

"Hi," I said again, taking a step closer.

Still, Gabe didn't say anything, but he did stop striking the bag, and pulled his gloves from his hands, placing them at the back of the garage and picking up a towel to wipe the sweat from his face.

"Hi," he said finally. "Is there something you wanted?"

"You haven't been to work in a couple of days."

"I've been sick." He picked up a water bottle and squirted some into his mouth.

"Yeah," I said, skimming my eyes over his body. "You sure look it."

Gabe threw the now empty bottle away and reached down to grab his t-shirt and pull it over his head. "What do you want, Lauren?"

I stepped closer to him and took a deep breath. "I've missed you."

Gabe snorted. "Sure you have."

I took another step forward. "You didn't call."

"Neither did you." Gabe paced back and forth across the concrete floor. He glanced at me quickly and then said, "I've missed you too," while staring at the ground. "But you've made it pretty clear how you feel, Lauren."

"I have?" I questioned.

"You don't want to be with me, I get it."

I almost laughed, thinking of all the times I had fantasised over him in the last couple of days. "I do. I just don't want to be with someone who sulks every time something doesn't go his way."

Gabe stopped pacing. "I'm not sulking."

"Well, what would you call it then?" I stepped dangerously close to him.

Gabe looked down at me, ran his tongue over his top lip, and then turned away. "I don't like having to hide like I'm your dirty little secret."

"That's not what you are."

"That's how it feels. I feel like you are ashamed of me."

"I told you it wasn't like that."

"Well, I'm telling you that's how it feels. If we could just be open and honest, this whole argument over Haleigh and Derek would have never happened."

"I'm just not ready for that. A few months ago I was engaged to Derek, having not long lost a baby. Did you stop to think about that? There's more going on in my life than just you."

Gabe chewed on his lip and reached out to take the tips of my fingers in his. "Come to the work function with me. With me, with me. Not as just a friend."

I took my hand away, feeling like he hadn't listened to a word I said. "You know I can't do that."

"Why not?" he pleaded.

"I just told you why."

"Well, maybe I should take someone else then," he said cruelly. "You know, just so people don't get the wrong idea about us."

I was getting sick of his games. "Fine," I said and started walking towards the door.

"Fine," he yelled back, slamming it behind me.

30

LAUREN

Our end of year work function wasn't exactly at the end of the year, but it was as close as we could get before everyone started taking time off over the Christmas break. Peta decided, instead of going somewhere for dinner, she would close the café early and simply have it there. She and Mark had been cooking all day and there were platters of food over every surface as well as crates of beer and bottles of wine. Music played loudly and I had even helped Peta decorate the café in Christmas colours, something she was usually firmly against, but to counteract the cheer, she had managed to somehow combine Halloween and Christmas decorations and insisted that everyone dress up to suit the strange holiday mash-up.

"So," Peta asked, stepping back and studying the fake black-needled Christmas tree we had just decorated with cobwebs, plastic spiders, silver tinsel and red fairy lights. "Everything okay with you and Gabe? You don't seem to be talking much."

I groaned. "So you noticed."

Peta patted me on the shoulder sympathetically and somewhat patronisingly, before saying, "A little hard dating a teenager, is it?" and grinned stupidly.

I laughed, but at the same time realised how close her words were to the truth. I had never had these problems with Derek. We had always trusted each other. Never had a need to be jealous, that was, of course, until the lying-man-stealing-bitch came onto the scene. Maybe Gabe's insecurities weren't such a bad thing.

Peta, momentarily distracted by Shrek applying frosting to the windows in the wrong pattern, turned back to me. "Is everything okay with you two?"

I let my shoulders slump and Peta walked over and pulled me into an embrace. "Just tell me," she said.

So I let it all out, telling her about our argument, how I threw my drink at him, and how we ended things with him slamming the door behind me.

"And you haven't heard from him since?"

I shook my head.

"Well, that explains why he's called in sick so much lately. I was actually beginning to worry about him." Peta glanced at her watch. "He'll be here soon though. He texted to let me know he was coming and, of course, apologised profusely for being sick. He blamed it on food poisoning."

I dumped myself onto a seat. "I wonder if he'll bring a date."

Peta pulled over a chair and sat opposite me. "Look," she started by saying. "Maybe this is for the best. Gabe, as gorgeous as he is, just isn't right for you. He's so much younger, and I'm not talking about years here, I'm talking about every aspect. The kid hasn't had a job other than this one. He doesn't own a house. And from what I can tell, he has no aspirations to change any of that. And why should he? He's only twenty-one." She lifted my chin so I looked her straight in the eye and then she repeated, "Twenty-one. You and he are poles apart. You need to find someone more suited to your personality, someone more in line with your way of life."

I felt like crying and my throat constricted tightly. "But I want Gabe."

Peta sighed deeply and pulled me in for another embrace. "Then Gabe you shall have," she whispered in my ear, patting my head gently. "No, seriously. Gabe's here."

I jerked back from her and glanced out the window. Sure enough, Gabe, along with Drew, Jordan and Kate pushed the door open. "Oh, god," I groaned, wiping away the tears. "How do I look?"

Peta ran her eyes over my face. "Terrible," she said bluntly.

I turned away from the group walking through the door and wiped under my eyes furiously. I didn't even know why I was crying, but I certainly didn't want to face them all like that.

"Hey, boss lady," Gabe said, embracing Peta. "You don't mind that I brought a date, do you?"

My head whipped around, but Gabe was standing with his arm slung over Drew's shoulder and grinning stupidly. He lifted his head in my direction, nodding in greeting. "Hey, buddy." His gaze only rested on me for a fraction. Beside him, Drew rolled his eyes.

"You're more than welcome, Drew," Peta said, flinging a tea towel over her shoulder. "You're practically part of the family anyway."

Gabe pulled a chair out and sat down. "Yeah, that's what I figured too."

More and more staff filed into the café with their partners. There were some staff members I had never met before, being university students that only returned to cover the Christmas break shifts. The music was loud, the food was great, and Gabe was friendly to everyone but me. Occasionally, he addressed me, but only to call me buddy, or mate. He appeared to be having fun, but perhaps a little too much fun. His smile was too bright, his laugh too loud. Everything about him was forced. Peta kept looking over to me with an 'I told you so' look on her face every time he sauntered past. At one stage, encouraged by Gabe's friendlier than usual demeanour, a rather intoxicated Jordan wrapped her arms around his neck and begged him to dance. He laughed, but a small sigh of relief escaped when he unpeeled her arms and stepped away politely, not even glancing in my direction. Unable to stand the distance between us any longer, I walked over and tapped Gabe's shoulder.

"Hey buddy!" he greeted loudly. Too loudly. "Something I can help you with?"

"Can I talk with you a moment?"

Kate leaned over and whispered something in his ear. Gabe threw back his head in laughter, before turning back to me. "Sorry, you were saying?"

I took a deep breath. "Can I talk with you a moment?"

"Sure!" Gabe smiled widely and took a large gulp of beer. "Fire away."

"In there?" I jerked my head towards the storage room.

Mock horror passed over Gabe's face. "I hardly think that would be appropriate now, would it? You know what sort of things people get up to in storage rooms, I wouldn't want anyone to think badly of us."

I glared at him, but he wouldn't meet my eye. He kept talking to Kate and Jordan and doing his best to make me uncomfortable.

Drew looked up and mouthed, "Sorry."

"Gabe," I warned.

"Oh, sorry." He turned to Kate. "Looks like I'm being summoned. Back in a minute. Get me another beer, would you?"

He followed me inside the storage room and I pulled the door shut.

"You can't have it both ways, Lauren. You can't be friends in front of everyone out there and then jump me in the storage room."

"No one is jumping anyone."

Gabe crossed his arms and leaned against the wall. "Shame. It could have been fun."

"What are you doing out there?" I asked.

"Having fun. That's what I'm supposed to do, isn't it?"

"You're acting childish."

Gabe's snide grin dropped. "Maybe that's because I am."

"What? A child?"

"You seem to think so."

"I don't think that at all. Believe me."

"Well, why don't we go out there and tell everyone? Why don't we just own it?"

"You know I can't do that, Gabe. Not yet. I need time."

Gabe lifted himself from the wall and pushed open the door. "Well, I will give it to you. I'm going to return to the party. I'm going to have a good time and I'll catch up with you later, maybe. Depends on how late this thing goes. I better not stay up past curfew."

"Gabe," I called after him but he let the door fall shut. "Gabe," I called again, pushing the door back open. But he had already sat down and was sculling the beer that Kate handed him.

The more Gabe drank the darker he got. His previous tactic of avoiding eye contact changed to glaring at me every chance he got.

During one such glaring match, Peta slumped to the chair beside me. "Having fun?" she asked.

I took in a deep breath. "I can't ignore him. Why can't I just ignore him?"

She patted my knee. "Beats me. Maybe it's got something to do with those eyes. The way he's glaring at you, although cold, is hardly innocent. If you are wanting this little thing you have going on here to remain between the two of you, you're going to need to stop the way he's looking at you. Even Jordan is suspicious. I caught her glaring at you also."

"Delightful. This is exactly what I wanted to avoid. I need to get out of here," I said and got to my feet.

"You can't leave me here alone."

"You're not alone. Shrek's here."

"He doesn't count," Peta said, getting to her feet. "Excuse me everyone!" she yelled loudly. The hum of chatter died down. "I think it's time the party moved on. Who's up for some dancing?"

Gabe leapt to his feet and held his beer bottle high in the air. "Maybe not dancing but I'm up for more drinking!"

Shrek shot Peta a look of confusion and I hissed in her ear, "What are you doing?"

"Getting you out of here."

"I meant away from Gabe."

"It will be away from Gabe. Stuck here in the café with everyone is drawing lots of attention. If you leave, it will only get worse. If we all leave together and go dancing, you can slip away after a while and no one will even notice. Besides, I'm in the mood for dancing," she sang.

Shrek walked out and wrapped his arms around Peta's waist. "What was that? I'm getting lucky tonight?"

Peta laughed and pulled away. "That's not what I said."

One of Shrek's eyebrows lifted. "But you did say you were in the mood for dancing, and you in the mood for dancing leads to the mood for—"

Peta covered his mouth with her hand. "Okay, okay. Yes, I get where you are heading. Keep your pants on and we'll see how things progress."

Shrek looked over to me and grinned around her fingers. "I'm in," he mouthed once she removed her hand.

The music at the club was loud. Deafeningly loud. Peta and I couldn't even talk above the blare of it. Gabe was quickly led by Kate and Jordan to the dance floor and Drew followed begrudgingly in their wake. Drew wasn't much of a dancer. He stood in one spot, sipping on his beer and nodding his head to the beat. Gabe, on the other hand, moved smoothly, but I noted, thankfully, that every time one of the girls got a little too close, he slipped away from them, laughing.

"You really need to stop watching," Peta yelled in my ear.

"Pardon?" I yelled back. I could barely hear anything over the music.

"Gabe," Peta yelled again. "You really need to stop watching him."

I took a sip on the bottle of some horrible premixed drink that had been shoved in my hand and nodded glumly. "I know."

"Well if it isn't Lauren Lees!" a voice boomed from behind. I turned to find Derek's workmate, Preston Jones, with arms open and waiting for an embrace. I stood and hugged him quickly, correcting, "Lauren Greer. It's always been Lauren Greer."

Preston grinned and slung his arm heavily over my shoulder. "So it has." His breath reeked of alcohol. "I'm pleased I ran into you."

I tried to shift away, but his arm was heavy and there was no escape. "Is that so?"

"Yes. There's been a lot of talk around the office since you left. You leaving Derek has done wonders for my sales results."

"Is that so?" I said again. I just wanted to get away.

He leaned closer and his breath was hot on my ear. "Derek is nothing without you. Your photography and marketing skills sure upped his game."

Gabe pushed his way through the crowd and grabbed my hand. "Excuse me a minute, mate," he said to Preston and pulled me away. "So I'm not allowed near you in public, but this guy can have his hands all over you?" he growled.

Even intoxicated, the scent of him drove me wild. I wanted to wrap my arms around his neck and pull him to me. Kiss him right there in front of everyone. But I didn't.

"He hasn't got his hands all over me," I insisted.

"So it's fine if I do this then?" Gabe pulled me to him and roughly crushed his lips against mine.

"Gabe!" I exclaimed, pushing him away.

Gabe stumbled back and held his arms out wide. "What?"

Preston stormed over and shoved his chest. "Back off!" he demanded, assuming he was protecting me from a random drunk man.

I grabbed Preston's shoulder and pulled him away from Gabe. "It's fine," I assured him.

Gabe's lunged at Preston, his punch landing squarely on his jaw. His eyes were wild as he turned to the crowd that had gathered as Preston fell to the floor. "Anyone else want a go?" he yelled.

No one moved. They all just looked on in bewildered confusion before Gabe threw his bottle to the ground, the glass shattering at his feet and stormed out of the club.

I ran after him. "Gabe!" I called but he kept walking. "Gabe, please stop! Talk to me."

"Leave me alone, Lauren," he yelled over his shoulder. "Just leave me alone."

By this stage, Preston's friends had followed us and caught up to Gabe, shoving him as he walked. Gabe's response was to wildly flay his fists around until one of them connected. The men backed off, seeing the power in his swing, even if he was rottenly drunk.

"Anyone else?" Gabe yelled into the night air. The men watching him took a step back. "Then I shall take my leave." Gabe bowed deeply in my direction. "Mrs Robinson," he said, then walked into the darkness. I started after him but Drew grabbed my arm, pulling me back.

"I'll go," he said. "I know how to handle him when he gets like this."

Peta came and wrapped her arms around me, pulling me away from Gabe's retreating figure. Police lights flashed in the distance and a siren wailed as the car turned around and headed towards the club. "Come on," she said. "Let's go home."

31

LAUREN

I stayed at Peta's that night, stuffed into the spare single bed in Henry's room. Thankfully, he didn't cry. But I did. I felt like I had lost Gabe but at the same time, I was so angry with him.

He didn't call the next day or turn up for his shift at work. I worked the close alone, thankful for the peace and quiet to reflect on my thoughts. I kept returning to Drew's words, 'I know how to handle him when he gets like this'. What did he mean by that? Was this sort of behaviour something Gabe did regularly? The jealousy I could have handled but the sulking afterwards was too much. I tried his cell phone multiple times before giving up and admitting to myself I was too old for these games. If he didn't want to talk to me, then why should I chase him? I wasn't the one who punched a stranger. I wasn't the one who threw a fit simply because I wouldn't go as his partner to the end of year work function.

Resisting the urge to throw my phone into the sink, I placed it carefully on the counter. I couldn't reward him for bad behaviour by repeatedly calling him and begging for him to talk to me. I couldn't chase him every time he threw his toys.

Just before I was about to shut the doors for the night, Drew walked inside. My heart jumped, hoping that Gabe would be with him but he was alone.

He stood before me, hands stuffed in his pockets. "Hey," he said.

"Hey," I said quietly and wiped at an imaginary spot on the counter.

"He's in hospital."

I froze. "What? What happened?"

"Those guys that he taunted last night followed him down the street and beat the shit out of him before I could find him. I've just been down there."

Without realising what I was doing, I began to untie my apron and walk to the front of the store.

"Wait," Drew called. "He doesn't want you there."

I sunk to one of the chairs and Drew came to sit beside me.

"Is he okay?" I managed to croak out.

"Fractured rib, but the rest is just bruising. He'll get out tomorrow, they think. He received a rather nasty knock to the head, so they want to keep him in another night for observation."

"He didn't call," I said, glancing over at where my phone lay discarded on the counter.

"He lost his phone. I spent all night searching for him, but it wasn't until I remembered last time that I thought of the hospital."

I stood. "I should go down there."

Drew reached out and pulled me back down to the seat. "His mother is with him. He's fine. Just give him a little time. He's feeling like shit about the whole thing."

All the anger I had been feeling earlier melted away. I hung my head and covered my face with my hands. "Does he do this a lot?"

Drew looked down. "Only when he goes dark."

"Goes dark? What does that even mean?"

Drew sighed heavily. "It hit him really hard when his brother died. For months, my life simply existed to follow Gabe around while all he did was drink, fight and fuck." His eyes darted to me in an apology. "Sorry. He kept getting in fights until there was no fight left." Drew looked down at the ground and then back up at me. "Can I ask what happened between you two? I haven't seen him this bad in ages."

"He wanted to tell people."

Drew frowned. "Tell people what?"

I lowered my voice, the words almost painful. "I didn't want people knowing we were together and he did."

"Oh," was all Drew said.

"Yeah."

After a long silence, Drew stood. "Look, he's got a heart of gold and I love him, but the gold just turns dark sometimes. We've all got a bit of darkness, Gabe's just not great at hiding his. And for whatever reason, this thing between you has hit him hard."

"I want to see him," I said.

"Just give him a few days to lick his wounds, okay?"

I said okay but as soon as he left, I quickly closed the café, leaving the cleaning of the cabinets for the morning staff and headed straight for the hospital. A nurse showed me to his room, scolding me for visiting after hours. He lay on the bed, shirtless, his chest covered in bruises and his eyes black. His lip was split and his jaw was painfully swollen. He didn't say anything to me as I sat on the chair beside his bed and reached out to take his hand.

He pulled away. "I told him to tell you not to come."

I placed my hand back in my lap. "He did. But I came anyway."

"You shouldn't have."

I shrugged. "Well, I did." I moved the chair a little closer. "Are you in pain?"

"I'm sorry," he blurted out. "I was stupid, again. I just can't seem to help myself. I never meant to do any of it. I never meant to punch that man, I just saw red when he shoved me away from you like that."

I placed my hand back on the bed beside his, but not touching. He moved his fingers a fraction closer and I took them, my heart swelling when our skin connected. "Gabe, I—"

The door opened and I quickly withdrew my fingers, earning a withering look from Gabe just as a lady dressed in long flowing clothing, and looking like something out of the seventies, stepped inside and looked at Gabe questioningly. "Gable?" she asked.

"Mum, this is Lauren. We work together. Lauren, this is my mother, Lynda."

She smiled sweetly at me as I got to my feet to shake her hand. She looked nothing like Gabe. Her hair was dark and streaked with grey, and the layered long skirts and flowing tops made her look like she should be adorned with flowers in her hair and driving a spray painted van.

"Nice to meet you," she said.

"You too." I wasn't sure what else to say. Gabe obviously hadn't told her anything about us, but I guess that was what I wanted. So why did I feel disappointed at being introduced to his mother as nothing more than a workmate?

Both Lynda and I stood awkwardly in the room, Gabe's eyes firmly on his mother and not me. Finally, he spoke. "I'll call you when I get out, okay, Lauren?" The way he said my name left me cold.

"Okay," I stammered.

"Nice to meet you," his mother called after me when I walked out the door. As soon as I was gone I heard her turn to Gabe and ask, "So who was she?"

"Nobody," he replied. "Just someone I work with."

* * *

After talking with Peta, she agreed I could have the next day off, so I spent it waiting for Gabe's call. It never came. Finally, at nine o'clock in the evening, I admitted defeat and was walking down to the bedroom, Smudge purring contentedly in my arms when the doorbell rang. I dropped Smudge and flew to the door, pulling it open, desperately hoping that it would be Gabe on the other side.

"Gabe," I breathed when I saw him. His hair was slicked to his face with droplets of rain and his white t-shirt clung to the swells of his chest. Even with the swelling around his jaw and the bruising around his eyes, I had never seen him look so sexy. He strode through the door forcefully and came at me, causing me to stumble backwards until I was pressed against the wall, arms caging me. His eyes were so blue, surrounded by the darkness, and they shone with an intensity that caused my knees to shake.

I reached out and stroked the swollen purple patch across his chin. "Are you okay?"

He didn't answer, but instead, closed his eyes as my finger traced his jaw, breathing heavily. I drew my finger across his skin and tenderly ran it over the swelling of his lip, careful to avoid the open cut, although it was clear of blood.

"Are you okay?" I repeated breathlessly.

Gabe tilted his chin, inching towards me until our lips met and we kissed. It was gentle at first, his lips brushing against mine like a feather, but as he leaned closer, pressing his body to mine, his kiss intensified and deepened. I was scared it would hurt him and tried to pull away, but he pressed harder, not appearing to notice the way his lip dragged roughly against mine. My breathing hitched as he pressed every inch of his body against mine. His hardness pressed into me, begging for attention. Moving his kiss from my lips, he trailed across my cheek and moved down until he came to the soft flesh in the curve of my neck. I winced as he sunk his teeth in and sucked hard, marking me, claiming me with his mouth. But I didn't protest.

Once content, Gabe drew back and ran his hand over the deep purple mark that now stained my neck, his eyes dark and hungry. His finger followed the line of my collarbone, leaving sparks of desire in its wake until it rested on the first button of my top. My heart was in my throat as he looked deeply into my eyes before they fell to my now heaving chest. Moving methodically, he undid each button and then slipped my shirt off my shoulders, allowing it to fall to the ground. Without speaking, he turned me around and unclasped my bra, my breasts swollen and heavy in anticipation. Falling to his knees, he pulled my pants and underwear down, his breath teasing my flesh with heat as his hands travelled down my sides and pulled my clothes out from under my feet.

Then he turned me around so I stood naked before him, my back pressed against the wall. He was still fully clothed as he bent his head and lay a trail of kisses from my neck down between my breasts, and over my stomach until he drew in a deep breath and groaned when he reached his destination. But he didn't touch. He inhaled deeply before standing back up and turning me around again so my front was splayed against the wall. He held me there as he kissed every inch of flesh from my neck to my feet, his hands roaming over the places his mouth wasn't.

For a moment, my awareness focussed on the open curtains of the window behind me, exposing us to anyone that chose to walk up the driveway, but it was only a fleeting thought as Gabe's mouth scrambled my brain. My chest rose and fell heavily the more he teased with his mouth. Not one inch was left unattended. I'm not sure when he undressed, but soon he was naked and pressed against my back, grinding himself against me as his mouth came back to my neck.

"I don't ever want another man to touch you," he growled in my ear. But in that moment, other men didn't exist. I wasn't even aware of them being on the same planet.

He pushed me harder against the wall, flattening my breasts against the patterned wallpaper. I gasped as his cock pressed into the cheeks of my buttocks. "I want you." Turning me around, Gabe slid down my body until I felt his tongue teasing me, begging for me to open to him. I reached down and ran my fingers through his hair, pulling and tugging the long strands as his tongue lapped, pushing him further into me until the intensity was almost too much.

"Stop," I panted, scared I wouldn't be able to resist the sensations that were now crashing against my skull, my chest, and pulsating in my very depths. But he only intensified his efforts, groaning gloriously as I cried out and dissolved over him, sliding down the wall and slumping to the floor. With no time to recover, Gabe dragged me under him and rose over me, his eyes dark and needy and determined. "I want you," he said again. "All of you. Only you." He entered me slowly and I arched off the floor, my insides tender and sensitive from their recent explosion. But Gabe didn't stop. He rocked in and out, staring down at me from burning eyes. "I don't care about the age difference," he said, as he thrust into me. "I don't care if I'm your dirty little secret." He fucked me slow but hard, grunting each time he thrust. "I want you."

As he started to move faster, my body responded, tightness and anticipation rising within me again. I reached up and ran my fingers over his glorious chest then over his shoulders, digging my nails into his back and leaving my mark. The hair that hung around his face jolted every time he moved, and I looked up at him, marvelling that this beautiful man wanted me. Not someone else. Not someone with perfect unmarked skin and flawless features. Me.

Tracing the bruising on his face, I pressed my hand to the swollen flesh of his ribs. He winced, but it only made him move faster and harder. He drove into me time and time again and I whimpered with pleasure. He was so hard, I started to quiver around his length, unable to control myself for much longer. Pushing into me, he held himself still, looking into my eyes. "I want you, Lauren. And I will take whatever I can get." And then he fucked me hard and fast until I couldn't stand it anymore and surrendered myself, crying out as wave after wave of pleasure pulsated through me. I dug my nails into his arms and my insides gripped against his hardness, the cause of his undoing.

He slumped over me after he came, breathing heavily. "I love you, Lauren Greer," he whispered in my ear. "I don't ever want to be without you, whether anyone ever knows it or not."

32

LAUREN

The next few days at work were filled with secret smiles and knowing glances. Gabe's bruising faded and he was content with the way things were between us. He stopped sulking and I did my best to relax a little, even allowing him to pull me into the storage room for make-out sessions when no one was looking. By the time Christmas approached, we were in a good place and I was dreading leaving him to go visit my parents, even if it was only going to be for a couple of weeks.

"I'm going to miss this," I said as we kissed, surrounded by bags of coffee beans and sleeves of takeaway cups.

Gabe nuzzled into my neck, cracking the door open and glancing out to the café to make sure it was still empty. His mouth had me hot and bothered and I desperately didn't want to stop. Sometimes, just the mere sight of him made me wet. I reached down and pressed my hand under the waistband of his jeans. He sucked in his breath as I wrapped my fingers around his hardened cock.

"Careful," he warned as I began to stroke his length, teasing and pleasuring him in ways I knew couldn't be continued. He pulled away a little but I gripped harder. "Seriously," he panted. "Careful."

I jerked him back to me and stroked harder, attaching my mouth to his earlobe and nipping the flesh with my teeth.

He sucked in air sharply. "Mark's going to walk in from his smoke break any minute. We should stop."

I removed his hand from where it was placed against the door and guided it between my legs, knowing the wetness and warmth he would find.

"Oh god, Lauren." His fingers moved over my swollen clit before sinking inside. "Lauren," he panted.

I moved my hand faster, wrapping it around his bulging cock which strained against his jeans until Gabe jerked his hand out from my pants. "Shit," he said, pulling away from me. "Shit, shit, shit. Mark's back." Gabe looked down at the large bulge in his pant. "What am I supposed to do with this?" he said, looking up at me. I reached over and ran my hand over him, delighting as he twitched in response. "You're not helping, Lauren."

I laughed and pushed open the door, grabbing an unneeded bag of coffee beans. "See you out there."

For the rest of the shift, Gabe couldn't keep his eyes off me. Every time I bent down, I would get back up to find his eyes attached to my backside or my chest. Every time I concentrated on a task, I would look back up to find him fixed on the way my tongue ran over my lips. And every time we found ourselves alone, he would stride over to me, forcefully bringing his lips to mine and shoving his hand down my pants, groaning each time he still found me wet.

After another close call when we repelled from each other before Mark's entrance, Mark stood leaning in the doorway of the kitchen and crossed his arms. "So?" he asked.

My heart raced in my chest, certain that this was the time we had been caught.

"What are everyone's plans for Christmas?"

Gabe breathed a sigh of relief and laughed even though there was nothing he should have been laughing about.

"I'm heading up to my parents' place for a couple of weeks," I said, turning my back on a chuckling Gabe. "You?"

"Home with the family," Mark said dryly. He looked between Gabe and me. "As much fun as it is seeing you two squirm and trying to hide it, I know."

"Know what?" I asked, attempting to look innocent.

"About you and him."

The grin that overcame Gabe's face was huge and he lifted an eyebrow at me. "I didn't say a word," he insisted. "I swear."

"He didn't," Mark agreed, reaching into his pocket. "Here." He extended his hand to Gabe. "I think I owe you this."

Gabe took the notes and fanned them out, laughing. "Cheers," he said. "This will come in handy for Christmas. There's a certain lady I need to buy for and she did kind of help me earn it."

I couldn't help but roll my eyes.

Our shift finished and it seemed no time at all before Gabe was leaning through the window of my car, planting a kiss on my forehead, my bags resting on the back seat.

"Do you have to go?"

"It's only for a couple of weeks," I said.

"It will feel like forever. You've got to send me naughty pictures, okay? I'll need to relieve the pressure while you're away and you are kind of leaving me with rather blue balls since we

TOUCHED

never got to finish what we started earlier. Unless—" He tugged on the door handle but it was locked. "Never mind," he muttered and feigned a pout.

We kissed goodbye and soon I was making the four-hour trip to my parents' house. Gabe interrupted my journey with numerous phone calls and the four-hour trip soon turned into five. It was dark when I finally pulled up the drive. Morgan and Alistair's car was already there so they must have arrived before I did. Mother came to the door before I cut the engine, and stood with arms crossed in the light of the doorway.

"You're late," she said. "Your father has been worried sick, afraid that you had driven yourself over the edge of a cliff by travelling this late at night."

I opened the door and hopped out, grabbing my bags from the back seat. "Hello, Mother," I said, leaning over to kiss her cheek and earning a wink from Dad as he came up behind her.

She swatted me away and threw a tea towel over her shoulder, reminding me of Peta, before retreating inside.

"How's my girl?" Dad asked, patting me on the back. He had never been much of a hugger.

"Your girl is wonderful," I said.

Dad lifted an eyebrow. "Wonderful, you say?"

"Wonderful," I repeated.

Morgan, Alistair and Madison appeared out of the lounge and Madi threw her arms around me. "Merry Christmas, Aunty L," she said excitedly as I hugged her back. Morgan merely nodded in my direction and Alistair stretched out to shake my hand.

"Did you bring me a present?" Madi asked, scanning the bag I carried. "I can go put it under the tree."

I looked to Morgan questioningly. "A tree?" Mother had never allowed us to have a Christmas tree growing up. In her mind, having a tree did nothing but distract from the true message.

"She's getting soft in her old age," Morgan whispered.

Mother, coming in from the kitchen carrying a tray of hot chocolates, squinted her eyes and shook her head at Morgan. "I heard that, young lady. Your mother might be getting old, but her hearing is just fine."

Christmas Eve was spent singing carols in our house. Mother would pull up a chair to the old electronic organ sitting in a corner of the lounge, and the notes of Silent Night and The First Noel filled the room. As much as I was dreading the time spent away from Gabe, it was good to be home.

Gabe texted through most of the evening, updating me on his mother's strange habits, the organic, dairy and alcohol-free egg nog she had made, the quality of the weed they smoked, the vegan meal for dinner. The way he explained it all had me thinking that it was my family that was the saner of the two. Mother kept looking at me disapprovingly each time my phone buzzed, but I ignored her looks and replied each time a text came through, trying not to smile at his comical descriptions of his mother.

"So," I said, putting the phone down, and turning to Alistair once the organ music had stopped. "How's the app coming along?"

Alistair's eyes lit up. "I sold it."

"Did you not notice the new car in the driveway?" Morgan asked proudly.

"It was dark," I replied.

"Made a pretty bundle on it too," Alistair said. "At first, I was worried as there were certain hurdles I just couldn't overcome, but then some developer got wind of it and offered to buy it off me.

They were way ahead of me in the game, anyway. In fact, there were a number of apps already out there, but they still saw the value in mine. I couldn't believe my ears when he mentioned the figure. It's done very nicely for us."

"Would have been better if you had you actually worked out those kinks," Morgan said, taking a sip on her second hot chocolate.

I could have murdered a wine, but Mother refused to have alcohol in the house.

Alistair swallowed and smiled tightly. "I'm sure your new wardrobe would disagree. And the jewellery. And the makeup. Oh, and of course the students who now have access to a whole lot of new instruments."

"They were ordered long before you sold the app, Al."

"But they weren't paid for," Alistair said firmly.

I smirked a little as he held his ground.

"We're all very proud of you, Alistair," Dad said, interrupting Morgan and Alistair's staring competition. "Aren't we, Morgan?"

Morgan took another sip of her hot chocolate and simply shrugged her shoulders. "Would be nicer if we didn't have the nuisance lawsuit to deal with now."

Alistair rolled his eyes and turned to me. "There's another developer claiming I stole his idea, all because we used the same graphic on one of our marketing packages. It will all wash over as soon as the judge sees the evidence."

"Hopefully," Morgan muttered.

I took out my phone and flicked through a text to Gabe.

Me: I love you.

His reply was almost instant.

Gabe: You don't know how much that made me smile.

I thought back to when I first met Gabe and how afraid I was that his interest in me was merely for his amusement. I had been scared I was nothing more than a challenge or that he would use me. And then my mind drifted to the way Gabe must feel, knowing that I wouldn't tell anyone about him. I was saying I liked him, but not enough for other people to know about it. My breath caught in my throat when it dawned on me that I was treating him exactly the same way I had been scared he would treat me.

With tears springing to my eyes, I excused myself from the room and dialled Gabe.

"Fuck, I miss you," he said as a way of greeting. His voice was light and happy and a little slurred. "Sorry," he said and laughed. "I'm a little wasted. Lynda grows some excellent weed."

"I need you," I said.

"Oh, babe," he said, and I smiled to myself, having never heard the word 'babe' out of his mouth before. "I need you too. Want to try phone sex? I think it would work a lot better on a video call."

"Get your mind out of the gutter."

"Believe me, it's not in the gutter. Do you want me to tell you where it is? What it's thinking of?"

"I want you to come up here."

"What do you mean?"

"I want you to come and meet my parents." There was silence on the other end of the phone. "Properly," I added. "As my—" I paused trying to think of the right word. Partner seemed too clunky, too old for the relationship we shared. Lover sounded weird and significant other just wasn't right. "My boyfriend," I finally settled on.

"For real?" Gabe asked.

"For real," I said and couldn't help the smile that crept into my tone.

"I probably shouldn't drive right now," Gabe replied.

"Tomorrow?"

"First thing," Gabe confirmed. "Lauren?"

"Yes, Gabe?"

"I love you."

"Love you too."

33

LAUREN

Christmas Day dawned bright and clear and cold. I woke up in my childhood room, dressed in the hues of pinks and purples I had chosen when I was ten and listened to the sound of the house rising. Madison was already awake and I heard her yelling at Morgan to get out of bed so she could start opening presents. Mother was already in the kitchen and the smell of filtered coffee crept down the hall. There was a text already waiting on my phone letting me know that Gabe had risen at the crack of dawn and would be arriving any minute.

I bounded out of bed, wrapped my dressing gown over my pyjamas, shoved on my slippers and opened the door. Mother was walking down the hall towards my room.

"Merry Christmas," I called cheerfully.

Mother's eyes travelled from my head to my toes. "You should get dressed."

"It's early, and Madison is ready to open presents," I replied.

"You're wearing your pyjamas."

"So I am," I said, tugging my dressing gown closer and ducking past her.

"Lauren wait," Mother said, following me. "There is something I should probably tell you."

I walked through the kitchen door to find Derek sitting at the table, just about to take a sip on a steaming cup of coffee.

"Merry Christmas," he said brightly.

"What are you doing here?"

Derek's eyes turned to my mother.

"He's here because I invited him," she said firmly, walking over to the stove and turning on the element. "Pancakes?" she asked.

"Why?" I demanded.

"Because it's Christmas morning and I always make pancakes for Christmas morning."

"Why is Derek here?"

"Sorry," Derek muttered, dropping his head to the cup of coffee. "She said you needed me."

"I needed him?" I glared at Mother.

"You two need to talk and I thought this would be the perfect opportunity."

Morgan took that moment to stroll into the kitchen, stopping abruptly when she saw Derek.

"Did you know about this?" I asked her.

Morgan held up her hands at my onslaught. "Nothing, I swear."

"For goodness sake," Mother uttered. "Would you stop being so dramatic. Derek is here because I asked him here. Once upon a time, he was part of this family. Now, I know you two have had your differences, but for the sake of the family, you two need to sort things out."

"There's nothing to sort out, Mother," I said darkly.

"Look," Derek said, scraping his chair across the tiles as he rose to stand. "Your mother said you were in trouble, she said you needed help and that's why I came, nothing else."

"Nonsense," Mother said. "You two were made for each other. You created a baby. God has given his blessing. You are supposed to be married."

Tears lodged themselves at the back of my throat and sprung to my eyes. I looked over at Derek, demanding he explained the truth.

"Clementine," Derek said, walking over to Mother and placing his hand on her shoulder. "I know you have done this with the best of intentions, but Lauren and I simply aren't right for each other and the time apart has helped us realise that."

"Is it because of your floozy?"

Derek swallowed a smile. "My floozy?"

"Your bit on the side. The other woman. Lauren told us all about her."

I looked at Derek and shook my head.

"No, it is not because of her. I'm not with her anymore."

"Well, what's the problem?" Mother asked bluntly.

Derek took a deep breath. "Lauren and I want different things out of life."

I closed my eyes, my thoughts returning to the baby that lay lifeless in my arms.

"We simply grew apart. We're just not meant to be."

I was grateful to Derek in that moment. There were so many other things he could have said. So many ways to hurt us both, but he chose not to.

But Mother persisted. "I still don't see what the problem is. Marriage can be hard work at times, but God looks favourably on those who choose to honour that promise you made to each other."

"We never made that promise," I said.

Mother ignored me and turned her attention fully to Derek. "Is it because of what happened to the baby?"

"Mother," Morgan warned, flashing a worrying frown in my direction. Morgan knew what had happened. Morgan had been there through the sadness and the tears. Mother had not.

The doorbell rang. Gabe. I flew out of the room and pulled the door open, scrambling into Gabe's arms the moment I saw him.

"You're here," I said, as the tears slipped out my eyes.

"I'm here," he repeated, pulling back from me and studying my appearance. "Are you okay?"

I drank in the sight of him and smiled through my tears. "I'm good now," I said. Gabe had on his usual baggy jeans and a t-shirt, and only half his hair was pulled back into a tie while the rest hung loosely around his shoulders. It made him look even younger. I grabbed his face between my hands and kissed him deeply.

"I'm sorry," I said, before pulling him inside.

Derek was still explaining things to my mother, Morgan was leaning against the kitchen table listening, a cup of coffee in her hands, and Dad was reading the paper and trying to ignore Derek when I dragged Gabe inside. I called for Alistair and Madison and they popped their heads in from the lounge

"Mother, Dad, Morgan, Alistair, Madison, Derek," I said, listing each of them. "I'd like you to meet Gabe."

Mother looked up mid-sentence, her mouth hanging open and staring at Gabe. "We've already met him," she said with a frown of confusion.

"Hi, Gabe," Madison sang and wiggled her fingers at him, skipping over to loop her arm through his. "What are you doing here?"

Gabe pulled away from her and I reached out to take his hand. "I'd like you to meet Gabe again because, he was, and still is my boyfriend."

Derek laughed. And then he looked between us and down at our joined hands and his face reddened with anger.

"But he's just a boy!" Mother exclaimed.

"I'm hardly a boy, Mrs Greer," Gabe started to say, but Derek cut him off.

"Seriously, Lauren?" he yelled at me. "Him? You're fucking him?"

"Language!" Dad yelled. "No one will speak in such a way about my daughter when I am present."

The corner of Morgan's mouth started to twitch.

"You can have more children," Mother implored, ripping my hand away from Gabe and dragging me over to Derek. "Look at him," she said.

I looked up at Derek's flashing eyes and winced.

"Mother, please," I said, the tears beginning to well again.

"I'm sorry you lost the baby, Lauren, but you can try again. You and Derek can work through this."

Tears and sadness mixed with anger swelled in my chest and I exploded. "Don't you get it?" I yelled at my mother. "It wasn't just the baby that died, it was part of me too!"

"Don't be so dramatic, Lauren."

"I'm broken." I sobbed. "I can't have children and Derek wants children. His own children. That's the reason he left in the first place, that's the reason he turned to the man-stealing-bitch. I can't ever give him children."

I ran from the room, leaving a dazed Gabe behind me. He didn't need this. He didn't need this introduction to my parents, my family, my brokenness. But in that moment, all the feelings that I had pushed down, returned with a vengeance. The pain. The guilt. The darkness. I ran into my room and slammed the door shut, falling onto my bed and letting the sobs spill out.

My door creaked open seconds later and the bed dipped with the weight of someone sitting on the edge. Gentle hands skimmed across my hair and pulled me from the bed, enveloping me in strong arms and shushing me gently.

"Lauren," Gabe said. "Lauren, it's okay, it's okay."

But the tears wouldn't stop and the sobs kept escaping, violently ripping themselves from my throat.

"I'm sorry," I finally managed to stammer.

Gabe held me close, his chin resting on the top of my head. "There's nothing to be sorry for," he assured me.

"This wasn't how it was supposed to go."

"Oh, I don't know," Gabe said softly and chuckled a little. "I thought it could have been a lot worse. Neither Derek nor your dad tried to punch me. That's got to be some sort of a bonus."

I let out a half laugh, half sob and sat up on the bed, drawing my knees to my chest.

"Do you want to tell me about it?" he asked.

"I'm not even sure myself," I said, my mind going back to the time I had tried to block out. I swallowed deeply and closed my eyes. "I went into labour early, the baby was distressed and there were complications during the caesarean. The doctor told me later that my likelihood of getting pregnant again had been dramatically reduced. I had what they called an inhospitable womb." I spoke quickly, the words rushing from my mouth in a hurry to be heard. It was painful going back there and the words burned in my throat. But they needed to be said. Gabe had to know what he was getting himself into.

Gabe moved up to sit behind me on the bed and held my hand in his, stroking his thumb in a circular motion over the soft flesh of my wrist.

I took a shaky breath and continued. "When I fell pregnant it was such a shock. Derek was so happy and I wasn't. I wasn't ready to have kids. I wasn't ready to settle down. Even though we never planned to have children in our twenties, the possibility of a child pleased Derek so much, I couldn't tell him how I truly felt. I resented the fact that I was pregnant. And then—" My voice tightened with emotion. "When everything started going wrong and the baby was in distress, I felt like it was all my fault. The baby knew deep down that it wasn't wanted and God cursed me for it." I stopped to draw in a deep breath, the burning sensation in the back of my throat intensifying. "The doctors had to perform an emergency C-section. I don't remember all that much, I think I blocked it out. But I remember the bed being wheeled into the operating room, I remember the lights shining down on me and the strange sensation as they cut my stomach open. It was weird. It didn't hurt but I felt all of it, the tugging, the pulling, the pressure when the baby was finally out. And then I started to feel faint. The light was too bright, the doctors spoke quickly and urgently, the tightness on my arm from the blood pressure machine increased to a point where it was extremely painful and that's all I remember. The pressure. The pain. Then nothing. When I woke up later, the doctor explained what had happened but I just remember watching his mouth flap open and shut and not hearing a word he said." Gabe put his arm around my shoulder and pulled me close as my voice faded to a whisper. "It was Derek who told me we had lost the baby. He wanted to try again and because of the guilt I felt, I agreed. We tried and tried but I never fell pregnant. I can't. Instead, he turned to her and she did." A choked splutter of laughter shot out of me. "Well, I guess, as it turned out, she didn't either."

Gabe held me tight as the tears fell. I clutched onto him desperately, drawing all the strength I could from him. "I'm sorry I didn't tell you," I said finally.

"You didn't need to," he whispered. "It was up to you to tell me when you were ready. Nobody but you could know when that was."

"And you don't hate me?"

"Why would I hate you?"

"Because I'm broken."

Gabe tilted my chin so I was looking at him. "You, Lauren Greer, are not broken. I fell in love with you. You," he emphasised. "Not your baby-making abilities."

"But—" I protested.

Gabe held a finger to my mouth. "But nothing," he said.

We sat in silence until there was a knock on the door and Morgan's voice called out, "Are you okay, L?"

"I don't want to face them," I said to Gabe.

Gabe reached down and wiped away the single tear rolling down my cheek. "Then we'll face them together."

About the Author

Sabre Rose writes about love and lust. Flawed people in messy relationships. Happiness and heartbreak. Loyalty and betrayal.

With stories as unpredictable as they are steamy and intense, Sabre draws you into the lives of her characters and their complicated families.

The ideas floating around her head range from delightful to dark, so sign up to her newsletter at

www.subscribepage.com/sabrerose

to keep up to date with her latest news and releases.

Social Media:

www.facebook.com/sabreroseauthor

www.twitter.com/sabreroseauthor

Website:

www.sabreroseauthor.com

Email:

sabreroseauthor@gmail.com

Other books in the Series

Tempted (Thornton Brothers 2)

Taken (Thornton Brothers 3)

Torn (Thornton Brothers 4)

Printed in Great Britain
by Amazon